Montana

By

C.J. Phillips

Trigger Warnings

This is a story about pain, ptsd, vengeance and forgiveness. There are many sensitive topics included within this love story. This story will also leave you on a cliffhanger. You have been warned. Please do not push yourself past your own limits. Your mental health matters.

- Gore
- Murder with knife
- Murder with gun
- Murder with machete
- Recalled Rape
- Recalled Torture
- Recalled Sodomy
- Recalled stabbing and shooting
- Many painful torture techniques
- Inappropriate use of kitchen tongs
- Intrusive thoughts winning during torture
- Military related PTSD
- Flashbacks
- Self inflicted wounds
- Death of loved ones
- Domestic violence
- Abuse of power
- Extreme Sexual Situations
  - Hand Necklaces
  - Blood Kink
  - Cum Kink
  - Primal Kink
  - Magic Mike inspired moments
  - Is it considered knife play if you are using a machete?

This book is dedicated to a multitude of people. Without them, it would not have been possible. Of course, Carrie for the unsolicited comma checks you would do over my shoulder at any given time.

Also, to the entirety of the MBBC, Morally Black Book Club, there is not one of you that I could thank enough for giving me the encouragement and confidence needed to continue to publish my psychotic little stories. Without you, it just would not have been nearly as much fun as it turned out to be.

To Maeve, you my darling, are a light shining brightly in the darkest of nights. Your spirit and your presence are a force to be reckoned with. Your very essence brought this character to life. I hope she does you justice.

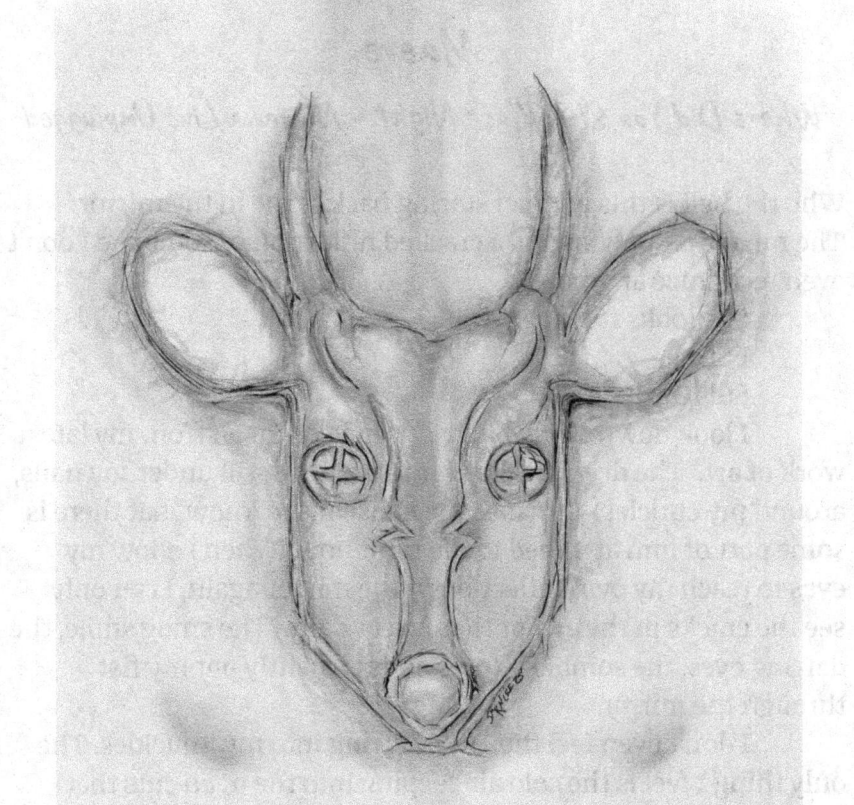

1

Maeve

Where Did You Sleep Last Night – Nirvana Live Unplugged

Who the hell is this woman staring back at me in the mirror? The mirror is showing me a cracked reflection of someone I don't even recognize anymore.

She looks fucking weak.

Filthy.

Sullied.

I look down at my hands, stained crimson from my latest work of art. The dried flecks of his blood are still under my nails, around my cuticles. It makes me nauseous to know that there is some part of him attached to me right now. When I allow my eyes to reach my own reflection in the mirror again, I can only see the cracks in the armor that I wear daily. The smug smile, the darting eyes, the somber expressions. I swiftly put my fist through the mirror.

I don't even feel the glass cutting into my knuckles. The only thing I feel is the cold air seeping into the open cuts that now cover my knuckles. I should feel something, anything besides the physical. I shrug into the mirror, letting my thoughts die in my mind. This is a shit motel anyways. They probably won't even replace the damn mirror. I turn the water on in the shower then slowly peel out of the clothes I am now going to have to destroy. Why I decided to take that motherfucker down while wearing my new jacket, I have no idea.

I really liked that jacket damnit.

I step into the shower and feel the sting of the scalding water on my shoulders and face. It feels like tiny little needles ripping through my skin, trying to get to what's beneath.

Looking down at the drain, I can see the rust colored water rolling off of me in waves. I can still smell the iron of his blood in my nose. I try not to gag as I stand here watching until the water runs clear then only then do I allow myself to wash my hair, my skin. I begin to scrub at the beds of my fingernails. Compulsively trying to get the remnants of that monster removed from my skin. The thought of even leaving a trace of him on me makes me more nauseous than before.

It should be a good 2, maybe 3 days before that asshole is found. I left him in the normal type of situation.

Naked, bound, face down in the mud.

My calling card on his back and the initials L. M. carved in his chest. Asshole had been messing with his underage step daughter.

I had caught wind of it while sitting at the only bar in this no name fucking town. He had decided that little girl was his right as her guardian. I decided otherwise.

I wash my hair twice and make sure there is no blood left anywhere on my skin. I check behind my ears, around my knees and elbows. I bring my hands back to my face and can feel myself frowning at them. I watch my fingers trembling under the stream of water coming from the showerhead. They tremble but I am uncertain if it is from nerves, fear or disgust. Disgust with myself just as much as with the man whose existence I removed from this reality. I only leave the comfort of the shower when the hot water runs out.

Cold showers don't wash away the filth and shame that lines my soul. I never even bother to turn the cold water on at all actually. Wrapped in a towel, I walk back towards the sleazy ass bed then grab the remote. There is no way I am sleeping under these blankets tonight. I will probably already have to douse my stuff with god knows what because of bed bugs.

3

I roll my shoulders, skin still tight from the scalding hot water then recline to lean against the headboard while I turn the tv on. It only takes scanning 3 or 4 stations to find a local news broadcast. I watch until the last second, but there is no mention of the small town deputy. I feel a smile fall over my face as I turn the tv off to veg out staring through the window.

The neon lights flicker in the darkness around me, their bright colors casting a cheap seedy glow over the motel's sign. The letters are mismatched and broken, some missing entirely.

The buzzing of the broken bulbs on the sign outside the window reminds me that I am not at the Five Seasons. Not that I could have afforded the Five Seasons anyways. The humming of the lights remind me of the sound of my mother cutting my dad's hair in the kitchen when I was younger. I remember walking in and seeing him in a chair in the middle of the linoleum floor, smiling from ear to ear as my mother would give him his signature tapered haircut. I smile thinking of them, but then let the smile fall from my face. Those days are long gone.

A musty scent lingers in the air, the scent of stale cigarettes, old booze and unwashed sheets. I try to keep from inhaling too deeply so I don't lose my supper all over the floor.

No matter, I will be gone by morning and this shithole town will be left in my past. I have been running for months now. Never looking back but still constantly peering over my shoulder. Still, no matter how many pieces of shit I take out I am still no closer to Lane Masters than I was 3 fucking years ago.

I just need him to mess up. Just once. Then I can find out where the fuck he is hiding. I have already found the others. The names are written in the little notebook I keep in my pocket.

4

Brock Sanders, died in battle in 2022. Kevin Lang, is currently occupying a suite at a mental health facility in Georgia. That leaves two. Chad Weathers and Lane Masters.

Chad is going to be easy to find but possibly hard to get alone. And I know the minute he sees me, dye job or not he is going to recognize me. I must say though, I am looking forward to the look that will be on his face. Will it be fear? Regret? Shame?

I don't really care which it is, he will die all the same. I have decided it is his time. The time for his name to get crossed off the list. I have been slowly making my way to Montana since I found out his address. I never imagined scouring old message boards with active and retired soldiers would be such a gold mine. But they lead me right to him.

The thought of him begging for his life is exhilarating. I can hear him, pleading for forgiveness. Begging me not to hurt him. God, I hope he fights back. I feel the smile as it rolls over my face. It is going to be glorious. I don't even care that I sound psychotic. Does that make me more psychotic?

I finally fall asleep after changing into clean clothes and getting as comfortable as I can in this shit hole room. I lay on top of the blankets, barely even using a pillow. It feels like my skin is crawling the entire time.

I wake up to horns honking and a baby crying. I stretch out my shoulders before slumping back down onto myself. The sun is shining in through the window but it doesn't make me feel like it used to. When I was younger, it was almost like the sunshine was an energy source. Like it fed me or something in me at least. I would wake up and smile into the window before running to the beach with my board. Now when the sun is shining, all I can think about is who can see me, who is watching.

I check my phone but there are no messages. I never really expect there to be. Only mom has my number. No one else even knows I am alive. I was listed as a MIA over 2 years ago. I am a ghost now. A shadow. I stand up, stretching my overused muscles as best I can. Dude was hefty last night. I had to work a bit harder to get him to fall than I would normally like.

Fuck, I need some coffee.

But first I need to make sure that piece of shit from last night hasn't been reported yet, or worse found. I click the tv back on to watch the morning news. Nothing yet.

I throw the remote on the bed, reaching down to pick up my duffle. With any luck, I will be able to hitch a ride and be near Augusta within 5 or 6 hours. With a bit more luck, I will be able to rid this world of Chad Weathers tonight. Then I can be back on the road again by morning.

I opt to stop at a local diner to get some food and coffee before I start walking the highway. I need food for energy and I definitely need caffeine. I didn't sleep worth a shit last night. I was shifting all night from the invisible ants crawling under my skin. And when I did finally doze off, all I could see was the jungle. The woman was lying on top of me. Her skin splitting open. I shake my head, trying to get the memories to fade away, but they never do.

It doesn't help my lack of sleep that I refuse to let myself doze off when I am hitching from someone. Last thing I need is for someone to get the slip on me.

I slide into a booth at some hole in the wall diner called Sandy's. I reach across the wobbly table to grab a sticky menu. I let my eye scan it quickly as I hear a waitress approaching. It is all the standard grease trap offerings you see at every mom and pop restaurant.

"What can I get ya hun?" My eyes slide up to the face of a woman tragically begging to still be 18 when she is obviously in

6

her 60's. The blue eyeshadow, red lips, and big hair is a dead giveaway for the unsettling lifestyle she is clinging to. Her obviously dyed blonde hair is rocking this Flock of Seagulls look that is just fucking comical. Does she even look in a mirror before she goes out into public?

I give her a slight side smile, "Coffee, black. And pancakes. Thanks." She nods at me as she writes it all down then snaps her gum while walking away.

I can feel eyes on me. I know I am always being watched, whether there is anyone ever really there or not is the real question. I just "feel" like I am always being watched. There are only a handful of people here. And though none of them are actually paying attention to me, I still feel like I am being watched. Being judged.

I have felt that way since I crossed the border back into the states almost a year ago. I know that I don't know anyone here. I have never even been to Montana before. But the need to always look over my shoulder is strong. Just one run in with someone who thinks I am dead and this whole mission will be over. My revenge will fall flat. It keeps me more paranoid than I feel comfortable being. I honestly believe everyone should feel some sort of paranoia. Even if they aren't running from their past. There is nothing wrong with being a little jagged. Frayed edges never really scared me.

I dyed my hair black hoping between that and my now pale, sallow exterior that I would draw less attention. I have always done nothing but draw unwanted attention with my blonde hair and blue eyes. Skin always perfectly tan from the hours I would spend chasing waves back home. But now, I know I look alot older than 22. And I definitely don't resemble a Barbie anymore. Unless Mattel has come out with Scary Goth Barbie, I think I am safe. I pull my hood tighter around my head, reluctantly waiting for my coffee.

I stare out the window at a young mother and child. She is trying to wrangle the kid into a car seat. The little girl is kicking and screaming at her mother. I feel another grin come over my face as I think, "That's right kid. Fight back."

The smile instantly drops when I hear Lane's voice in my head saying the same words back to me. "*Fight me bitch.*" Now is not the time. I can not have a flashback right now.

I grip the sides of my head in my hands tightly but luckily enough the waitress picks that exact moment to come back, dropping off my order. I finish up as quickly as I can, dropping $20 on the table then leaving. I have a gut feeling that there is going to be a lot of walking today.

It starts raining about a half hour into my hike when some nice woman stops offering me a ride. She says she can take me as far as Great Falls.

I immediately flinch not wanting to be anywhere near a military town but it is a necessary evil I am going to have to deal with today. I thank her then stare out the window the entirety of the trip. She seems nice enough. She is content with carrying the entire conversation which makes the ride easier for me. I think I only say 5 words the entire drive.

She is going on and on about her son. How he is about to graduate from some university. Going to be some kind of new age hippy dippy farmer or something. I barely hear her words as I fake a smile and nod towards the windshield.

It takes about 3 hours but then I am free of the woman and her hippy dippy son. I am finally walking northwest up 15, that much closer to Augusta. I let all the wonderful things I am going to do to Chad roll around in my head.

I can't wait to hear him scream, watch him suffer. Remind him of what he did when he held me down for Lane to rape, stab, mangle then leave for dead. Remind him of the face he left laying in that ditch after he put a few rounds in my chest. I reach up, touching the circular scar on the left side of my chest. It doesn't hurt anymore except when I think about that night. Then it stings like it is just starting to heal.

I finally catch another ride, after I veer off towards Sun River. This time it is an older man in a pick up. I throw my duffle in the back then jump in bed of the truck myself. I smack the inside of the truck bed loudly to let him know I am in and he can go.

I actually let myself doze off for a bit then. No one within reaching distance of me. And I will definitely wake up if he stops the truck or starts to slow down.

Still though, I set an alarm on my watch for a half an hour just in case. Once again, there are no real dreams. Just memories. The old man slows down just outside of Augusta about 5 minutes after I wake up. I grab my bag, give him a short wave of thanks as I start to make my way in town.

I come across a bar about a block in. I look at my watch and huff – it's only 5 pm. Hopefully, I am here early enough. I am still holding out hope that I will be able to find him easily. There is only one truck out parked in front and it is definitely not the truck I have written down in my list. This one looks like it has seen much better days. I glance at it as I step up closer to the building, there is a license plate on the front reading, "Mustang in a Chevy body." I snicker at the plate, yeah....sure.

I slip through the front door of the old, dilapidated tavern. The outside has faded, chipped paint that looks like it has been flaking off for decades already. The inside isn't much better with grimy windows that barely allow a sliver of dim light to filter in.

The air inside is musty and stale. It smells like a disgusting combination of stale alcohol and unwashed bodies. I find a booth that allows me to see the front door easily but also have a good view of the surrounding area.

I throw my duffle in the seat then slide in touching the sticky table that is coated in a layer of grime and gristle. I quickly pull my hand back trying not to imagine what all has been done on this table.

An old man probably knocking on death's door yells across the bar to me, "What are ya drinking?"

I look up and notice I am the only other person here. I pull the hood down and give a half smile, "Whiskey, neat."

He nods his head geriatric forehead at me. I watch him as he pours the whiskey into my glass. He looks tired, with a faded bandana wrapped around his head keeping the length of his hair pulled back. He could win a Willie Nelson look alike competition hands down. He waves as he sits the glass down on the bar for me to come get. I do a quick glance, making sure there is actually no one else in the room, then move quickly to recover the drink and go back to my seat. I leave another $20 on the counter and glance up at him, "Keep the change."

He slides the money off the counter with a small smile as I turn back towards my seat, "Thanks a lot little missy."

I feel my shoulders tighten at the remark.

I keep walking to my seat reminding myself that he is not my target. He is not Chad. Even though his words make me want to punch him in the fucking throat, I contain my rage. He is from a different time. Hell, he probably meant it as a compliment and not the narcissistic snarl that I heard in my head.

I try to bottle the anger deep inside. Let it continue to build for Chad. I keep a close eye on my watch as people start to filter. I have already put my hood back up just in case. I sit here swirling the amber liquid around for over 2 hours before I hear a familiar voice,

"Come on boys. I am buying the first round."

I quickly look over without turning my head. My eyes follow the figure that just walked in the door and up to the bar. It is definitely Chad. He has lost some muscle though, which is only a blessing for me. Since he last saw me, I have gained about 35 lbs of nothing but muscle. I definitely don't have that little girl body he would remember.

I have cut my long blonde hair again into a shorter bob and dyed it black. I now have tattoos covering both arms and most of my thighs. From the reflection in any mirror, I look about as hard as they come anymore.

Honestly, most days I look like I have just walked out of a prison. Between the black clothes, dyed hair and sunken in face I am sure my own mother wouldn't even recognize me.

I continue to watch him as he carries his beer over to a pool table then starts a game with one of his friends. Some young looking chick walks up to him. She starts throwing herself at him, laughing at everything he says. It is disgusting. I sit here wondering if she would continue to throw her pussy at him if she knew what he really was? What lies beneath that fake smile and painted facade that screams down home good ole boy.

As I try not to throw up all over the table, I pull my phone out to check my notes again. He drives a blue Ford F150. License plate 5 498621. Single, lives alone about 3 miles north of town. I look back up at him and determine enough is enough. I grab my duffle as I silently slide out of the booth and make my way out the front door to find his truck.

I glance around the parking lot, making sure no one is watching. Just for precaution, I check out the front of the building. Quickly noting no cameras. I throw my duffle in the back of his pick up then stealthily climb in. I lay still and quiet in the bed of the truck for what feels like days. I did luck out that there was already shit back here so I just shimmy myself under some of the planks of wood to keep out of sight.

The sun has just started to go down when I feel somebody getting into the cab. He grunts and shuts the door, jostling me and all the crap he has back here.
Game on.
I smile to myself as I double check my thighs again to make sure my knives are still strapped on. I can feel my pistol still lodged down the back of my jeans. I am ready. I let a full teeth smile come over my face as I feel the truck roar to life then back out of the parking spot.
It really is only about a 5 minute trip to his house. I lay back here, waiting a solid 15 minutes more after hearing his front door slam before climbing out of the back. His house is nothing at all to write home about. Just a dilapidated single wide trailer on a small parcel of land. Albeit, beautiful land. The home itself has seen better days though. The siding is cracked, there is no underpinning left on the bitch, honestly it just screams that a creeper lives inside. I move slowly around the side of the trailer until I catch a glimpse of him through the window. He is sitting in a recliner watching tv with yet another beer in his hand.
He really hasn't changed too much besides the weight loss. He still has the stocky build, luckily though he is not much taller than me. I can see he now has a few USMC tattoos on his arms. I chuckle to myself, like he fucking deserves to have those. I should filet them off his skin.
The sun is already setting low on the horizon as I look around to see what kind of distraction I am going to have to cause to get him outside. There is no way I am trapping myself in a single wide with him. He may have lost some bulk but there is

no way in hell I am going to let him think he can contain me anywhere.

I move slowly around the front of a barely held together wooden porch then kick over a metal trash can. I run around it quickly to crouch in the shadows of the porch until he comes out to check the noise. I hear him stomping through the house then a screen door slamming.

"Fucking raccoons." His voice is just as I remember it. Dark and gravelly. He continues to grumble as he walks down the porch steps looking out into the yard for the culprits. He is facing me now as he leans down to pick up the trash can. He starts to stand to put the lid back on the can when he catches my movement.

I stand up at the same time as him.

He looks me up and down, no clue what kind of insanity is standing in front of him, "Who the fuck are you? What are you doing on my property?"

I feel that maniacal grin come over my face again as I pull my hood back then stare at him, tilting my head a bit to the left, "What? You didn't miss me, Weathers?"

The fear that punches through his face is fucking beautiful. I knew it was gonna feel this good. His eyes are blown wide like he is seeing a ghost. I see his hands start to tremble, like he suddenly can't keep them still. I can feel the lightning zipping through my veins as the adrenaline and vengeance starts to take hold.

He drops the trash can and starts to back up, hands spread out wide before him, "Carrie, what the fuck? I thought you were dead? They said you were gone. Missing."

I smile wider as I pull the gun from my back, "Oh, I am. I have been missing for years now. Dead too. Can't you tell?"

Chad is looking all around him but quickly realizes there is nowhere for him to go. No weapons for him to grab. I laugh out loud as I turn then point the gun at his head. He clenches his eyes shut like he is bracing for the bullet that is about to pierce his brain at any moment.

I shake my head at him. No, this won't do. I need him to be more scared, or at least grovel for his life or something. How am I supposed to enjoy this if he just gives in right away?

He hears the click of the safety as it slides back on then and only then does he slowly open his eyes to look towards me. I carefully replace the gun in the waist of my jeans then cross my arms across my chest, staring at him as I slightly tilt my head to the right. I see a sigh of relief roll over his body. I smile again because he thinks he is safe for the moment. Oh, how fucking wrong he is.

He still has his hands in the air, trembling with his eyes trained on me, "What do you want?"

I take a small step towards him, grinning maniacally again, "I just wanted to see what you were up to. Ya know, for old times sake."

His eyes continue to scan his immediate area but are landing on nothing of any help. His entire body seems to be trembling now. I smile as I watch him starting to crumble in front of me. I take another small step towards him, "What? You act like you haven't missed me at all, old buddy. After all that quality time we spent together down south."

Chad is shaking his head back and forth. The panic is starting to overtake his movements. His body is jerky like his muscles are screaming for him to run but his pride is telling him it is just a feeble fucking female in front of him. I grin again, "Use your fucking words, Weathers. I want to hear what you have to say."

I take another step towards him, now just barely out of his grasp. He looks down towards the ground quickly then back up to me, "I didn't want to do it Carrie. I did what I was told, what I was ordered."

I nod my head back at him. I know this all already. He was only following orders. I knew that was going to be the bullshit lie he tried to use on me. I look back up just in time to see his fist flying towards my face.

What a dick!

I quickly move to the right to miss his punch, just barely. It came close enough to my face that I can feel the wind of it as it sweeps by my cheek. I grab the knife from my right thigh holding it up at shoulder height, protecting my core with my other arm. If he wants to play, then we will play. Chad turns back around diving at me again. I quickly take the knife and plunge it into his side 3 times. Not anywhere that will kill him, but I bet it hurts like a bitch.

Chad grabs his side as he tries to stand back up to his full height. I watch him looking at the blood on his fingers and I smile again,

"What is that supposed to intimidate me? I wasn't scared of your slow ass 3 years ago. I am sure as hell not scared now."

He touches his left side again with his right hand seeing the blood that comes back on his fingers. Then his eyes are right back on me, crazed like I remember, "I am gonna fucking finish you off this time."

I laugh rolling my eyes as he lunges at me again. I quickly dodge him, "Yeah yeah, like I haven't heard that one before."

He recovers quickly coming at me again. I was anticipating that but not him lunging at my knees. His arms wrap around my thighs as he takes me down hard. The wind is knocked out of me. Before I can get my hand up he is on top of me punching me in the face.

After the first fist to my temple, I block him with one hand as I try to make the knife hit its mark again. He quickly

15

knocks it from my hand and tries to swing at me again. I grab his shirt pulling him closer as I head butt him in the nose.

I hear a crunch when I make contact with his face. I feel the blood as it pours out of his nose, coating my own. I can smell the copper tinge of his blood as it rains down on me. The smell is fucking nauseating. I feel like he is leaking his soul all over my skin and it fucking burns. He falls over to the side as I try to wipe his blood from my eyes before he comes back for another swing.

I can now feel the adrenaline coursing through my veins. It is like heroin, burning through my vessels trying to find a release. I quickly sit up, grabbing the pistol from my waistband again. I train the aim right between his eyes.

His hands shoot up in front of him again, "Please Carrie please. I am sorry. I was just following orders. I didn't want to but he made me. You can't just kill me out here like this. I have lived with it every day since that night."

I laugh out loud again as I roll my shoulders then click the safety off. "You mean you didn't want to when you were laughing at me? When you and Lang jumped me then knocked me out? Or maybe it was just when Lang stripped me down? No, I bet you are meaning when you were telling Masters to fuck me harder?

"That's what you were made to do? Or are you talking about after, when he had finished carving me up? When you dumped my body in that ditch to die. When you fucking put two rounds through me. Is that what he made you do?"

I crack my neck in both directions quickly as I do another once over on him, "Plus, what exactly did you have to live with every day? Did you have to spend months learning how to be a human again? Were you left for dead with no one and nothing? No. That was me, Weathers."

Chad has tears running down his face but I don't believe them for a second. He isn't remorseful, his fucking nose is broken. That is the only way this piece of shit would ever cry. He can't feel real human emotions. He doesn't even know what empathy is.

His eyes blow wide as I take a step closer. I can feel the psychotic smile cover my face as I stare from the pistol to his head. I can see the flashes of the memory of his smile in my head as he pinned me to that metal table. I take the silencer out of my back pocket and screw it onto the barrel, "Just lay there and take it like a good little bitch."

One shot to the forehead is all it takes. I watch the spark leave his eyes. I watch him piss himself. I watch the shock and horror as they litter his expression. Now etched onto his face for all time. The bullet hole has a small trickle of blood rolling from it as his body slumps down to his knees then face plants into the dirt before me. I smile again as I put the safety back on, unscrew the silencer then slide the gun back into my waistband.

I reach down for the knife on my thigh, quickly realizing it isn't there. I search the ground near me but I can't see it. I try to take a deep breath and realize that it is getting more painful to breathe.

One glance down shows me that in our scuffle, he has grabbed my knife and shoved it into my side. Just between two of my lower ribs.

Motherfucker.

I lean over his body, screaming down at his corpse, "You stabbed me with my own fucking knife? What the hell man?" I kick him hard in the side but he has no reaction. I kick him again for good measure, "Fucking dick!"

I leave the knife in my side so I don't bleed out in his driveway. I use my foot to roll him over onto his back. His dead eyes stare past me towards the starlit sky above us. I use my other knife to cut his shirt open and flay it out. I quickly carve the initials L. M. on his chest. I roll him over and pull up his shirt to carve my calling card into his back.

I run the blade through his skin, watching the small lines of blood form as I etch the red brocket deer head into his back. I continue to huff into the night as I shape the large sun behind the deer then mark the wavy lines coming from it. It isn't perfect but it is close the fuck enough. I take my time trying to stand back up. My side radiating a sharp pain into my ribs.

Only one more to go before my list is complete.

I put my knife back in my leg holster as I stumble over to his truck. I reach in painfully, grabbing my duffle then slowly walk towards the road. I turn left to head further away from town not looking back at the massacre I am leaving behind.

I have to try to find an abandoned barn or something. Somewhere to hole up and tend to my wound. There is blood seeping out from around the knife. The wound itself is smooth, showing he had just slid it right in there with no hesitation.

But the air around me is starting to smell metallic, like the wound is emitting the odor of copper and rust. Bitterness is all I can taste.

I should just be thankful it is not a deep wound but the blood loss is starting to make me worry. Every step I take I can feel myself becoming weaker. Doesn't help that I probably have a concussion from the headbutt present I gave him. I have to get the knife out then somehow cauterize the wound. Maybe I will luck out and it will just clot itself. I know that no major organs were hit but the dying out adrenaline mixed with pain is making me extremely weak and tired.

I follow a wooden fence line towards what looks like an old barn or something. My breathing is getting rougher. I see a farmhouse up on the left with no lights on but I am sure there is no way that I can make it all the way there. Also, I am a bit worried that I still haven't felt any pain from the knife wound itself. Just the radiating pain of its surroundings.

I stumble as I feel myself starting to roll down a small hill. Great, here I am laying in a ditch again, probably about to die. I lay on my stomach and do a quick ground shuffle out of the ditch so that I can lean up against a fence post. At least if I am going to die, it isn't going to be in a fucking ditch. The last thing I remember is pulling the knife out of my side, then the world goes dark.

2

James

I Found – Amber Run with Freya Ridings

The last thing I feel like doing today is checking the fucking fenceline. But if another goddamn horse gets out I am going to lose my shit. These mares get spooked by anything it seems. This last one probably saw a leaf fall from a tree and booked ass over the fence.

Chad has already called me once this week to let me know one of my mare's was in his front yard. That is all I need is to lose out on a paycheck because a pregnant mare died somewhere. It luckily didn't take much to coax her back onto my property but this shit is getting old.

I step out onto the porch to take in the view. The only good thing about this place is the view. Though, the memories of growing up here still haunt every corner and shadow. Granted, it is a lot better than the view I was accustomed to for 4 years overseas. If I never see another desert it will still be too soon. I pull my arms across my chest one at a time, stretching out my shoulders and biceps. I quickly crack my neck as I stretch my shoulders out. I let out a heavy sigh as my clenched fists fall to my sides.

I let my eyes roam over the driveway then across the fields towards Chad's house. I don't see any horses running wild which is a good sign but I am still going to ride the fenceline to make sure nothing is broken and there are no fresh hoof marks in the dirt. I catch a glimpse of Chad's broken down trailer as I sigh then roll my shoulders forward. I have always been envious of the stories Chad would tell. His biggest assignment had been

20

in South America so it was all jungles and tequila. While mine had been IEDs and warm beer.

One good thing about Chad though, he never asks me about my real time overseas and I never ask him about his. We all have our history, our stories. But neither of us want to hear the others. Only once did he get drunk enough to start to touch on the subject of his time in the jungle. Thankfully though, he pulled himself together and shut that shit down. I have enough demons of my own, I don't need his living rent free in my head as well.

I stretch out to my full 6' 3" letting my muscles try to wake up. I really should have made some coffee. But hopefully this won't take long at all and I will be back home, in the comfort of my solitude.

Not out looking for a fucking runaway horse all god damned day again. I trudge around the front of the house then out to the barn to fire up the four wheeler. I quickly maneuver the ATV towards the back of the property. I will work my way from back to front, that way when it is over it is a straight shot back inside.

I hate being outside anymore. I hate that anyone can see me at any time. I guess after knowing that snipers are trained on you at any given moment, being well seen is more of a fear than it used to be. I know all that is behind me. I know that there is no one hunting me now. But it is still a deep seeded fear that I try to keep hidden from the world. Hell, I even try to hide it from myself.

I catch myself at all times of day and night, tracing the horizon with my gaze. I know there is no one out there with a mark trained on me. I know those days are behind me. But that doesn't keep me from scanning for hide sites or checking the trees for a cuckoo.

21

I make my way across the back forty then head west, back towards the road. Luckily, none of the fence is broken and I haven't seen any fresh trail marks. The creek has a nice little gurgle going to it today though. Must be from all the rain we got yesterday.

I continue to scan the horizon when my eyes fall across something leaned up against a fencepost. Fuck! Did something kill one of my horses?

I stand up on the ATV, placing a knee on the seat as I accelerate quickly towards the black mass huddled on the ground. The moment I see two legs splayed out in front of it, I start to panic.

Someone jumped the fence and passed out on my property? What the hell?

I turn the ATV off and saunter towards the person, giving the dude a light tap on the boot with my own, "Hey Buddy? This isn't a Holiday Inn. You need to get movin'."

I watch his leg twitch from the movement of me tapping his foot but other than that there is nothing. Not a sound, not even a breath. I step around in front of the guy and see the red puddle beside him. It isn't a huge amount but the color of it against the yellowing grass at the edge of the field shows me enough blood has been lost to account for this guy being passed out. Fuck me.

"Hey man, are you alive?" I quickly check for a pulse on his wrist. I pray to whatever god might be listening that there is at least a pulse. And it is there but it is faint. His hands look small but that isn't what catches my attention. They are completely coated in dried blood. The dark crimson is stark against his extremely pale skin.

His knuckles also look busted open on one hand. This dude's breathing is pretty labored as well. I can't see his face but I

22

can only assume that it is messed up as well. His build looks alot smaller than me so I reach down and pick him up.

As his head falls back, the hood of his jacket falls off and I see the face of a broken porcelain doll. Her skin is so pale it makes her look like Snow White. So pale you can trace the veins in her neck with your eyes. She has some green forming around her right eye like she has been hit hard in the temple.

Her bottom lip is busted as well leaving a small smear of blood down her chin. Her hair is short and pitch black, obviously a box job since there are light roots starting to show. Her eyelashes are long, lying across her cheeks like blankets.

She is fucking covered in dried mud too. Like she had rolled around in it or something before passing out against my fence. I glance around the post she had passed out against. I can see where it looks like she dragged herself out of the small ditch that leads to the creek. What in the actual fuck happened here?

I quickly carry her over and lay her gently across the back of the ATV rack. Panic hits me quick. What do I do? She is wearing all black. She has a knife strapped to her fucking leg. She obviously is not wanting to be found. She looks like she has had the hell beat out of her and there is a puddle of blood next to my fence. Seriously, what the fuck do I do?

I turn around running back to grab her duffle, thinking maybe there will be some kind of ID inside. Under the bag, lays another knife and a pistol. I look from the ground back towards the lifeless body draped across my four wheeler.

What in the hell is happening right now? I feel like I am stuck in an old episode of the Twilight Zone. This kind of shit just doesn't happen in real life. Especially not out here in the middle of fucking nowhere.

I quickly open the duffle and stuff her shit inside then sling it over my shoulder as I jump back on the four wheeler. I have one hand on her abdomen to hold her in place while the other is on a handle steering the ATV back towards the house. I try to avoid holes and bumps so she doesn't fly off the back, getting anymore injured than she already is. I pull the ATV right up to the back porch steps. I nervously slide off after grabbing the key out of the ignition.

I carefully lift her off the back of the four wheeler, trying not to jostle her as best I can. I have her duffle bag full of fun in one hand and her cradled bridal style in my arms. I sweep her in the back door, throwing her bag on the floor by the sliding doors. Quickly, I turn the corner into the dining room to lay her out on the table there. I unzip then pull her hoodie off of her. Her skin is so white it is almost clear.

Does this chick ever go outside?

I start looking her over for wounds. There has to be a reason why she is out cold. I check her neck, nothing. I check her head, even though she is covered in blood there is nothing other than that black eye and a busted lip. I pull the bottom of her tank top up to see there is a knife wound on her side.

I look from the wound back up to her resting face, "Fuck. What happened to you honey?"

I run into the office off to the side of the dining room to grab my old medical kit. I quickly start to clean her wounds, praying that there isn't anything worse going on inside that I can't take care of. I clean and stitch her up, barely taking a full breath the entire time. After she is completely made whole, I do another once over on her to make sure there aren't any other bloody wounds that need tended to.

I look around the table. I breathe heavily seeing there is now blood and debris everywhere. I sit back in the chair, trying to figure out what I am going to say to her when she wakes up. 'Hey ma'am sorry but you're bleeding all over my dining room table, kindly leave.'

Quickly, I realize I am in over my head. Just sitting here staring at a lifeless body laying on my table. I take a deep breath as I hear a knocking at the door.

I stand up feeling fear gripping my throat. I check myself to make sure that I don't have blood all over me, then slide the pocket doors shut to the dining room as I turn to head to the front door.

I pull the wooden door open then push the screen door out while I shield my eyes from the light, "What's going on today Bob?"

Why the fuck is the sheriff on my front porch?

I look behind him, seeing his car going with lights blaring. I look down the road a bit then see lights going wild over at Chad's house as well. A ricocheting fear starts flying through my chest.

Bob lets out a heavy sigh as he turns to look the same direction as me, "Well, shit James. Looks like someone went and killed Chad Weathers last night. Whoever did this got him good. His nose was broken, he'd been stabbed. Then they shot him right in between his fucking eyes. They even carved him up. There were some initials on his chest and some kind of animal carved into his back. Have you seen anyone or heard anything this morning?"

I don't know why but I shake my head back at him, "No, sure haven't Bob. I even rode the fence line this morning. Didn't see a thing."

Bob nods his head back at me as I feel sweat starting to run down the crack of my ass. What the hell am I doing? This chick most likely murdered my fucking neighbor last night and I am going to let her just lay on my dining room table?

I let out a sigh as I look back towards Bob. He tilts his hat towards me, "Well, if you see anything or hear anything, you know where to find me."

I smile back at him as he makes his way back down the porch and into his patrol car. I look back over at Chad's then quickly move back inside. I shut then lock the door behind me, finally able to let out an anxious breath.

I have to find out what the hell happened last night. I have to know if this girl has something to do with Chad's murder. And if so, why?

I roll my shoulders as I walk back towards the dining room. The stress riddling my body is starting to make all my muscles tight, like they need to react at a moment's notice. I haven't felt that level of tension in years. I slowly pull the pocket doors open to see an empty dining room table.

I look towards the door but her jacket and bag are gone. I turn, looking out into the backyard but I don't see anything suspicious. The atv is still here and the barn door is still shut from this morning. My eyes sweep the perimeter for any type of movement but there is nothing. She can't be outside, she wouldn't have made it very far. I would still be able to see her hobbling through the field if she took off that way.

I look across the table towards the living room then slowly start to make my way towards the doorway. I quickly clear the confines of the room with my peripheral then duck my head back into the dining room. I reach over and grab one of my mother's brass candlestick holders off the mantle just in case. I would really hate to break the candlestick holder but I don't know how crazy this chick is. Also, I know she has a gun because I was the one to put it back in her bag. The bag that is now missing along with her. I silently kick my own ass over that one.

I make my way into the living room, slowly moving past the couch. I look to the left of the stairs to see the bathroom door open and two boots sticking out. I put the candlestick holder down on a side table and slowly move forward.

She is slumped over on the floor, leaning up against the vanity. Her breathing has become a bit heavier than before as well. I stop about 3 feet away as her eyes come up to meet mine.

Her eyes are the clearest shade of blue I have ever seen. They are almost white. I lean against the window sill, letting out a long breath, "So....you new around here?"

She flips me off as she tries to lean forward, unsuccessfully. I take a step forward and she instantly pulls a pistol out from behind her. She points it straight at my head. There is zero expression on her face. She isn't even grimacing at the pain I know has to be riddling her body right now.

I put my hands up as I take a deep breath, "Is that the same gun you killed Chad with?" She doesn't even flinch. She is not surprised that I know or that I am questioning her. She looks exhausted and her arm is wavering like it is taking all of her strength just to hold it up.

"Weathers had it coming." Her voice is barely more than a whisper. It flows over me as I look her up and down again. Her breathing is still shaky at best but I think all in all she will be alright. Then a thought hits me. The way she had said his name.

Weathers? Why the fuck was she calling him by his last name? I let my eyes roam her mud covered arms for a moment as I realize this chick is covered in ink. I had been so focused on her not dying on my dining room table, I didn't even notice the tattoos until now. Granted, most of the work looks shotty but still, it's ink. I have seen worse. Full sleeves and even one on her neck. On her right bicep, I can see what looks like a skull with a combat helmet on. The realization hits me like a mack truck.

I take another calming breath, as I tilt my chin towards her bicep, "What branch?"

She lets out a sigh as she drops the gun to her lap, "What are you talking about?" Her voice is just as broken as her movements. She sounds like she is even annoyed with just

27

questions. But excuse me honey you passed out on my property and my neighbor is dead. I think I have the right to ask a few questions.

I take another step forward before squatting down in front of her, "You are covered in tattoos, you are barely able to move but still trying to keep a gun trained on my forehead. You have two knives strapped to your legs and your boots are laced pretty fucking perfectly. You even have your pants tucked into them. You look like the poster child for an Army commercial."

She gives me a slight side smile and with a ragged breath sighs out, "Marines."

What the fuck?

She must not be from around here then. I know everyone that has served from this area. Hell, I spent most of my training with them. I cross my arms in front of me again, "How did you know Chad?"

She slides the gun down to the ground and lets it rest there, taking her hand and wrapping it around her side. She takes in a deep rattly breath, still never even wincing, "I had the displeasure of serving with him."

I tilt my head to the side a bit, "Special Ops?"

She blinks hard, still staring at her boots, "Once upon a time."

I nod my head back at her, scared for the answer that I am about to receive, "Did you kill him?"

She looks back up at me with those piercing eyes again, "Like I said, he had it coming."

I nod at her again. I don't know what the fuck is going on but I don't feel like she is here for me. I let out a heavy sigh, "Are you going to try to kill me?"

She doesn't hesitate or even blink, "Were you in my regiment?"

I give her a soft smile, "No, I definitely was not. Pretty sure I would remember you."

She gives me a thumbs up back with a sarcastic smile, "Then you're safe."

I let out a held breath into the space between us. I squat back down in front of her again, "I don't know what is going on but I don't think you killed him just for shits and giggles. Obviously, you feel like your reasons were warranted. Am I right?"

She looks past me out into the living room, "They were definitely warranted."

I give her another small nod, feeling a bit naive but for some reason I believe her, "Okay then. How about I help you get up and we get you into some clean clothes and laid down for a bit, huh?"

She looks back over me again, her eyes scanning me for some unknown evil, "How do I know you won't try to kill me as soon as I am asleep?"

I stand back up reaching a hand down to her, "Well considering I was a field medic, I spent my time saving lives, not taking them. Plus, I don't want to have to replace the flooring for the blood so...."

She gives me a small chuckle which seems like a rarity, then takes my hand. I help her up then lean her against the wall next to me. I reach down to grab her jacket, duffle and gun. I stuff it all back into her bag then turn to pick her up.

Her hands come down on my chest as her eye's blow wide, "What the fuck do you think you are doing?"

I give her another soft smile, "I am picking you up and carrying you up the stairs. I don't really want to stand here and watch you suffer while taking 5 hours to make it up there. Okay?"

29

She lets out another heavy breath as she lays her head back on the wall. She closes her eyes like she is debating something within her own mind, but then slides her arm over my shoulders, behind my neck. I lift her up like she is nothing. She is easily around 150 pounds but I swear to god it is pure fucking muscle. This chick must hit the gym daily.

I move her upstairs then into the spare bedroom right across from mine. It is the only other room close to the bathroom. When my mother passed, I didn't even bother to redecorate so it is covered in powder blues and doilies.

I have a feeling this chick is going to love it. I smile to myself as I sit her down on the bed then sit her duffle on the floor next to her.

I give her another once over, noting she is still covered in mud and god knows what else, "Do you want to take a shower? Get cleaned up?"

She looks down at herself then nods. I stand up to go get her a towel when I hear her ask, "Why are you doing this for me?"

I slowly turn back around, pinned under the gaze of those clear eyes again, "Because it seems like whatever went down between you and Chad was something that is A, none of my business and B, probably deserved. I have been on the receiving end of some bullshit before and honey, you are covered in it."

She nods her head back at me, training her eyes back on the floor in front of her as I turn to go get her a towel. I come back into the bedroom to see her still trying to get her first boot off.

I toss the towel on the bed beside her, "Do you need some help?"

I squat in front of her and reach for her boot but she quickly recoils from me, "No, I got this."

30

I stand back up, watching her attempt to bring her knee up again but can tell her side is killing her.

"Oh for fucks sake, just let me help you." I reach down, taking her foot in my hands, quickly unlacing the boot then pulling it off. Jesus, even her socks are black.

She reaches up and smacks my hand away, knocking the boot to the floor. My eyes lock with hers again as her lips curl up on her face, "I don't need your fucking help."

I smile down at her as she tries to lift the other leg. I again quickly reach out and grab her foot. But instead of letting me unlace it, she rears back and kicks me right in the gut.

I fall back hard onto my ass, "What the hell was that for?"

She reaches down with one hand and starts to pull the laces free, "I said I didn't need your goddamn help. The last thing I want is some man trying to fucking undress me."

Her words cut through me. Now I am really starting to wonder about her and Chad. I let out a breath then stand back up, "Don't flatter yourself honey, you're not my type. I like my girls with a conscience."

She pulls the boot off dropping it to the floor before looking back up at me, "I guess I really don't have anything to worry about then do I?" Her expression remains completely emotionless. She tries to stand up but is still shaky. I reach out to help her but she recoils again.

I let out another breath, looking up at the ceiling then back down into her face, "Okay, let's get one thing clear here. I am only trying to help you get cleaned up so you can rest and get the hell out of my house. I am not trying to fuck you or anything okay? I am just trying to help speed up this process a bit."

Her eyes search mine for what feels like forever when I see her subtly nod her head at me. I feel like her accepting help is another one of those rarities, just like her smile. I nod back then reach down to pull her socks off. She braces herself on my arm as she stands up and starts to unzip her pants with one hand. I look at her left hand to see that her pinky finger is jutting out to the side. Opposite of the side it should be.

I quickly reach out, taking her hand in mine, "Jesus fuck, why didn't you tell me your finger was dislocated?"

She looks down at it then back up at me without even batting an eye, "I was just gonna fix it in the shower."

I look from her finger to her face then reach over and grab the towel, "Bite down on this."

She opens her mouth, biting down hard on the towel as I yank the finger back into its normal spot. She doesn't even make a sound. She just stares at my face the entire time, never even blinking.

I reach down to unbutton her pants and finish sliding the zipper down. She throws the towel back down on the bed then stares past me like nothing has happened. The baggy jeans fall from her slim waist into a heap on the floor. I see she has a few more tattoos on her thighs.

And who would have guessed, black underwear.

I grab the hem of her shirt as her eyes shut completely then she raises her arms to the ceiling. She isn't wearing a bra. I quickly point my eyes away from her chest and grab the towel for her. Seeing just the hint of a few scars on her chest as I avert my eyes.

I motion towards the bedroom door, "The shower is just out in the hall to the left." She takes the towel from me covering her chest with it as she turns to walk towards the door.

Her back is covered in scars. It looks like she has been whipped at some point. Underneath the clutter of marks though, there is something deeper. It looks like some kind of animal etched into her skin. But it is too hard to tell through all the

32

scarring on top to see what it actually is. The scars are dark and raised, crisscrossing her skin in long, jagged lines. They seem to serve as some sort of painful reminder of a past she doesn't seem very willing to share with me. Hell probably not with anybody.

She rounds the corner into the bathroom, leaving the door open. I quickly cross the room into the hallway then step up beside her in front of the vanity. I reach into the shower, past her to turn the water on. She takes a small step to her right, "No need to turn the cold on. Just let the hot run through."

I slowly look up at her then back at the spigot, laughing into the tub, "Okay, but it's your funeral."

I step back watching her step out of her boy shorts then into the shower. She pulls the curtain closed and I am left standing here trying to figure out what the fuck is going on. I pick up her underwear then go into her room to grab her other clothes.

I throw them all in a chair by the door then stand in the doorway of the bathroom while steam pours out from every single angle of the shower curtain. I lean into the doorframe and I can hear her breathing heavily. I listen to her pick up a bottle then set it down. I am trying to keep my eyes trained on the floor and not her silhouette that is shadowed behind the thin white curtain separating us.

Something really messed up has happened here. She is covered in blood, way more blood than just hers. I am already figuring out in my head that she most likely broke Chads' nose. That has to be where the majority of the blood came from. So basically, she was beaten then stabbed last night. And she still came out the victor. But for the life of me, I cannot figure out why or how.

I look back towards the curtain, seeing her shadow. She is just a little thing. Though I can tell the black hair, oversized black clothes, they are all a facade. She is hiding more than what

33

went down last night. She is lost. You can see it in her eyes. The thousand yard stare. I have seen it before. Hell, I have felt it before.

There is just something more about her. I feel like I am supposed to help her. I don't normally take in strangers bleeding to death but I immediately knew I had to jump into action this morning. It honestly felt like someone tapping me on the shoulder saying, 'Hey, do this or you will regret it for the rest of your life.' I let out another sigh as I look back into the shower curtain.

"Are you okay in there?" I know I am hovering, but I really don't want her to pass out in the shower and drown or something.

I hear her weakly from behind the curtain, "Yeah I am good. Almost done."

I step back out into the hall with my back to the door as I hear the water turn off. I keep looking down the hallway towards the stairs, hoping she doesn't shank me with my back turned to her like this. I hear her step out of the shower then shuffle around a bit. I turn around when I hear her step towards me.

This girl is fucking stunning. I was right about her hair, it is easier to tell now that it is a horrible box job. Her skin is almost glowing, it is so pink. She had literally not turned the cold on at all. She is covered in bruises but just the shape of her face, her stance, she is beyond beautiful. But more than that, she is familiar. I just don't know why. I move back a step to let her walk in front of me and back into the bedroom.

I pick up her bag, motioning to it with my free hand, "Do you want me to get something out of here for you to wear?"

She nods towards the bag in my hand, "There should be another pair of underwear in there. Maybe a clean shirt."

34

I shake my head, doubting there is actually anything clean inside but open the bag anyway. I pull out a pair of what seems like cleanish underwear then quickly note that the only other clothing in the duffle is definitely dirty.

I hand her the underwear, "Here, take these. I will go get you a tshirt and some shorts to wear."

She snickers at me. I quickly look down at her face, "What?"

She smiles again pointing towards my chest, "Do you really think I can fit into any of your clothes? They are just gonna fucking fall off of me."

I look down at myself then back at her. She isn't wrong. I shrug my shoulders, "At least I can get you a tshirt. That should work long enough for me to wash your clothes."

The smile falls from her face again, the hard shell exterior coming back over her, "I didn't ask for you to wash my clothes. You don't have to do that."

I huff as I roll my eyes and turn to walk from the room, "I know you didn't ask, I offered. Get dried off." This chick is so fucking broken. She acts all tough and shit but I can see the cracks in the exterior. She is barely holding it all together, whether she realizes it or not.

I walk across the hall grabbing her an old t-shirt. I even make sure to grab a black one. It's an old Nirvana shirt, she will probably be comfortable in that at least.

I walk back into her room as she has her clean underwear on and her back turned towards me. With her skin clean now, I can definitely see some kind of symbol has been carved into her back, but she also has a couple bullet and knife wounds as well.

I look at her eyes as she turns back around towards me. She is covering her chest with her arms, "Don't fucking pity me."

I shake my head at her, "I don't."

35

She reaches over grabbing the shirt from my hands before turning back around, "Don't fucking lie to me either."

I continue to shake my head as she pulls the shirt over her head, "I wasn't."

The shirt drapes down her body to her mid thigh. I walk around her then pull the blankets back on the bed for her to lay down. With a heavy sigh, she lays down onto a pillow so I can cover her up.

I grab her clothes and wet towel then head back towards the door. Still completely unable to wrap my head around the past few hours. I hear her let out a small sigh, "Hey, you got a name?"

I turn around from the doorway, staring her back down, "Yeah. Had it since birth."

She flips me off again but smiles this time while she does it, "What is it then?"

I smile back at her with my hand on the doorframe, "James. My name is James. And you?"

The smile falls from her face as the shadows start to fall back across her exterior, "Maeve. Just call me Maeve."

I give her a quick nod, accepting this small token of whatever it is she is offering, "Well, Maeve, get some rest. I will come check on you in a few hours."

Before she can argue, I quickly shut the door then head down the stairs.

3

Maeve

Ghost Town - Layto, Neoni

I will not lie, it is glorious to sleep in a bed that isn't lumpy or infested with god knows what. I can feel the crisp clean sheets covering my body. The pillows are soft and don't smell like cheap cologne or shame. I don't even want to open my eyes afraid it will all disappear if I do. I sink my head further into the pillow just trying to hold onto this dream a bit longer. I wake up almost forgetting about where I am. I take one look around the room though and quickly remember that I am in that old farmhouse.

James had brought me here apparently after finding me passed out against his fence this morning. I turn my head to look out the window. The sun is still pretty high in the sky so I assume it is probably mid afternoon at this point.

I reluctantly push the blankets off me. I take a deep breath before I attempt to swing my legs around. I instantly feel a sharp intake of breath as my muscles stretch around my injuries. Pain starts to radiate from my side. I wince as I look down, pulling up the side of my shirt to see James' handiwork on my side. It is a pretty clean fucking stitch. I am grateful for that at least. Hopefully it will help keep it from getting infected. I don't really care about the scar it will leave. I have millions of those anyways.

Jesus, I'm sore. I clench my teeth as I try to roll my shoulders and stretch my legs but every single muscle in my body feels like it has been put on a speed cycle in a washing machine.

I still can't believe I let Weathers get the fucking drop on me. I feel my side then test my lungs by trying to take another

37

deep breath. At least the stabbing pain is starting to fade, I may have lucked out and there isn't any serious damage internally.

I stand looking around the room a little closer. There is little old lady knick knacks fucking everywhere. Why in the hell does everything smell like baby powder? Is that a doily covering the entire top of the dresser? Where the hell am I?

I wonder whose room this had been before I arrived. Hopefully, I am not putting some poor grandma on the couch because I took over her space.

I open the dresser drawers but they all seem to be empty. Well, at least that makes me feel a bit better. No one actually lives in this room. James just doesn't know how to decorate like a grown ass man.

I smile thinking of the different levels of shit I can give him about that. I promptly let the smile drop from my face. I am not going to get comfortable, I am not going to get attached. I am out of here first thing. I still have work to do. I hate that I even let him get through my first wall of defenses. But there is something just grossly trusting coming from him. The way he averted his eyes when I stripped to shower. The softness of his tone when he was talking about my wounds and how I should be taking it easy. It was somehow comforting but he is still just a man. And I don't trust men. Ever.

He just seems like, I don't know, empathetic? Maybe it is just my mind playing tricks on me though. I have yet to meet a good man besides my father. I am sure he has his flaws, though I have never seen them. But all men are flawed, somehow.

I walk across the room, half expecting the door to be locked and me to be trapped in here. I let out a slow breath as I test then turn the doorknob slowly, pulling the door open.

The hallway is empty, nothing but a long rug running down the hall as a way of decoration. I take a small step towards the open door across the hallway from me. I peek my head around the corner fully expecting to see James standing there but the room is empty.

His room actually looks like someone from our age group lives in it. Greys and dark blues covering the walls and bed. Mahogany furniture scattered around the room. I back out slowly moving down the hallway towards the stairs.

There are two more doors but they are closed. I walk by them, leaving them shut. I don't want to seem intrusive or nosy. I instead make my way down the creaky old stairs to the empty living room. I can see out the window and down the dusty drive. There are no cars out front. Just brown fields as far as I can see.

I explore a bit further into the home. I vaguely remember the dining room. The table I had rolled myself off of then shuffled on my hands and knees to the bathroom by the stairs. The table is cleaned off again. There is a door off to the left that seems to lead to some type of office or maybe a small library.

To the right is a set of pocket doors that are pulled completely open. I cautiously step through seeing a very dated but comfortable kitchen. He has one of the old formica tables with the matching red chairs. If I had to describe the vibe, it would be country chic. I smile to myself as I look around the kitchen, his wife or girlfriend must have done the decorating. I don't see any man our age choosing willingly to have antique looking but still new appliances. The room's theme seems to begin and end with the table and chairs.

I smile around the room again, feeling something else settling into my gut. Is he married? I have seen touches of woman's decorations here and there but not an actual human person. I would have thought he would have said something if there was a wife waiting to murder me when I woke up. Why am I even worried about it? It's not like I am in any shape for a relationship.

I look out the screen door seeing a huge barn behind the house with the doors standing wide open. It seems familiar to me but I know I have never been here before. To the left of the barn is a pasture with horses running through the breeze.

This place is peaceful. It is hard to think about all the things going wrong in the world while watching those horses carelessly running around. I let a smile hint onto my face as I step out the screen door onto the back porch.

The breeze is gentle, causing the tall grass and wildflowers to sway in perfect unison. Beyond the pasture, the wide open plains create a waving sea of green and gold until it meets the blue sky that stretches endlessly above. The smell of freshly cut hay mixed with hints of pine and cedar is intoxicating. The air has a crisp and clean scent to it, like it has been filtered through a mountain spring.

I can feel that same breeze brushing against my skin, bringing a slight tingling sensation as it lifts a strand of my hair and caresses my neck. The breeze itself is warm as it dances over my skin, making goosebumps raise in its wake.

I can see myself in a place like this someday. If I ever find a way to settle down in one place at least. Instead, I just stand here watching the horses when out of my peripheral, I see James walking towards the porch from the barn.

I instantly put my guard back up. It is just a natural reaction when I am approached by anyone. It doesn't even have to just be a man in general. He casually steps up beside me on the steps, turning to look at the beautiful beasts as well, "How are you feeling?"

His voice is gruff and deep, like he has been working out or something. I turn to look at him, seeing the sweat running down his temple from the band of his backwards baseball hat. I watch that one bead of sweat, trying to figure out why everything about him is so damn intriguing. As I feel myself relaxing a bit, I give him a soft smile, "Much better. Rested."

He nods while turning to look back at the pasture. I clear my throat lightly, "I will get changed and get out of your space. But thank you for helping me, letting me rest."

James turns his head back towards me briefly then looks back across the field again, "You don't have to run off right away. You are still healing. At least stay for dinner, get a good night's sleep. Then if you still want to leave in the morning, I can take you wherever you wanna go."

My guard instantly goes right back up again. People are never nice for no reason. Men are especially not nice for no reason. I notice my muscles all tighten like they are getting ready to take flight and get me out of danger. I take a step backwards, fully intent on running, "No, I appreciate it but no. I don't want to intrude any longer. I will feel better just getting my things and leaving."

James lets out a small sigh as I see his shoulders fall just a bit then turns back towards me, "Well, at least let me get you fed first. When was the last time you ate?"

I glance over his shoulder towards the barn, closing one eye while thinking back, "Yesterday morning I think, before I left Jordan."

James' eyes go wide, "You came all the way from Jordan yesterday? How the hell did you get here? Do you have a car somewhere you need me to go get for ya?"

I don't like the questions. He already knows too much, even though he knows nothing at all. I shake my head, "No, I hitched the whole way."

He nods his head as he looks down towards the steps, "Your clothes are clean and folded on the couch. If you want to leave, I won't stop you. But I do hope you decide to stay a bit longer. You need rest. Plus, I am afraid you just walking out of here won't look good. There are still a lot of cops over at Chad's place."

My eyes fly to him as fear clenches my heart, "What do they know?"

James lets his shoulders shrug, "Nothing as far as I can tell. They don't seem to have any leads at all. Chad wasn't really liked that much so I am guessing they figured it just happened sooner rather than later."

I smile to myself when he says that. He has no idea the things Weathers was capable of. But I know, first hand. I look back out at the horses, "They are beautiful. They seem so happy, free."

I can feel his eyes on me. I turn back to see two golden orbs staring back at me. How had I not noticed his eyes are a shining amber color? His skin, bronzed from the sun.

I could only assume his hair is dark to match his eyebrows, I haven't seen him without a hat on yet. James is handsome, though that isn't something I am looking for. I don't know if it is something I will ever be looking for.

You can tell by just looking at him that he takes care of himself. Every bit of 6 foot tall, he is stocky. He is honestly built like a brick wall. He probably keeps fit by working the farm.

I look back towards the horses, afraid I have stared a bit too long at him. I nod my head again, "I will stay and eat something. See how I feel after that."

I can feel James smile towards me then turn towards the screen door, "How does pizza sound?"

My taste buds kick in quickly at the word pizza, "Heavenly."

James smiles back at me then walks into the house leaving me standing on the top of the steps staring into the pasture. I wish I could be as free as those horses. But then I quickly realize, they are caged, they just don't know it yet.

Some day they might. Some day they might fight for their freedom too.

I stand out here watching them run through the breeze for another 5 minutes. Finally, I take another deep breath then turn to head into the house with James.

He is standing at the counter rolling dough out with his bare hands. I feel my jaw drop a little, "I thought you were just gonna throw a frozen one in the oven or something?"

James turns his head towards me while giving me a disgusted grimace, "Please. I am not eating some frozen piece of shit from the store. If we are having pizza, we are having good pizza. How do you feel about mushrooms?"

I let a hint of smile grace my face, "Mushrooms are fine."

He gives me a small smile back as he goes back to kneading the dough. I pull out one of the formica chairs and sit down with one knee up. I wrap my arms around my leg resting my chin on my knee, just watching him at work.

"How long have you had this place?" He looks up and out the window in front of him as he continues to knead the dough, "I was born and raised here actually. My mom passed on a few years back and she left the land and house to me. I didn't really plan on staying here forever but it's hard to say no to a free house and property. I figure if I ever get tired of it I can just sell it and move on."

I look around the room. It all makes sense to me now. This house looks like it has been decorated by a woman. It sends a zip of happiness to my stomach as well that he hasn't mentioned a wife or girlfriend yet. But I can feel the tension in the air since he mentioned his mother.

"I'm sorry. About your mom." I am sincere. My parents are still alive but not in my life. No one is really in my life. It is safer that way. For everyone.

43

James glances over his shoulder at me quickly then back at the dough, "Thanks. She uh, had cancer. She found out while I was overseas. I had been stateside for about a month when she finally passed. I was pissed as hell that she didn't tell me sooner but, what can you do?"

I feel sorry for him. He seems like a good man. Which I am definitely not used to. I put my chin back down on my knee, just watching him as he works. He finishes rolling out the dough then adds the toppings and slides it onto a piece of stone before pushing it in the oven.

He walks over to the sink and washes his hands all the way up to his elbows. I smile at the familiarity of it. I have seen medics do that hundreds of times out in the field. "Old habits die hard" I think is the saying.

James walks over and pulls out a chair across from me. Before sitting down he looks over at me, pointing a finger in my direction, "You want a beer or soda or something?"

I nod back gratefully, "Soda would be great. I don't really drink."

He lets out a chuckle then pulls a Coke from the fridge. I reach for it, smiling at him, "What's so funny?"

He pulls a beer out and twists the cap off while sitting down across from me, "Ex military, covered in ink, possibly a cold blooded murderer, who doesn't drink? That just seems comical to me."

I flip him off as I take a drink of my soda. He just laughs louder at me. I sit the can back down and glance towards him, "Why don't you have a little wifey running around here? Are you gay?"

His eyes go wide again and the beer seems to be teasing his nostrils, "Uh, well. No, not gay. Just haven't found the right girl yet I guess."

44

I nod my head back at him, "I wasn't sure. You had said I wasn't your type so I just assumed."

His eyes are laughing at me again, "So because my type isn't some butched out chick with a shiner and a stab wound that means I am gay?"

I laugh out loud at him. I feel a full smile cover my face. A real smile. I can't remember the last time that happened. He seems to recognize as well that it is an anomaly.

His eyes begin to scan my face so I quickly look back down at the table, "I'm sorry about everything. I had every intention of being long gone from here by now. Things just didn't go as I planned last night."

James tilts his head towards me, then takes another swig of his beer. He sits down the bottle, turning it slightly in his hand, "Why did you do it?"

My eyes meet his and instantly everything starts flooding back. I blink repeatedly but can't get the visions out of my sight. I stand up quickly. My body jerked in response to the visions, "I am gonna run to the bathroom. I will be right back."

Before he can say a word, I take off through another doorway leading to the living room. I can not lose my shit on him right now. He is the only nice thing I have going for me. I make it to the bathroom barely able to shut the door right before it all starts rolling through my head.

Maeve
4 years ago

Mom and dad are still freaking out. I will be fine. Yeah it will be tough, I will get my ass kicked a lot but this is what I am meant to do. I am not meant to be some freaking barbie doll trophy wife in this god forsaken town.

45

I want to make a difference. I want to help people. Sure, I could have gone into healthcare or law but the Marines is something I have always admired. Girls are finally able to go into infantry, special ops. That is what I want to be, G.I. Jane and shit. I smile as I hug them both goodbye then grab my duffle to walk towards the gates. Today is the beginning of it all.

I have my long blonde hair pulled up into a tight bun. I never wear makeup so I don't have to worry about that being an adjustment. I have always been a tomboy. I wanted to play football not softball. I wanted to beat all the guys at pull ups, not pick out a new nail color with the cheerleaders.

I never fit in back there. I want, no I need a challenge. So as soon as I turned 18, I signed up. I thought the recruiter was going to laugh me out of the building when I told him I wanted to go into the special forces.

I know I don't look like much. 5 '5 " with blonde hair, blue eyes and a California tan. But I know what I am capable of. I know what I want. When I passed all the physical then mental tests, he seemed impressed if not surprised. I have always known I was going to make it.

I pull my duffle higher on my shoulder as I start marching towards the bus taking me to the base. There is a man marching up and down a row of recruits screaming at them at the top of his lungs. I throw my bag into the storage bin under the bus and fall in line.

Everyone else seems scared shitless of this dude but not me. I want to be drilled. I want to be hardened. I have waited for this my whole life. Strict rules and regiments have always been something I

force on myself so this is a welcome change, having someone else set
them for me.

"What the fuck are you smiling at Barbie? You look like you
are in the wrong place! You don't get to smile anymore! Your ass is
mine!" I wipe the smile off my face and look straight ahead, "Sir, Yes
Sir!" The Sergeant quickly moves onto the next recruit as I keep my
eyes trained on the side of the bus in front of me.

I stare at the mirror in front of me, trying to regulate my
breathing. I can not lose my shit on James. He doesn't deserve it.
He wasn't there. He isn't one of them.

My freak out moment just clarifies my thoughts. I need
to get out of here as soon as possible. I don't want to hurt him.
He doesn't deserve that kind of added stress. He is too good for
me anyways. Even if there was any part of me to share, it would
just be broken, shattered pieces of who I used to be. He should be
with someone who can love him the way he deserves. It doesn't
matter if I am attracted to him. It doesn't matter that he is the
first man I have ever *been* attracted to. I am no good for him. No
matter what my heart and stomach are telling me. I splash some
cold water on my face then quickly dry it off with a hand towel.

I can smell the pizza now, he must have just pulled it out
of the oven. I make my way back towards the kitchen completely
oblivious to the fact that I am still only half dressed, wearing his
clothes.

4

James
Death of Me – Amira Elfeky

Maeve has seen some shit. I knew that already. She is skittish. She always seems on edge, like she can slip away at any moment. I have watched her muscles tighten in her shoulders a dozen times since I first found her. It is easy to tell that she has lived through something traumatic, just by watching her eyes dart across the room as she clenches her fists and teeth. She seems to always be ready to defend herself somehow. I had thought it was safe to ask her about what happened but as she quickly stood up and took off out of the room I realized we were not that friendly yet.

Can't say as I blame her. I have secrets too. Dark ones that I don't let people know about. Probably never will. I drain the rest of my beer then pull the pizza out of the oven. It looks and smells delicious. I laugh to myself thinking she was expecting a frozen pizza.

I did not live through hell for 3 years just to come home to frozen fucking pizza. I can eat like a king now and make sure I do as much as humanly possible.

I pull out the pizza cutter and start cutting the pie into 8 slices. I can hear her slip back in behind me then pull the chair out to sit down. I have to show her I am not afraid of her, that I am not the bad guy. I don't jump at the noise she makes, I just go about my business.

I pull a couple of plates out of the cabinet then load each one with a few slices of pizza. I turn around handing Maeve a plate, noticing she has slicked her hair back a bit. Her eyes seem a bit clearer now, maybe she did just need to use the bathroom.

48

I had assumed she was having a flashback, maybe just needing a minute to calm down. I know that is what I have to do when it hits. I have to just shut down and hide away. Being around people just seems to make it worse. My therapist told me I need to talk it out, so I fired him.

I watch her face and body soften as she looks at the food in front of her. There is almost a full smile across her face at this point. Maeve reaches for her plate smiling at the pizza, "This looks delicious James. Thank you so much!"

I smile back at her as I sit down at the other side of the table. One little smile from her and my day is made. I need to shake this kind of shit out of my head. She is just passing through. She is scared to death of me.

Oh yeah, also she murdered my neighbor last night. Probably not the smartest idea to become attached. But there is just something about her, yeah she is broken but there is something else. Something just screaming at me like a siren in the night. I just can't decipher what it is screaming about.

I dig into my food, trying to hold back a bit so she doesn't stare at me. I know I eat like a caged animal. I look up and she is already one slice down with sauce covering the lower half of her face. I belt out an audible laugh as she looks up at me with wide surprised eyes.

"I thought I ate like a vagrant but apparently you hold the title of the Queen of Vagrants."

I quickly hand her a paper towel as she grins from ear to ear then starts wiping sauce from her chin. She swallows her food as she looks back up at me, "Sorry. I usually eat alone so I don't really need manners."

I smile back at her, "I get that. I never really go out or into town unless I absolutely have too. I kinda fell into my happy place out here and have no real desire to go anywhere else."

49

She nods at me while taking another bite, "I can understand that. It is so fucking peaceful here. I could stand out there and listen to the silence for hours."

I give her a soft smile back, "Yeah, I get that. When I first got back, every single little noise set me off. It was rough because I was in Great Falls for a while with my mom in the hospital. I brought her home about a week before she passed. She said she wanted to be near the horses when she went. But being in that city after just getting back from overseas, it was fucking rough."

She nods as she looks back out the screen door towards the horses, "I can understand that. I could look at them all day. Your mom was a smart woman." I smile back at her in agreement.

I get us both the last few slices and then sit back down. Eating a bit slower now, I don't really want the openness of our conversation to end. She seems to be opening up a bit now that we are comfortable. I don't want to spook her but I have so many questions.

"So, where are you from originally?" She wipes her hands on her paper towel then picks up her can of soda, "California."

I look at her in amazement, "So, do your parent's own a sunblock company or something?"

She laughs out loud sitting the can back down, "No, they are vampires just like me."

I smile at her, taking another bite of my pizza. I like this side of her. She is opening up a bit and showing that she does have a sense of humor. I think that is one of the biggest surprises from her. I just assumed she was going to be brooding and tormented the whole dinner. She has slowed down her eating as well and leans back in her chair, just staring at me. I feel like she is judging something in her mind. And I feel like I am failing the test.

I wipe my hands on the paper towel as well and stare back at her. She gives me a slight smile then starts picking at her pizza, "No, the whole pale skin thing is kinda new. I uh spent a lot of time in the hospital. I didn't get out much. When I was finally able to get out, I didn't really want to be around people. I know it's hard to picture but I am not really a people person, if you can believe it."

I clasp my hand over my heart with a gasp, "Really? I never would have guessed it." She smiles again as she flips me off.

"Were you wounded in action or something?"

The smile slips from her face again as she looks back towards the screen door, "Or something."

I nod, okay, not something she wants to talk about. I can do that. "Where did you do your basics?" She picks the pizza back up, taking a small bite, "Camp Lejeune."

I whip my eyes back at her, "MRTC? You were really specials? I was just fucking around earlier."

She smiles again, "Yeah, I really was."

I wad up my paper towel, throwing it on top of my pizza, "Small world."

She smiles back up at me, "You too?"

I nod gently, "I wasn't MRTC material but yeah I was there for a bit. Started my medics training there, finished up overseas. Fallujah."

She blinks heavily a few times, "Yeah, I luckily didn't make it over there. I was sent to South America."

I remember the stories that Chad had told me, he had never mentioned her before. A part of me doesn't even want to dare to wonder why. It makes me want to justify what she has done. Even if it isn't justifiable.

"Is that how you knew Chad, were you in the same regiment?" Her shoulders lock up tight. She robotically jerks herself into a standing position, grabbing both of our plates. I have seen that type of knee jerk reaction before. Trauma response is what they call it.

She quickly walks to the trash to dump the plates then turns to set them in the sink. I stand, walking up behind her. Not too close but close enough for her to hear me, "I am sorry. I didn't know it was such a touchy subject. I won't bring it up again."

Maeve slowly turns and looks up at me, "How well did you know Chad? Were you friends?"

I shake my head back down at her, "Not really. We were neighbors, he wasn't raised here. He only moved here after he left the corp. I know who he was, had seen him a few times in town at the bar, that's about it. Like I said, he wasn't a very likeable guy."

She stares at my chest, seemingly lost in thought again before she whispers, "Yeah, I know."

It is killing me not knowing what has happened. Then it hits me like a ton of bricks. She is skittish around me, she was a female in special ops, probably an all man regiment besides her. She was afraid earlier I was trying to fuck her. I feel my heart rate tick up just thinking about what she could have possibly been through. Anger flies into me out of nowhere.

Something very fucked up has happened to her. I quickly take a step back to give her some more space to breathe. She looks up at me then turns around to start to wash the dishes. I step up beside her looking down into the sink, "You wash, I dry?"

She smiles back at me, "Yeah, that sounds good." I nod my head and grab a towel.

We grab our drinks to head out to the back porch after the dishes are dried and put away. I sit down on the porch swing while Maeve sits down on the top step stretching her short legs out across the porch.

I take a swig of my beer then look over at her again, "So, California?"

She smiles back then looks at the horses, "Yup. Ever since I got back I have just been traveling from town to town. Not really sure where I am gonna end up."

I tilt my head towards her a bit, "You didn't go home when you got back?"

She lets the smile fall from her face a bit, "Yeah, no. I haven't been back home."

I lean forward bracing my forearms on my knees, "No family to go back too?"

She looks back towards the horses, "No, I have family there. It's just a long story. I just, I am not ready yet."

I let it go. I understand all too well what she means. I lean back and chug my beer, "I am gonna go toss this and take a shower. Are you gonna be okay by yourself?"

She gazes up at me smiling, "Yeah, I'll be okay. Can I ask you something first though?"

I stop in my tracks as my breath catches in my chest, "You can ask me anything Maeve."

Her ice blue eyes seem to stare into my soul at that. She still seems hesitant but there is a softness in her eyes when she looks at me now. I am trying not to let it eat away at me. Trying to convince myself that doesn't mean she actually likes me. She lets out another soft sigh, "Is it okay if I do just crash here tonight? I don't really know where I am going next."

I smile back down at her, "You are welcome to stay as long as you like." I quickly turn, walking inside. I have to put some distance between us before I do something stupid. Like fall for her.

I take the stairs two at a time. What the hell is wrong with me? This chick obviously has issues, she has basically told me she murdered my fucking neighbor yesterday in cold blood and here I am offering her a place to stay.

There is just something about her. She seems so goddamn familiar. I have racked my brain all day trying to pin it down but still have no clue where the feeling is coming from.

I grab a towel, tossing my boots to the foot of my bed. I throw my hat onto the top of my dresser then pull my shirt up over my shoulders to toss it into the hamper. I turn to head to the bathroom and see Maeve standing at my bedroom door, eyes wide.

"You okay?" I am worried that something or someone has spooked her. I let my eyes scan her face for some hint of the problem. Her eyes seem to roam down my chest and abdomen before they whip back up to my face. I let a small grin come over my face when I see her cheeks turn pink before she turns, running into her room, loudly slamming the door behind her.

Was Maeve just checking me out?

I chuckle to myself as I step in the bathroom and get the water to a manageable temperature to step into. I stand there letting the water run over me. I wash my hair, still trying to place where I might know her from.

I close my eyes thinking back to her standing at my bedroom door. Her eyes had slowly grazed down my chest and then like she had even surprised herself they whipped back to meet mine. I let out a breath thinking of her face. The way her cheeks turned pink. I can feel my own chest getting tight as I think about her. My body is beginning to react on its own from the thoughts running through my mind.

Wait, did she stand a bit taller when I asked if she was okay? Was she pressing her thighs together? Thoughts of her

54

cling to me like stubborn cobwebs that I can't seem to sweep away.

No, she couldn't be thinking about me like that. She has made it abundantly clear that she is not interested in me. I lean my face back into the water and let the sight of her back into my thoughts.

Before I even realize what I am doing, I have a hand wrapped around my dick and am giving it long hard strokes thinking about her cheeks turning pink. Thinking about her squeezing her thighs together.

Was she wet for me? Was she hot and wanting me?

The thought of her slick pussy wanting me is making me speed up my strokes. I have one hand planted on the wall in front of me as I lean over myself and start tugging on my dick erratically. I picture her face in my head, her mouth falling open, her eyes closing in ecstasy. I hear her soft little moan in my head then I am quickly emptying myself into the tub. I hear a grunt leave my body as I finish, praying to god she didn't hear it too.

I finish my business, turn off the water then step out of the shower. I wrap the towel around my waist as I run a hand across the steamed up mirror. I stare at myself for a long moment. It has been a long fucking time since someone interested me.

I smirk at my reflection, hopefully she decides to stay a bit longer. I am not going to push myself on her though. I am completely content living out my little fantasies in my head. I just want to know her, the real Maeve. I grab another towel that is hanging on the rack and quickly run it over my head to somewhat dry my hair.

I hang the towel back up on the hook, scooping up my dirty jeans and underwear before stepping out into the hallway. I look to my right to see her bedroom door is open again. I peek inside but she isn't there. I see her duffle still sitting in the chair and let out a deep sigh of relief.

She didn't take off.

I smile to myself as I turn and head into my room. Shutting the door behind me, I look up to see her standing in front of my full length mirror. She is only wearing her underwear. She is covering her breasts with one arm while the other is raised up over her head as she looks over the stitch work I had done on her earlier.

I let my eyes roam over her body, the curves of her athletic legs. I watch her as she slowly turns to look at her wound a bit closer. I can see the toned, defined muscles of her abdomen flexing as she bends sideways to get a better look. Each and every line of her body is highlighted, from the curve of her biceps to the sleek lines of her legs.

She sees my reflection in the mirror behind her and her cheeks start to turn pink again, "I'm sorry. I thought you would be longer. I was gonna try to find another bandage to change this but wasn't sure where they were."

I quickly nod at her, trying to rein in my thoughts, "Yeah, no that's fine. Let me grab one."

I turn back out the door and into the bathroom, trying to talk my dick into going back into hiding. Now that I have flipped this fantasy switch in my head, I am quickly realizing it is going to be hard to turn it off.

I grab another bandage out of the cabinet then head back into the bedroom. Maeve is still covering herself but has turned towards me. I stand here, taking deep breaths, trying to steady myself before approaching her. She steps up to me and turns slowly so her side is facing me. I quickly unwrap the bandage from its paper, placing it on her side gently. Smoothing down the edges so it is a firm seal.

I really fucking hope she can't feel the tremble in my hands. The heat from her warm skin under mine feels like little shots of electricity running up through my fingers and into my arms.

Maeve smiles back at me sweetly, "Thank you James."

My eyes trail up her body then meet hers, "You are welcome Maeve."

She turns her back to me as she grabs the tshirt off the end of the bed. She slowly lifts it back over her head then glides it down her body. I watch her in the reflection of the mirror. The way the fabric slides across her skin. The way the muscles in her abdomen flex and stretch as her hands go up above her head. I am in a trance, completely unable to resist the vision in front of me.

I know I should turn away but I just can't bring myself to do it. She looks back up into the mirror and sees me watching her. She takes in a deep breath and I see her shoulders shaking a bit.

She turns slowly, taking a few steps towards me. Her eyes hold mine the entire time. She starts to blink rapidly, "I uh, I am gonna go ahead and go to bed. Thank you for everything today James. Truly. It is more than I deserve."

I suck a deep breath in through my teeth, "You deserve so much more Maeve."

Her face falls to the floor. I take a step closer. I put my finger under her chin to lift her gaze back up to my own, "Truly, you deserve everything."

Her eyes flit across my face before she starts to walk around me. She stops beside me, gently placing her hand on my chest.

My breath catches in my throat as I turn to her and she says, "So do you, James." Then she is gone.

57

5

Maeve

BURNED - Britton

Maeve
4 Years ago

I have been here for months now and it is not getting any easier at all. There are only a handful of females left in the training program. It seems like each week another one drops out. Not me though. I am not going to give up. Nothing is going to stop me from getting to where I want to be. Where I deserve to be. I have worked my ass off, getting into better shape, spending hours on end running the obstacles by myself. Rain, shine, it doesn't fucking matter. I am going to master all of these fucking exercises then those guys are going to have to eat their words.

I have been called everything but a decent human since I have been here. Some of the older ones call us BAMs. That one doesn't really bother me as much as it does the others. But the guys that will whisper that we should just bend over and take it like good little bitches, that's the kind that pisses me off. I finally got tired of it last night and told Weathers he didn't have the equipment to satisfy me, that I had seen him in the showers and laughed all the way back to the dorm. The black eye that is in full bloom shows just how he felt about that jab. But that is fine, he has a matching black eye as well.

But today is a new day. I am going to ace this fucking obstacle and I am going to move on in my training. I grab my stuff then run to the latrine to take a quick shower and put my hair up in a bun. I round the corner, seeing them immediately. Weathers and Lang are standing there in full gear waiting for me. I start to back out of the room as I quickly realize Sanders is blocking me from leaving. I feel my heart start racing and my palms have become sweaty. They could literally do anything to me right now and it would be my word against theirs. I try to hold my ground against them but they are fucking intimidating and they know it.

I stand tall, not letting them see the fear that is eating at me. Lang pulls a bowie knife from behind his back as my eyes glaze over. I watch the knife as he twists and turns it under the harsh lighting. The blade gleams against the walls around me. What the fuck are they gonna do?

I wake up a half hour later, my clothes in ribbons all around me. My long blonde hair cut from my head laying all over the floor. I look in the mirror at the short choppy bob I am left with and the cuts down my arms. I let one single tear slip down my face.

I jump awake as lightning shoots across the sky outside. I am sweating like crazy. I throw the blankets back and pull my legs over the side. I brace my feet on the side rail of the bed then put my head in my hands.

I can feel my breathing all over the place. I can feel myself falling into a panic attack. I try to breathe through it quietly but that is not something that is easy to do. I quickly stand up and start pacing the room. Storms always fucking do this to me. Spending months in a jungle, fighting for your fucking life will do that shit to you.

The storms there were chaotic. You would have torrential rains and rolling thunder within just minutes of sunny clear skies. Thunder rolls across the fields again shaking the entire house. Before I know what I am doing, my legs are carrying me out into the hallway. I place an ear to James' door but don't hear anything.

Another clap of thunder hits and I scream. I quickly bend over, instantly trying to catch my breath with my hands on my knees. You are okay Carrie, you are good. You are not there. You are here, you are in Montana, you are at James'. You are safe.

I feel myself starting to calm down just a bit when James' bedroom door flys open and he is standing there with a fucking 9mm in his hand.

I stare up at him. He is wearing nothing but his boxer briefs. His muscles are pulled tight across his chest. There is a vein protruding from his neck, beating at the same pace as my heart. His eyes are almost as wild as his hair.

He quickly grabs me pulling me into his side, "What's wrong? Is someone in the house?"

He is looking past me down the hallway. I inhale deeply trying to catch my breath only to smell his scent. It is musky, a hint of male and cedar. His skin is warm against mine. I can feel a trace of something running up my side where our bodies are meeting. It feels nerve wracking but somehow right. Like I am supposed to be there. Supposed to be here.

I let out a small breath, trying to smile, "No. I am sorry, I didn't mean to wake you. I was just scared by the storm. I don't do well with them after being in the jungle for so long. I am good though, you can go back to sleep."

He runs his hand down my arm then reaches over, putting the safety back on the gun. He looks me over as another clap of thunder hits and I clench up into his side.

I can feel him smiling into the top of my head, "Oh no. The big bad wolf is scared of the storm?"

I grin into his side then reach up and tweak his nipple with my thumb and first finger. He yelps as he jumps back a step laughing at me.

He smiles again then pulls me in closer, "Come on, you can sleep in here with me. I will keep you safe."

I clench up even harder at that. "No, no, that's okay. I mean I will be fine. I will just walk around the house until it passes."

James stares down at me seriously now, "Maeve, it's the middle of the night. You are exhausted. I promise I will keep my hands to myself. Just get in here so you can actually get some sleep tonight, okay?"

He is serious. I stare past him towards his bed as I take a deep breath. I trust him. I don't know why but I do. I have become pretty good at detecting assholes. He is the furthest thing from that. Something about him just tells me that he won't hurt me. That he is on my side.

Another part of me wants to know what it would feel like to lay down next to someone, willingly. I may be psychotic at times but that doesn't mean I have never thought of meeting someone. Maybe even falling in love. I just never thought it would be in the cards for me.

I take a hesitant step into his room as he pushes the door shut behind us. I slowly walk around the bed to the far side then pull the blankets down. I see him put the gun back into the top drawer of his dresser, mentally keeping track of where his weapons are at all times.

I steady my breathing a bit more, "Do you have maybe another t-shirt or a tank top I can wear? I am kinda sweating like a whore in church in this one."

James barks out a laugh as he walks back over to his dresser. He reaches in then tosses me a wife beater. I turn around, quickly changing. I turn back around to see him already under the covers with his eyes closed.

I smile as I crawl into bed beside him. I lay on my side, closing my eyes trying to force myself back to sleep. Another roll of thunder shakes the house and I feel my body tense up again.

James reaches over, pulling me close into his side. I look up at his face but his eyes are still closed. The sound of his easy, steady breathing is somehow soothing to me. I let myself relax again. I place the side of my face then my palm on his chest. I listen to the steady beat of his heart pull me into a relaxed state.

The next clap of thunder hits and lightning lights up the room. But before my body has a chance to react, he is hugging me a bit tighter then rubbing his hand up and down my bicep. I smile into his chest, nuzzling in a little closer.

At some point, I fall asleep. It is still storming outside but I feel this calm roll over me. I have not felt this much peace in years. My brain is finally quiet.

The voices, the yelling, the memories, it is all gone.

I wake up a few hours later and James is spooning me. We have rolled at some point, now he is holding me tightly with my back against his chest. It just feels right. It just feels meant to be and I don't know why.

He is my calm.

I slide his arm over me as I stealthily attempt to step out of the bed. I tiptoe to the bathroom. After peeing, I look into the mirror not liking the face staring back at me. My hair, the greenish shiner, my stance, my memories, all of it is torture.

I know I am going to have to leave. I will do nothing but bring trouble. The last thing I want to do is to make anything harder on James. He has quickly become someone, something I don't want to fuck up. I make the decision right then to leave in the morning. No matter what.

I slowly make my way back into the bedroom. James has rolled onto his back and is looking at me as I try to be quiet, sneaking back across the room to get into bed.

I give him a side eye as I crawl back into bed, "I'm sorry. I had to pee. I didn't mean to wake you up."

He smiles, turning his head towards me, "Honestly, I thought you were either sneaking out in the middle of the night to disappear or looking for a knife to kill me while I slept."

He is smiling but I am not. I look deep into his eyes, meaning every single word I say, "I wouldn't do either of those things to you. You have not done anything to me like they did."

He rolls his body towards me, "They?"

I close my eyes tightly, realizing my words, my mistake. "Chad is not the only one that deserved it."

I feel him let a breath out onto my chest, "How many have deserved it?"

I open my eyes but can't look at him. I quickly sit up, turning my head in the other direction. I feel him sit up beside me, "Maeve, you don't have to say anything. Really. I trust you. Whatever you have done, you have your reasons. I get that. More than most would."

I slowly turn my head back towards him. Why does he make me feel like it is all going to be okay? Like this is all just a fleeting memory that will soon be gone and forgotten. James is staring at me with an intensity that is igniting a flame in my chest. Before I can stop myself, I am kissing him fiercely. He wraps his arms around me tightly as he pulls me deeper into him.

I wrap my arms around his neck, losing myself in his lips. I feel his hands move to my side so I turn towards him completely. I lay him back on the pillow as I continue to move my tongue around his.

63

The voices are gone again. There is quiet. There is peace. I smile into his lips and I feel him smile back. I roll my body then slide a leg over him until I am straddling him. I can feel his rather impressive length beneath me. He is so hard. I grind myself into him as I continue to kiss him deeply. I never wanted to feel this with someone. I have never needed to be this intimate with anyone.

I feel a moan leave his throat. It makes me smile, knowing that I am the one causing him the kind of pleasure that would lead to that reaction. But now, I don't know what to do with my hands. This is not something that I do. This is something I have never done on my own, not consensually at least. I pull back looking into his eyes.

He can see the fear in mine, the hesitation. James puts a hand on each side of my head as he smiles at me, "It's okay Maeve. This doesn't have to go anywhere. We can just lay here and hold each other. We don't have to do anything you are not comfortable with."

I smile down at him, "It's not that I don't want to, I just don't have a lot of practice in this department."

His confused eyes search mine before it seems like a light bulb goes off, "Are you a virgin?"

I let out a soft laugh, "No, but that doesn't mean this is something I know how to do."

I roll myself off of him, letting out a heavy sigh as I stare at the ceiling. This is not something I really want to talk about right now but he deserves answers if he has the balls enough to ask the questions. A part of me hopes he's ball-less right now though.

James rolls onto his side placing his hand on my abdomen, "How many people have you been with?" He apparently has balls after all.

64

I turn towards him, staring at his adam's apple as it raises in his throat, "One."

He nods his head, "Okay, just a guesstimation then, how many times do you think you guys fucked?"

I close my eyes, trying not to think about it, "Once."

I feel his hand grip my tank top as I open my eyes to look at him again, "How long ago was that?"

I let out another sigh, then answer, "3 years ago."

James looks over me, past me towards the room behind me. I look up at him as his gaze returns back to me, "Did you cum?"

I feel my face instantly turn red. What the fuck is wrong with me? Why am I fucking embarrassed right now? I try to hide my face and I hear him laugh.

He pulls my chin up to face him as he searches my eyes with a smile, "I am going to take that as a no then?"

I nod my head at him in agreement. I see the adam's apple move in his throat again. I look back up at his face as a devilish grin creeps onto his cheeks.

6

James

Feel Nothing - The Plot In You

I smile back down at Maeve. I lean in, our lips touching in a gentle, yet passionate kiss. The warmth and scent of her skin envelop me. I pull back, "Will you let me make you cum?"

Her eyes fly wide as her breath hitches in her throat. I smile again, "I am not going to fuck you. But will you let me make you feel good?"

Her eyes seem to be scouring my face then with a shy smile she slowly nods her head yes. Her hands tremble slightly as they grasp my neck, pulling me closer. I smile back at her then move in for another kiss. Our tongues dance together in a sensual rhythm that is leaving me breathless. I can feel her hands wrap tighter around the back of my neck holding me close to her.

She smells like lilies. Lilies wrapped in vanilla. My hand glides up her bare skin, stopping at the small of her back before traveling back across her abdomen and up her stomach. Her kissing becomes more insistent as I slide my hand up then cup her perfect breast. She gasps softly, arching into my touch.

Maeve is panting into my mouth. I smile back at her as I open my eyes to look down at her. Her eyes are closed tightly, her mouth is slightly parted. She is stunning. I roll her nipple between my first finger and thumb. She moans, turning her head back towards my face.

I let my thumb rub over her pert nipple a few more times before trailing my hand back down her stomach. She opens her eyes and looks up at me as my hand slides into the top of her boy shorts. Her eyes are searching mine for some kind of answer to a question she hasn't even asked.

I slide my middle finger onto her engorged clit and her chest heaves towards me. She moans loudly into my mouth and I pull back to watch the intensity in her eyes as they widen with pleasure. It's like nothing I have ever seen before – utter bliss written all over her face. She lets her legs and mouth fall open at the same time. Her eyes try to roll back in her head.

I lean in kissing her gently again as I start to circle her clit. She moans into my mouth and I pull back again to watch her falling apart, but her eyes are closed.

"Maeve, look at me." She slowly opens her eyes staring into mine. I start circling her faster, "Tell me if it's too much okay?" She nods her head yes to me.

I smile as I then slide a finger inside of her. I watch her as she bites her bottom lip nervously. Her eyes shut tight again as I smile at her again, "Eyes on me baby, okay?"

She opens her eyes again, staring at me as I slide a second finger in. She lets a moan out into the room around us as I watch her losing herself in the moment. I growl under my breath, "Fucking perfect."

She pants again then starts fidgeting with her fingers, "James, I don't know what to do with my hands. I just don't know.....God that feels so good."

I feel like a god. I am watching this creature come undone with just the touch of my fingers. Her right hand lands on my abdomen as I start to pump in and out of her. I quickly pull my fingers out of her then reach up to pull her underwear down over her hips.

She lifts up, yanking them off herself, instantly spreading her legs for me again. I smile at her insistence as I kiss her nipple through the tank top. I slide my fingers back into her and she pushes her chest further into my mouth. I lean up a bit then

67

lift her shirt just high enough for me to suck her nipple into my teeth.

She lets out another raspy moan, "Oh fuck James." I smile as I circle her nipple with my tongue and her clit with my thumb. She opens her eyes looking back towards me with a lust filled gaze. I feel her hand go back to my abdomen then her little hand slides into the top of my boxer briefs. She quickly grabs my cock and starts moving her hand up and down.

My eyes fly open, "Baby, you don't have to. This is about you." She smiles as she bites her lower lip looking back at me, "Shut the fuck up and let me make you cum all over my hand."

I almost lose myself just to her words.

I start pumping my fingers deeper into her then hook them inside. I know damn well I am going to hit a spot that is going to push her over the edge. What I don't expect is for her to go completely fucking feral on me.

Her grip on my cock tightens as she starts pulling on me faster. Before I can even try to control it, my hips start to buck into her hand.

She arches her back then looks at me, "Fuck this."

She pushes me onto my back then immediately pulls my underwear down just enough to see what she is doing. She can see me hard and throbbing for her. She grabs the briefs on both sides then slides them down to my ankles. I quickly kick them off then watch her pull the tank top over her head.

I slide my hand back over to her abdomen but she picks it up and puts it on her tit. At the same time, she slides over top of me and starts grinding her bare pussy on my dick. I bite my lip and growl, "God fucking dammit, Maeve. You are so fucking wet." She smiles as she leans down to kiss me again.

I kiss her back fiercely, with as much fire as I can muster, gripping her hair tight in my right hand. She is going to make me cum just by rubbing herself on me. She pulls back smiling, "Do you have a condom?"

I search her face, trying to judge the situation a bit better, "We don't have to Maeve. Seriously. This is enough."

She smiles at me like a jackal, "I fucking need you inside me James."

I reach over into the nightstand drawer pulling out a condom. All the while, hoping to god they aren't expired. She snatches it from my hand then tears it open. I look down and watch her slide off of my now wet dick so she can roll the condom on.

She looks back at me, hesitantly, "Tell me if I do something wrong okay?"

I smile back at her, "You can't do anything wrong. Just get on top of me okay?"

She slides back up my body and I grip the base of my dick. I look back at her face, "Now rise up and slide down onto my dick okay baby?" She quickly nods and raises up onto her knees a bit.

I feel her slide down onto my dick slowly. She is so fucking tight. The heat rolling off her pussy onto me is torture. Her head falls back as she starts to slide up and down on my dick. I just lay there, watching her face as she takes me in.

She smiles then rolls her neck towards me before opening her eyes, "Fuck James, you feel so fucking good. You are so big."

I smile at her as I put my hands on her hips. I thrust up into her watching her eyes fly open again as her mouth hangs wide. I grab her ass and slam up into her again.

She starts moving quicker on me and I know she is close. I can feel her pussy fluttering around my dick. I reach around with my thumb and start rubbing it quickly over her clit.

She starts slamming into me, "Oh fuck, fuck, fuck James."

I feel her pussy clench onto my dick as her body stills. Her eyes are huge, staring at me. Her mouth is hanging open as I

69

smile and grab her hips again. I grunt as I start thrusting myself up into her.

I pump into her 3 more times and then I feel all of her clamp down on me hard. "Oh my fucking god James. Harder. Harder, please harder!"

I grit my teeth as I slam myself into her quick and hard. Two more thrusts and I am spilling into the condom, "Fuck me Maeve. Jesus fuck. I'm coming. I'm coming."

She is riding me hard again trying to let the waves roll out of her body, "James, James, JAMES!" she rides me hard for another minute before her hips stop rolling into mine.

I still am not able to open my eyes. I have never cum so hard in my life. I have felt chick's cum on me before but this is something else completely. It is like I couldn't breathe without her riding me at that moment.

It has never felt this right before. I have my hands on her hips. Slowly pulling her up and down my dick just a little bit more. I open my eyes and see her smiling at the ceiling with her eyes closed.

I stop moving her as she looks down at me, "James, I...didn't know it could be like that."

I smile back at her running my thumb over her bottom lip, "Me either baby. It has never been like that before."

Her cheeks turn pink again, "Did I do it right? For you I mean?" I smile, feeling myself still pulsating inside of her.

"Maeve that was fucking perfect. I have never cum so hard in my life. Ever."

She smiles again as she leans down to kiss me. I roll her over onto her side then slide out of her with a hiss. I reach down to pull the spent condom off of me then roll over throwing it in the trash can beside the bed. I roll back over and see her smiling widely with her eyes closed, her hips still moving a bit on their own.

70

"Did you finish baby? Why are your hips still moving?"

She smiles as she looks at me, "I am just remembering what it felt like having you inside me."

I growl pulling her into another hard kiss. I slide my fingers over her clit as I growl into her lips, "Give me one more baby. Cum all over my hand."

Her eyes go wide as I start rubbing her clit in tight circles. Her mouth is open so I stick my tongue deep into it as I drive my fingers into her again and hook them. I am rubbing my thumb over her clit when I feel her hands wrap around my wrist.

I open my eyes to see her face clenching up. I move my fingers in and out of her quickly, hooking them inside each time. I feel her clamp down on my fingers again as I look at her face, "Look at me baby. Eyes on me. I wanna watch you fall apart."

Her eyes fly open, her pupils are dilated until they are almost completely black. I continue to pump my fingers into her as I feel her fingers flying over her clit as well. I look down and almost cum again just watching her help me finish her off.

"James, oh fuck me, James!" She screams my name again before slamming her lips into mine. She kisses me hard while she finishes out on my hand.

I feel her hand stop moving over her clit and I open my eyes. She is smiling again but is looking right at me, "I am so fucking glad I passed out on your fenceline."

I bark out a laugh as I pull my fingers out of her and bring them to my mouth. She watches my lips as I slide those two fingers into my mouth, tasting her on them.

I moan as I close my eyes, sucking my fingers clean. I open my eyes and look at her, "Me too baby. Me fucking too." I pull her in close as we both pass out again.

I fully expect Maeve to be gone in the morning. But instead I wake up to her and I still tangled up together. I pull her a bit closer and kiss her temple. She gives me a soft smile then opens one eye and looks at me.

I smile down at her, "Good Morning Maeve." She lets out a yawn as she pulls back away from me, "Good morning."

OH, she is not a morning person.

I smile again, stretching out my legs then turning to sit up. I look over my shoulder at her, "I am going to go make a pot of coffee. You want some?" That gets her moving.

She sits straight up in bed looking at me, "Please god yes!" I stand up, completely naked, still smiling at her, "Watch how you talk to me young lady."

Her eyes go wide as she glances up at my face then I can see her visibly relax when she realizes I am just joking with her. I need to remember to watch how I joke around with her. I don't want to spook her.

I quickly step over to the dresser to pull out some clean underwear and jeans. I slide them both on then pad out of the room barefoot to go downstairs and make some coffee. I can hear her moving around upstairs, smiling at the ceiling.

I wonder to myself if maybe she would want to help out with the horses today. I can teach her how to feed them then maybe she can brush a few down while I clean out the stalls. I sit two mugs on the counter when I hear a knock at that door. I walk through the house, glancing at the stairs but seeing them empty.

I unlock the door, pulling it open to see the Sheriff standing there again. I lean into the door frame, blocking his view into the house just in case, "Good Morning Bob."

He smiles back at me then back down to his phone. He quickly puts it away as he slides his hat off, "Heya James. So it looks like whoever did this to Chad sure did book it out of town."

I smile towards the sun then look back down at Bob, "Oh really, can't find any trace of the guy?"

He nods back at me, "Yeah, I mean we found some evidence. Shoe prints, alot smaller than Chads but that and there was some blood found on one the trash cans. I wouldn't even of fucking tested it but it was so far away from the body, I figured it wasn't his.

"I was right, it wasn't his but other than that, there is nothing. It was like the fella that did this just vanished. I wanted to come back by and make sure you hadn't seen anything else yesterday. Or maybe if you remembered hearing something?"

I stand back up, stretching my shoulders, "No. I didn't see or hear anything. Wish I had an answer for ya Bob."

He nods at me again and slides his hat back on, "Yeah. Alright. Well, I will get out of here, let you get to work. I will update you if I hear anything else though."

I stand there watching him get in his car and leave. I wait until he turns out of the long drive then head back into the kitchen to pour two cups of coffee.

I hear Maeve step up behind me, "So, how do you take your coffee?"

I hear the formica chair slide across the floor as she pulls it out, "Black please."

I smile to myself, shocker.

I turn around to sit her mug in front of her. I quickly note that her duffle is on the floor beside her. She is wearing black jeans, tucked into her boots. She has on a black tank top and her hoodie is now laying on top of her duffle.

I grab my cup and sit down across from her. Not saying a word. She is gonna leave this morning. Last night apparently had meant nothing to her at all.

73

7

Maeve

Move Me – Badflower

I am standing at the top of the stairs hearing James chatting with the sheriff again. They can run all the tests they want on my blood, my dna. It will never come back right. They will see it belongs to some Marine that went MIA almost 3 years ago. Never seen or heard from again.

I listen to James lie for me, about me. I can't do this to him. He deserves more, better than what I am doing to him. I turn back towards my room and quickly gather my stuff. I feel empty now. Like I had something, so close to perfection and it has just slipped right through my fingers.

I think for a minute about leaving him my cell phone number. That would make 2 people that know about me but I quickly dismiss the idea. It is better to just cut all ties and walk away while I still can.

I start down the steps after noting for sure that the Sheriff is really gone. The house somehow feels overwhelming now. Like the memories of last night are now secrets hidden deep within its walls. I round the door into the kitchen to see James pouring coffee into a few mugs. I sit my bag down and place my hand on one of the chairs.

James's voice is gruff again, "So, how do you take your coffee?" I have a hand on my throat, praying my voice doesn't crack. I pull a chair out to sit down, "Black, please."

I see the back of his head nod in acknowledgement as I sit down at the table. James turns to me and sits the mug down in front of me. His eyes go quickly to my bag on the floor, then he notices I am fully dressed. He grabs his own mug as he leans back in a chair across from me. Just staring at me.

I take a drink of the coffee, leaning back in my own chair. I can't look at him. It is physically painful just having his eyes on me right now. I know he can see my hands trembling. He nods towards my duffle on the floor, "Where are you gonna go?"

I glance down at the bag then out the screen door, "Not sure yet." He takes a long drink of his coffee then sits down the mug.

He leans forward onto the table, "You don't have to leave. You can stay a bit longer."

I shake my head, "That will only complicate things."

He huffs and I look up at him, "What things? What the fuck would it complicate? No one knows it was you that dealt with Chad. You said yourself, no one even knows where you are so no one else is looking for you. Why can't you just give yourself a break and maybe find some peace for a minute?"

I take another long swig of the coffee before setting the mug down. I look up at James' hardened face. He thinks I am leaving because of last night.

I let out a long breath, "Look. Last night was amazing. It was, in all honesty, the best night of my life. But this, whatever this is. It won't work. I have too much shit going on. I have too much shit still left to do."

James nods at me then stands up and puts his mug in the sink, leaving his back to me.

I stand up taking a small step towards him, "Seriously, James. I am not lying. Last night meant more to me than you will ever know. I have never had anyone be nice to me before. Not in that way. I let my guard down and that is just something I cannot keep doing. I don't want you to get hurt."

James turns back around as he leans into the counter, staring me down with his arms crossed over his chest.

75

I take a few more steps closer to him, then go up on my tip toes and give him a soft kiss. He takes his arms down and braces them on the counter on either side of him.

But he doesn't kiss me back.

I look down at his chest as I move to turn around. He quickly grabs my bicep and spins me back around. He kisses me deeply, fiercely. I put my hands on either side of his face and kiss him back with just as much passion.

We pull away from each other and I can feel some type of emotion making my chest tight. I have to get out of here.

James looks past me into the dining room, "I hope your absence brings you some kind of peace Maeve. I really do."

I give him one last smile then turn around. I stare at the wall in front of me for a moment before hesitantly picking up my duffle and head towards the front door. I have to get out of here before he reads the truth on my face. The truth being that I don't really want to go. I step down the porch but for some reason decide to turn around and look back towards the house. James is not there. I let another long breath leave my body as I pull the duffle over my shoulder then walk down the dusty driveway.

I turn right out the driveway, walking away from town, away from James. The dirt from the driveway is still clinging to my boots, as if trying to send me off with a reminder of what I am leaving behind. Maybe I can hole up near the mountains for a bit. I think a few nights on the hard ground in front of a campfire will do me good. Get whatever this feeling is to die down in my chest. I don't bother to turn around again.

I continue trucking northwest until my legs decide it's time for a break. I come across a paved road, which is fucking surprising to find out here in the middle of nowhere.

I let myself rest for about 5 minutes before continuing on. A car stops about a half hour later. It's a young girl, about my age, asking if I need a ride somewhere. I lean down into the passenger window and see she is sporting the same color of shiner that I have.

I thank her, throwing my duffle into the backseat then get comfortable as I buckle up in the seat next to her. She doesn't speak much. Can't say as I blame her.

She is super nervous. I can tell just by her mannerisms. She has been hurt, that's obvious even seeing through the bruises. She keeps her long blonde hair parted on one side so it hangs mostly across her bruise bloomed eye. She has the same type of busted lip as me too. Her eyes remind of a scared animal, always jutting around trying to keep a look out at every angle. She is me. Just a few years ago.

I look out the window for the first few minutes then give her a side eye glance, "My name is Maeve by the way."

She gives me a small anxious smile, "Sarah."

I nod back out the windshield, "Nice to meet you Sarah." She gives me a quick glance then turns back to the road.

I lay my head back on the headrest and look out the window. A few minutes pass when I hear Sarah ask, "What happened to your eye?"

I turn back to her, giving her a soft smile, "I know I am supposed to say I walked into a door or something but honestly, dude was an asshole. He busted my lip too." She watches me as I point to my mouth giving her a small smile.

She stares wide eyed at me then turns back to the windshield. I can see her knuckles turning white she is gripping the steering wheel so hard. I lean my head back and give her another soft smile, "Boyfriend? Husband? Or Father?"

She glances back at me then at the rearview mirror. She lets out a long sigh, "Boyfriend."

I nod my head, "You have time to get away then. He isn't blood so you don't have to worry about that. He isn't legally tied to you so that helps. Boyfriends come and go. You just have to be strong just for a little bit, then you can break down after he is gone."

Sarah glances back at me quickly. I can almost hear the wheels turning in her head as she points to my face, "Was he your boyfriend?"

I shake my head back and forth, "Nah, just someone from my past. I am not worried about him anymore though."

She smiles, "I wish I didn't have to worry about Alan."

I look back to her, "Is this the first time?"

She refuses to meet my gaze. I sigh again, "Is this the worst that he has done?"

She still refuses to turn to me. "Sarah, you can trust me on this. I am a complete stranger. You do not have to worry about me running off and talking to someone. I am not from here, I won't be back here. I am just passing through. Use me as a sounding board, seriously. Nothing you tell me will be something I have not either lived through or heard of before. I promise."

Sarah gives me a quick look then pulls over on the side of the road. She quickly turns the hazards on then turns to me in her seat.

"He is just so fucking mean. He gets so jealous, over nothing really. I said hello to the mailman. That's what this is about." She points to her eye then quickly looks down at her shaking hands.

I reach out and put my hand over hers, "You can always leave. Do you have somewhere else to go?"

She shakes her head vigorously back at me, "Not really no. I tried to leave before. I told him I was leaving. He pushed me down the stairs. I broke my arm in two places. I am just scared to death that I am going to end up pregnant or something and be stuck with him forever."

I slowly rub a small circle on top of her hand with my fingers, "Does he force himself on you?" She looks away quickly, as I see a tear roll down her face.

The anger that rolls through my veins is like lava. Another fucking man that thinks it is okay to force himself on her just because she is a female. Just because she is smaller than him, not as strong. I feel that pull, that familiar pull of needing to fucking destroy someone. The plan starts to formulate immediately.

I reach into my pocket for my phone. I pull it out smiling at her, "What's your full name? I will find you on facebook and send you a friend request. Then if you ever need help or just someone to talk to you can reach out to me."

She smiles gently back at me, "But if you are leaving the area how would you be able to help?"

I give her a quick grin, "Sarah, if you can't tell I don't really stay in one place very long. That doesn't mean I wouldn't come back if you needed me. Us girls gotta stick together, take care of eachother."

She gives me a broad smile, leaning forward a bit looking down at my phone, "Sarah Holmes. My name is Sara Holmes, if it asks the area it should say I live in Gilman. It's just northeast of Augusta."

I grin back quickly, typing her name into my notes, "Are there pictures of the douchenozzle on there?"

She blurts out a laugh, "Yeah, there are pictures of me and Alan. His name is Alan Archer. He isn't hard to find. He lives on social media."

I smile back, "Okay. I will definitely find you there. Then if you just need to talk or whatever, I will only be a message away."

She smiles and squeezes my hand back, "Thank you so much Maeve. I don't really have any friends. Alan doesn't really let me talk to anyone or go anywhere without him. Today is a complete fluke. My dad needed me to run something to my cousins for him. That is the only reason Alan let me leave town today."

I give her another nod as I put my phone back in my pocket, "Well, I am glad he did. I never would have met you if not. I think this might be a great friendship we are starting here."

I hate lying to her. I have no intention of sticking around. But I have every intention of getting her out of her current situation.

She pulls back out onto the road but after about 10 minutes I see that we are getting much closer to the mountains. I point to the side of the road on an upcoming curve, "Hey Sarah, can you let me out up here? I am gonna get some air, walk the last few miles to the next stop."

She glances around outside then back at me, "But we are in the middle of nowhere."

I smile back at her, "That is kinda how I prefer it."

She gives me a worried smile but pulls over. I reach in the back grabbing my duffle then lean back down into the window as I shut the car door behind me, "I will reach out to you in the next day or so okay? I just have to find some wifi first. I am really glad I met you Sarah."

She smiles back at me, "Me too Maeve. I will talk to you soon!"

I back away from the car waving at her as she drives off. I step down off the side of the road and pull my phone back out. I pull up a map, I guesstimate I am about 15 maybe 20 miles away from Gilman. It is going to be risky being that close to Augusta but it is obvious that Sarah is not going to be able to get herself out of this situation she is in.

I wait until I don't see her taillights any longer then turn back around. I start the hike back in the direction I have just been running from. I know I don't have to do this. I also know that wanting to do this probably makes me crazy. Okay maybe not crazy for wanting to do it, but definitely crazy because I will go through with it.

As much as I want to put some distance between me and James, I know there is no way my brain is going to let this go. It is like an itch that just needs to be scratched.

I can get in, take care of the fucking problem then be out again before Sarah even knows what happened. I hear my stomach rumble then I quickly rub my hand over it. I should have eaten some breakfast or something before I left this morning. I am fucking starving. Hopefully, I can kill a squirrel or rabbit to cook later.

I plan on finding a little wooded area somewhere between here and Gilman. Camp out for the night. I walk about 7, maybe 9 miles when I find the perfect spot. No houses nearby, there has been zero traffic down this dusty road.

I walk about a hundred feet into the woods and find a flat spot to camp out for the night. I would say I still have an hour or two of daylight before it gets too dark. I lay my duffle down then set to finding something to eat for the night.

I spend the majority of the night just sitting there leaning against a tree wondering what James is doing at that exact moment. I stare at the fire, listen to it crackle and pop. Letting the memories of the night before relive in my head.

I don't know why I did what I did, knowing damn good and well that I wasn't going to stay. Yeah, maybe if the sheriff hadn't showed up I would have stayed a bit longer but I would have left eventually. I am not good for him. I am not good for anybody. I'm toxic. Anyone with working eyes can see that.

I am sure he will forget all about me soon enough anyway. I barely fucking know him and he knows literally nothing about me. Not even my first fucking name.

8

Maeve

The Kill – Thirty Seconds To Mars

Maeve
3 years ago

"ALRIGHT! Fall in." I stand here hands behind my back, feet at shoulder width apart. I look straight ahead, desperately trying not to look towards Captain Masters. I am the only female left. They all make sure I know they don't want me here. But I have made it. I made it through training, I am now preparing for my first mission. We are set to head to South America soon. Everyone is going to be getting a weekend leave before we head out. I have decided to stay on base though, I need my head in the game.

I continue staring straight ahead, no expression on my face at all. Captain Masters is pacing back and forth in front of us. There are only 5 of us going. There is a cartel somewhere in Brazil that is dealing in arms trading, as well as selling women and children into the trade. Our only mission is to infiltrate and erase them. I have been training for this. My sniper skills are pretty solid but I do my best in hand to hand. I am prepared to kill. I am prepared to rid the world of these assholes.

Captain Masters gives us all the usual shit. Don't do anything stupid in the next 48 hours. Be ready at 0400 Monday morning. Yada yada. I continue to stare straight ahead when he stops in front of me. He looks down at the 4 other men to my right then leans into my ear, "Are you ready for the real fun to start?" I feel a shiver run *down my spine but I don't waver. I am not going to show weakness, not to anybody.*

I wake up with a start. I am sweating like crazy again. The dreams are getting more and more real. I honestly wake up thinking I am back in basics again. About to leave for South America.

Why the fuck is this all coming up now? It has been years. Is it because I am almost done with my list? Does this mean my work will be coming to an end soon? I highly doubt it. There will always be Alans' out there. There will always be someone else that needs to be taken care of. But maybe the pull won't be as strong?

I had been able to snare a small rabbit last night so at least I was able to eat before I fell asleep. But dreams of James riddled me all fucking night. The sound of his laugh. The dimple in his cheek when he smiles. I can still hear his voice as he was so gentle with me, so kind. I feel something run down my face and realize it's a tear. I need to get him out of my head. I don't have time to deal with this right now. Or maybe I am just weaker than I thought.

I search facebook and finally find a picture of Sarah's house that she shares with Alan. It is a small little ranch style home sitting far from the neighbors even though it is considered in town.

I plan to finish my hike to Gilman today, hopefully making it there in enough time to get a good glimpse of the layout. I am gonna get in, do what needs to be done and get the fuck out.

No need to play with my toys this time. One bullet to the head will be all it takes. I feel the smile pull over my face as I picture little Alan begging for his life. I really am messed up. I shouldn't enjoy this as much as I do. But it is justified, at least in my mind.

This is for Sarah.

I finally stroll into Gilman about 6 hours later. I have taken my time, there is no real need to rush. I don't even bother sticking my thumb out. No reason to. I have all the time in the world.

Lane still hasn't shown his face so there is no reason for me to scatter across the wind yet. I find somewhere secluded and sit behind some bushes across the street from Sarah's house, just watching it. There are maybe a dozen houses in this town total. If it is even big enough to be considered a town.

I watch Sarah and Alan walk around the living room. At some point, Sarah even sits down with a book. 2 different times I see Alan walk by and knock the book out of her hands. Laughing as she picks it up. Laughing as she flinches at his approach. Sarah never cracks a smile.

It is Tuesday night so hopefully they will go to bed early. Maybe, hopefully, they both have to work tomorrow. I watch them start turning lights off around 9 pm. I reach into my bag and pull out my lockpick set. Then my pistol. I check the rounds, make sure it is loaded.

I sit there for another half an hour watching for any more signs of movement. Then I wait a bit longer. I want him completely out of it before I make my way onto the property. He looks like a pretty big dude. I don't need any more fucking suprises like I had with Chad. I just need to get in, get this shit done then get the hell out of here. I stand up, hiding behind a small tree. I check the perimeter, there are no neighbors close by but I still make sure the silencer is attached tightly to the pistol.

The street light is my only worry now. I look down the road both ways before taking aim and shooting out the light. I wait another 10 minutes to make sure no one comes out their doors to check on it before I make my way across the street and around to the back of the house.

I pick the lock and slip in quietly through the back door. There is a kitchen to my left then the hallway opens up to a large living room. I do a quick perimeter check but there is no one there.

There is another hallway off the other side of the living room. I hug tight to the wall, pistol in hand. I have pulled my hood back up, tight around my face so no one, especially Sarah will be able to recognize me. I am not too worried if she does though, she doesn't even have my real name. I never friended her on Facebook like I had promised either. I will be a shadow that even Peter Pan himself couldn't catch.

I make it to the first door down the hallway and press my ear up to it. I don't hear anything, no snoring, no movement. My breath catches in my throat as I see a shadow run across the wall in front of me. I let out a silent sigh when I realize it is just the passing of a car outside playing tricks with the light. The next door is on my right and slightly open. A quick glance inside determines it is just a bathroom.

That leaves one last door on the left. I put my ear up to it and hear a slight snore. This is it. This is the bedroom. I slowly turn the knob and pull the door open.

There he is, Alan. He is lying with his back to me so all I can see is his back slowly moving as he breathes. Sarah right next to him, laying on her back face pointed at the ceiling. They both seem to be asleep. I silently take a few steps towards the bed. I hear the floor make a small creak then Sarah turns her head towards me.

Shock rolls across her face as she sees a hooded figure making their way across her bedroom. I lift a gloved finger to my mouth making a hushed motion but I can see her fear getting the best of her. She is gonna freak the fuck out and wake him up. This has the potential to get real fucking messy really quick.

I do the only thing I can think of at the time to calm her down. I pull my hood back so she can see it's me. Just her friend staring back at her. Her eyes fall wide again but then she gives me a slight nod of her chin.

I take 3 more slow, quiet steps towards her and see that he has one arm draped over her with a hand locked on her wrist. I look back to Sarah and her eyes keep going from Alan's face to the gun and back again. I see her arms are covered in bruises that look like handprints.

The anger rolls through my veins again like heroin. The burn of it enters my blood, fueling me forward. I look at Sarah and motion for her to look away. She nods her head slightly then turns her face to look towards the wall.

It is over just a few minutes later. Alan will not be hurting anyone ever again. He never even woke up. I take the silencer off and slide it into my back pocket. I turn the safety back on the gun then slide it into the waistband of my jeans. I had hoped for a quick clean kill. But unfortunately for Sarah she is now covered in blood and what looks like possibly brain matter. I had crouched down behind him and tried to shoot away from Sarah so the bullet didn't go through him and into her. I guess in the process that caused a bigger mess than I had intended.

Sarah turns back towards me and looks at Alan. Not one tear is shed. I don't even think she has a clue that her arm and neck are covered in leftover Alan. She turns back to me, "Thank you Maeve."

I nod back at her, "Give me about a half hour then call the police. Tell them an intruder broke in and killed him. Tell them the bruises you have are from them. Give me a bit of head start."

87

She smiles again and nods her head. She slides out from underneath his arm and stands up. She walks around the end of the bed. She stops as I give her a small nod then turn to leave.

I feel her hand on my bicep and turn back to her. She engulfs me in a hug, only then do I hear a small gasp as the tears start to fall. I run my gloved hand down the back of her head, "It's okay Sarah. You are free now."

She pulls back smiling at me again, "Thank you."

I smile back then reach up and touch her busted lip, "You are gonna want to find a way to bust that back open. Make it look like you fought back."

She nods and touches her lip, "I can do that."

It doesn't feel right leaving him there in the bed. I want to strip him down, leave my marks on him. It doesn't feel complete without it but I don't want to fucking traumatize her anymore than I already have. I have to trust in the power of a woman's intuition that she isn't going to call the cops on me as soon as I walk out the door.

I turn strolling back through the living room and out the back door. I grab my duffle from the ground near the bushes then head back out into the darkness. I walk for a few hours before I find another spot to curl up for the night.

It still feels so incomplete. I should have left my mark. But hopefully, Sarah will be okay. She definitely would not have been had she seen what I truly am. What I truly wanted to do.

I lean up against a tree, again about 100 feet from the road. I pull the hood tight around my head as I let myself drift off to sleep.

Maeve

3 years ago

88

I had no fucking idea how god damn HOT this place would be. We aren't in a fucking desert or something. It is just muggy and humid and sticky all the fucking time. We had been dropped at our mark yesterday around this same time. We have one location we are to all meet up at in the next 2 hours. I am happy to travel on my own until then.

Then I don't have to look over my shoulder all the goddamn time. Wondering which of the guys is going to jump out at me first. The only solidarity this team seems to have is men against women. I just have to keep my head down, not start shit and get through this mission.

I meet up with them at the designated time. Captain Masters goes over the plan, again. "We are only to drop the men. The women are most likely being sold into trade so they are not targets. Unless one of them attacks you, just ignore them. There will be about 20 men either around or already inside the warehouse. Take them down however necessary then get the fuck out. Does everyone fucking understand me?"

We all stare at him then whisper, "Sir yes sir" Captain Masters nods and we all head off to our marks.

I slowly, carefully step down an embankment. It looks like a small ditch before it goes uphill and to the walls of the building. I keep my eyes trained on my horizon when I feel my foot slide into something solid. I look down and see 2 dead eyes staring up at me.

She has to be no more than 25, maybe 26 years old. Her swollen stomach tells me she isn't the only person that died in this ditch. I reach down and check her pulse already knowing what I am going to find. Her clothes have been ripped to shreds and are laying all around her.

I look at her chest and see a strange carving. I look up and check my surroundings again before I lean down closer to her. There is some kind of animal carved into her chest.

It looks like some kind of goat head or maybe it is a deer head. There are all these squiggling lines jutting off at different angles from it. The mark is already in the process of healing though. She had it long before she was put in this ditch. I close her eyes with my hand then slide my night vision back over my eyes. These bastards are going to pay for this.

90

9

James
Chokehold – Sleep Token

I spent the first day debating on whether or not to go after her.
She didn't see me but I watched her walk down the driveway
then out of my life. Fuck, I don't even know her last name.

Even if I wanted to find her, and I do, I have nowhere to
even start. Not that she even wants to be found. So, I just spent
most of that first day pouting around the farm. I take care of the
horses and clean their stalls. Then I just sit at the doors of the
barn looking out over the property.

Why the hell am I brooding so fucking much? There isn't
anything between us. There were no promises made. It just feels
like I had something so close for just a second, then it slipped
away somehow. She needs to just be a fucking memory. I
continue to pace around the barn and the property like a lost
fucking puppy.

By the third morning being alone, I decide I need a drink.
A real drink. Beer just isn't cutting it right now. I drive into town
to the bar for some whiskey. I am on my second glass when I
hear two old timers at the end of the bar talking about some body
that was found.

I already know they are talking about Chad. Great, just
something fucking else to make me think about her. I down the
rest of my glass then sit it silently back on the bartop. I look over
to get the bartender's attention when I hear one of them mention
Gilman.

That piques my interest. I listen a bit closer, some guy
has been shot in his sleep with his woman laying in bed right
next to him. She had suffered minor injuries in the scuffle. She

is apparently too shaken up to give a straight story though. Only that the guy was dressed all in black and took off out the back door after shooting her boyfriend.

I know in my gut it isn't just some random guy. I know for a fucking fact it has to be Maeve. I quickly throw some cash on the counter and practically ran to my truck.

I fire it up then head north towards Gilman. It is a really small community not far at all from Augusta. There is no fucking way it was anyone besides her. It isn't hard at all to find the house they were talking about. There are cops lining the entire road and caution tape marking off the perimeter.

I park across the street and watch the cops going in and out. I scan the surroundings but there is no one that looks out of place. Just some cops and a few nosy neighbors. Maeve isn't around here anywhere. She probably took off like a ghost into the night. She is pretty talented with her escapes.

I watch as a beat up Honda pulls in behind me then I see an older man walking a young woman up towards the tapeline. I roll down my window to try to hear what they are talking about.

The old man leans over to one of the officers, "When will she be able to get back inside? At least to get some clothes. She will come stay with me until you are all done here but she needs some god damn clothes at least."

The girl he is talking about is beaten all to hell. She has a busted lip and a black eye. Her arms are also covered in bruises that look an awful lot like large hand prints.

Way too large to be Maeves'. Maybe I am wrong. Maeve wouldn't have beat the fuck outta some girl just to kill some random guy. Or would she? I shake my head, knocking the thoughts away. She wouldn't. Not a woman. Dude yeah, this girl no way.

The girl turns away from the old man and starts to walk back towards her car. She reaches into her pocket and pulls out a pack of smokes. She lights one up then gently touches her lip.

She must have busted it back open when she pursed her lips to light the smoke. Without even thinking, I grab a handkerchief and jump out the truck. I walk a few steps up to her then hand her the bandana to wipe her mouth with.

She gives me a questionable look but takes the gift. I put my hands in my jeans pockets and turn back towards the house, "What happened here?"

She looks back at the house then towards me, "I don't wanna talk about it."

I glance at her then back at the house, "Oh, Sorry. I didn't know if maybe you knew the people that lived there or something."

She glances back at me then towards the house again, "Yeah. I know them."

I nod at her then look back towards the cops on the sidewalk, "Hopefully everyone is okay."

She lets a small smile fall over her face, "The girl that lives there, Sarah. She will be just fine."

I can see the shadow over her eyes. I take a wild shot in the dark as I cross my arms over my chest, "Well, that's good. I don't want some crazed maniac running around. I would have to follow my girlfriend around like a golden retriever."

I let out a small laugh while still looking at the house. I hear the girl behind me take a deep drag off the cigarette then exhale, "No. No crazed maniac on the loose. Your girlfriend should be safe."

I smile gratefully at her, "Maeve will be happy for that at least. I won't have to keep tabs on her."

The girl throws the cigarette down and stomps it out before stepping up close to me, "Did you say Maeve?"

I smile towards the house, my suspicions officially being confirmed, "Yeah, you know her? I mean it's not a big town, I wouldn't be surprised if you did."

She smiles back towards the house, "I know a Maeve but I don't think she would be your girlfriend. The Maeve I know isn't from around here."

I nod, still not looking towards the girl, "Yeah, my Maeve isn't originally from here either. She is from the west coast. Short girl, about your height actually. She has short black hair, always wearing this old beat up zipper hoodie. She has the clearest blue eyes you will ever see though."

The girl reaches up and grabs my bicep. I look down at her hand then up to her face. She looks towards the police then takes a step closer to me, whispering, "Can you tell her that Sarah says thank you. Please?" I nod at her then look back at the house.

I take a deep breath, then roll my neck on my shoulders, "How long has he been beating you?"

I feel her hand pull back abruptly. I turn to her, "Don't worry. I am not going to say a fucking word."

I look down at her arms, her lip, her black eye, "This *is* his work though isn't it?"

She looks into my eyes then nods her head yes. I take another deep breath then close my eyes, "Did she get out okay? Did he hurt her?"

Sarah turns, putting her back to the house and faces my truck, "He didn't even wake up. She just snuck in and then I thanked her and she left out the back door."

I let out a shaky breath and feel the tension release from my shoulders. Thank fuck she didn't get hurt this time.

I smile back down at Sarah, "Thank you. I haven't seen her since the day before yesterday. I just wanted to make sure she is okay."

Sarah looks back over her shoulder then back to me again, "She said she is going to head back north. I am going to bet she walked a few hours then found a place to crash. If she started back out this morning, she shouldn't be more than maybe 15, 25 miles away at best. She went North up 287 towards Sun River. I would check the side roads though, I doubt she will stick to the highway."

I give Sarah a huge smile, "You are my new best friend Sarah."

She smiles back at me as I turn and run back to the truck. She steps up to the window, "If you find her, tell her to come around and see me sometime. It would be nice to have a friend around."

I give her a quick nod and smile then turn my truck North. I follow 287 north for about 45 miles. Just to make sure she didn't stay on the highway, but Sarah was right. If she thought she might get spotted she wouldn't be on the highway. Luckily, there is not much traffic, but whenever I do encounter vehicles I do a double take just to ensure they aren't blocking her view from me.

There is a small service road that runs along Sun River, maybe she would take that and cut over to another road. I quickly turn around and drive back another 20 miles before I turn down the service road.

I let my eyes scan the landscape but I don't see her anywhere. I come to the end of the service road then angrily slam my palm into the steering wheel. She is really gone.

I let out a deep breath then look to the right. There, walking down the side of the road is a small figure all in black, duffle bag slung over her shoulder. My heart slams up into my throat.

I quickly turn out onto the road then slow down as I get close to her. I roll down the passenger window, "Hey, need a ride?"

Maeves' eyes cut to mine and she seems to freak out. "No, I am good. Please just go."

She starts walking faster. I speed up then pull over in front of her. I leave the truck running as I throw it in park then jump out and run up to her. She stops in front of me but refuses to look at me.

I pull her in close to me then hug her fiercely, "Are you okay?"

She pushes back on my chest as she pulls her duffle up higher on her shoulder, "Yeah, I am fine. Just leaving town is all."

She steps around me, then continues past my truck and down the road. I take a few steps towards her then lean against the hood of the truck. I have to get her to turn around. I have to get her to stay.

I am not going to beg her but I need her here with me. I have to keep her safe. I have no idea why, I just do.

"Sarah says thank you, by the way."

Maeve stops dead in her tracks then turns around to face me. I can see the shock and alarm on her face. Her eyes are everywhere at once. She looks in my truck, then down the road, then down the sideroad then back to my face.

Maeve lets out a hard sigh, "So what? Are you here to take me in?"

I shake my head as I take a few more steps towards her, "No. I just wanted to make sure you were okay. That you weren't hurt this time."

She takes another step towards me then drops the duffle to the ground, pulling her hood back. Her black eye is now nothing but a yellowing bruise around her eye. Her lip is looking a lot better as well.

She crosses her arms over her chest, "So, you find out I am running around just killing random people and you want to know if I am okay? Some might say you are just as crazy as me."

I laugh at her as I shrug my shoulders, "Crazy is as crazy does."

She throws her hands up in the air, "What the fuck does that even mean?"

I laugh again, "How the fuck am I supposed to know, I'm crazy, remember?"

She barks out a laugh as she looks back down the road she has been walking. She turns back towards me, taking a step closer, "Why aren't you afraid of me?"

I step even closer to her, bridging the distance a bit more, "You haven't given me a reason to be."

Maeve tilts her head up towards me again, "I have killed two people within a 10 mile radius of where you sleep every night. How is that not a reason?"

I take another step closer to her, no more than a foot away from her now, "You also slept in my bed, in my arms and never once did I feel like you were going to hurt me. Maybe yourself, but never me."

She blinks heavily and looks away. I reach up, touching her chin, pulling her face back towards me, "Hey. What you are doing, whatever this is. It's not you. Well, it's not all there is to you. You are going through something. I just want to help."

She stares deep into my eyes, like she is searching for some kind of truth, "I can't be helped James. I am way too far gone. I don't want you to be involved. I don't want any of this to fall back on you."

I drop my hand from her chin then give her a quick smile, knowing damn good and well that my dimples are showing, "Why is that? Because you like me? Because you think I am cuuuuute?"

Maeve barks out a loud laugh then flips me off. I laugh right along with her then pull her shoulders into my chest to hug her again. This time I feel her arms wrap around my waist as she leans into my hug taking it deeper.

I run my hand over her head then kiss the top of it. "Maeve, I will not for a minute try to pretend that I know what is going on in that head of yours. And you may think you are too far gone but I don't believe that. That is not what I see when I look at you. But Chad, well, he was a dick. In my heart, I 100% believe he had it coming. Then after meeting Sarah, I also believe whoever that guy was, he also had it coming.

"Do I think what you are doing is safe or smart? Fuck no. But I don't think you are some crazed murderer just running around shooting people for no reason. I don't know what has made you this way. I don't know what you are running from, or fuck even towards. I just want to be with you wherever you go. I just want you."

Maeve lets out a loud sigh then pulls away from me. I look down into her face and see a lone tear run down her cheek. I didn't even know she knew how to cry. But that one single solitary tear speaks volumes.

She is in there somewhere. She does have emotions. She does have a conscience.

She is just lost. I look deep into her eyes, then cradle her face with my hands and kiss her deeply. I feel her hands come around my neck pulling me in closer. I tilt my head and let my tongue explore her mouth. Her mouth is dry, reminding me of the texture of sandpaper. I immediately wonder if she has even eaten or drank anything the past few days.

I pull back after a few minutes, giving her another small smile. She looks down at my throat, "I don't know how to do this. Any of this."

98

I smile at her again, "Me either. Maybe we can just figure it out together."

Her eyes search mine for a minute then she gives me a small smile. I pull back then step around her picking up her duffle. I walk back past her then put it in the back of my truck before opening the door and looking out the open window towards her,

"Come on. Get in. Let's go home."

Her eyes blink quickly then I see her take a deep breath. Her hands go into fists then she seems to shake them out a bit. Like she is nervous. Maeve then nods her head before walking over to the passenger side of the truck.

I climb in then wait for her to slide in and shut the door. I reach up and put the truck into drive. Before taking off though, I reach over, wrapping my arm around the back of her waist.

I pull her close to me on the bench seat then quickly cut the truck in the opposite direction back down the road towards the house. I don't dare look at her. I don't want to spook her again. About a mile down the road, I smile as I feel her hand slide onto my thigh. I kiss the top of her head again then hurry on back home.

Not a half hour later, I am pulling the truck up to the barn. Maeve slides out the same time as me, smiling as she sees the horses in the pasture. I reach into the bed of the truck and pull her duffle out.

I smile as I watch her walk over to the fence then fold her arms on the top rung and sit her chin on her hands. I walk towards the back porch, leaving her and her thoughts with the horses. She comes inside about 20 minutes later as I am preparing some steaks for the grill.

She takes her hoodie off and slings it over her arm, "I am gonna go put my coat and stuff in my room."

I give her a quick nod then move to step outside to put the meat and potatoes on the grill. I grin to myself knowing that when she reaches the top of the stairs she is going to see her duffle sitting on the end of my bed. Hopefully, she will understand the invitation.

It doesn't take the steaks long at all to sear and finish cooking. I check the foil wrapped sliced potatoes, making sure they are tender enough to throw some cheese on. I hear the screen door open and two little feet pad over towards me.

I smile as I sprinkle the shredded cheese on the taters then close the foil back up. Two hands slowly slide around my sides, linking back up at my stomach. I reach a hand down placing it on top of hers as I look out over the sunset.

I feel her cheek press into the middle of my back as she squeezes me a little tighter. I start to turn and feel her pull back a little. Maeve is standing behind me, wearing my nirvana shirt, legs bare to the breeze.

I smile at her then lean down to give her a kiss, "I hope you are hungry."

She smiles back up at me, "Famished." Her eyes hold mine, unblinking as she kisses me back.

5 minutes later we are sitting down at the table, plates loaded up ready to feast. I reach into the fridge then hand her a coke as I grab a beer. Maeve leans forward a bit, "Do you have any ketchup in there?"

I reach in grabbing the ketchup, then setting it squarely on the table before sitting down. "I have never seen anyone use ketchup on cheesy potatoes. Not sure how I feel about that."

She smiles as she shakes the bottle, "It's for the steak."

I drop my fork loudly onto my plate, in complete shock and honestly a bit of disgust, "Are you fucking insane?"

She looks up at me shocked. I reach over and yank the ketchup from her hand, "These are fucking ribeyes not a god damn hamburger."

Maeve laughs out loud. She tries to reach back over the table for the ketchup bottle, "I know!"

I stand up and back up to the counter, ketchup held high above my head, "NO! I will not allow this!"

Maeve is laughing maniacally while trying to climb me like I am a tree. I turn around and try to get the window open to throw the ketchup outside into the dirt. Before I can even get the latch undone, I feel a hand tightly gripping my balls and I freeze.

Maeve leans in close to my ear, "Drop the fucking ketchup James or I swear to god I am going to separate you and your best friends."

My eyes are large enough they probably look like they are about to pop out of their sockets. I slowly bring the ketchup back down and sit it on the counter, "You know we could have just talked about it. You didn't have to threaten my balls."

Maeve plants a kiss on my cheek then releases my boys and grabs the ketchup, "I don't like to beat around the bush with shit. Plus the food is getting cold. Nobody likes cold steaks and ketchup."

I hear her walk back to the table as I gulp, loudly, "Obviously."

I turn around and sit down, still a little scared but mostly disgusted as she squirts ketchup into a pile on her plate.

I lift my fork, "Can you at least try a bite without the tomato massacre juice before you defile that fine cut of beef?"

Maeve smiles up at me then cuts off a piece of steak, promptly sticking it in her mouth. I watch her lips wrap around the fork then slide the meat off.

Maybe I shouldn't have asked her to do that.

Maeve smiles again, "It's really good. Nice and tender."

I give her a half grin then cut into mine. I am not going to survive this, whatever this is. I watch her enjoy her dinner, only dipping the steak into the ketchup when she catches me staring. We sit back and just enjoy the silence a bit before I stand up, grabbing our plates to head to the sink.

I sit them down as she appears right beside me. I look down at her smiling, "I wash, you dry?"

Maeve smiles back at me, "Sounds good."

We finish the dishes then head to the back porch to sit for a bit. She takes her normal perch on the back step as I sit on the swing. I look over at her and she catches my eye. I smile again then get up, walking over to the steps with her. I sit across from her stretching my legs out beside hers. I lean my head back against the post just staring at her.

Her skin is still pale but there is more to it now. She just seems to glow a bit. I hope it is because she is happy to be here. I don't know if it is true or not but my brain really wants it to be.

She tucks her hair behind her ear as she turns back towards me, "What?"

I give her a soft smile, taking in her expressions, her mannerisms, "Nothing, just looking."

She smiles again, still hesitant, "What ya looking at?"

I let out a deep sigh, "Just this crazy beautiful bitch sitting on my back steps."

She barks out a laugh, it is deep and guttural almost like a duck call. I sit up, "What in the actual fuck was that?"

Her eyes are huge and she is trying not to laugh again. She has her hands slammed around her lips so she doesn't let another whatever that was slip out, "No seriously, there must be an animal dying somewhere! We should try to save it!"

I lunge for her shoulders as she laughs again, trying to scoot away. I grab her pulling her back to my front as I lean back against the post staring over top of her head at the horizon.

She lets out a small breath, "I feel like none of this is real. Like it's all gonna just fall out from under me at any time."

I wrap my arms around her, "I won't let you fall."

She turns her head, nuzzling her face into my chest. I cross my fingers and decide to jump in, "Why do you do it?"

I can feel her shoulders tense as she shakes her head, "I guess I look at it as a form of payback. I don't just kill random people ya know. Only the ones that deserve it. The ones that have hurt others, knowingly, willingly."

I rub my hands up her arms, "How many have there been?"

She lets out another sigh then turns to face me, putting a leg on either side of me, "Probably too many. So far there have been 12."

I try to keep my heart in check as I look out over her shoulder. I am really not sure what to ask next. Or how to feel about what she has just told me. She grabs my hands, looking at them as she traces the lines of my palm with her finger,

"It's only men that have hurt women or children. I just can't stand the thought of what they are doing. That they are just getting away with it. It isn't right that they are using their size, their everything to hold these women, these children down. It's not fair."

I watch her fingers as she traces those lines, like she is unable to look me in the eyes. I look back out over her shoulder, "My dad left when I was 12. He was a mean old bastard. He used to beat the shit out of me and my mom. I had a little sister. She was 3 years younger than me. She died when she was 6, I was 9. Dad was never the same after that. He started drinking, then started hitting. Mom always said it was the only way he knew how to get his anger out. He died in a bar fight when I was 18. Me and mom were never sad again after that day."

I can feel her eyes on me, then feel her finger start tracing my palm again, "My parents are great. Like so in love it's disgusting, kind of great. They were high school sweethearts. Mom is a librarian. Dad, he is a tax attorney. They have a pretty good life. I am an only child though. They tried for years to get pregnant so once they had me they just stopped trying. I like to say it was because perfection had been met."

I give her a laugh then watch her staring at my open hands. She continues, "They were not happy at all when I decided to join the corps. Mom, I swear, cried for weeks on end. Dad wasn't surprised, I had always been a tomboy, but he was more scared I think. They had gone through so much to have me. I think they thought I was just trying to throw my life away or something. I wasn't though. I just always liked the structure of the military. Everything had its place. I get nervous when things are not organized. Even my thoughts."

I pull her hands up to my mouth gently kissing her knuckles, "I get that. I like having all my ducks in a row too."

Maeve smiles at me then turns back around to lean into me again. A few minutes go by then I hear her say, "Every time I always say that was the last one. Then something will happen, I will hear a rumor, or like with Sarah. I just met her by chance. She was too weak to fight back on her own.

"I knew if I didn't do something she would suffer for the rest of her life. I try to tell myself it's okay, it's what I was trained to do so why not do it? But I wasn't trained to just murder people all willy nilly. It scares me that I can justify it so easily in my head."

I kiss the top of her head again then place my cheek on her crown. I can understand a lot of her thought process. I too was trained to do what she does, maybe not to her extent but I

104

understand how it feels to stand by helpless when you could obviously help. I trace her shoulders with my fingertips, "Do you think if you got some help with it, the organization of your thoughts, that you would be able to stop?"

She seems to hold her breath for a minute, "Maybe, but not yet. I am not done. Not yet."

I lift my face looking down at the back of her head. "Why?" She shakes her head back and forth, "I'm just not."

I give her a quick nod, "Okay. I won't push. Just know, if you need to talk to someone, about anything. I am here."

Maeve turns back around giving me a soft smile. She looks at my lips then my eyes as she leans in and gives me a kiss. I smile at her as she pulls back, "But I do have one more pretty serious question for you."

Her eyes narrow a bit and she pulls her knees in tight to her chest, "Okay?"

I clear my throat and lean forward a bit, "It's actually a two part question. One, do you own any clothing that isn't black and Two, is that your last pair of underwear?"

She grins from ear to ear shaking her head, "Well, One yes all I own is black, with my extracurriculars it has been a necessity. And Two, the last clean pair, yes."

I lean back into the post and snap my fingers, "Damn."

She sits up a bit straighter, "Why?"

I smile deviously back at her, "Well for one, you would look fucking sexy as hell in something red. With your skin so porcelain, it would probably make my balls drop all over again. And then, if that is your last pair of underwear I would feel bad if I ripped them off your body at some point. I don't want you to have to walk around going commando."

I watch her cheeks turn pink as her eyes seem to twinkle a bit. She stands up then reaches under the shirt, pulling her underwear down slowly then stepping out of them. She stares at me the entire time, smiling, then tosses them into my lap as she sits back down. "There, now you don't have to worry about destroying them."

I feel my jaw hanging open. I look down at her boy shorts laying in my lap then start to smile at her. I pick them up then stuff them into my back pocket. She smiles at me again then turns her back to me leaning up against me again.

I grin mischievously as I reach down grabbing the hem of my shirt she is wearing and start pulling it up so she isn't sitting on it anymore. I smile wider when I feel the goosebumps that raise up on her skin when she feels my hands touching her bare hips.

I continue to raise my hands until they are wrapped around her breasts, then I lean in and kiss her neck. She leans her head to the left to give me more access. She presses her hands into my thighs as she scoots back closer to me.

I kiss her neck then move up to her ear. She lets out a soft moan when I nibble on her lower lobe. I open my eyes to see her chest heaving, I whisper into her ear, "Why are you breathing so heavy?"

She smiles but doesn't open her eyes, "I don't know."

I smile back, "Do you like my hands on your tits?"

She grins again, opening her eyes to look out into the darkness. The only light now is falling out onto the porch from the kitchen. The light being cast across her profile is the most beautiful sight I have ever seen. The way the shadows dance across her skin as she smiles into the night.

Maeve looks back over her shoulder then leans in and gives me a kiss. She pulls back with her eyes shut tight again, "Yes."

I let a hand slip down to her hip bone and she sucks in a quick breath, "What do you want me to do Maeve?"

She shakes her head but keeps her eyes closed, her words shaky, "I don't know. Anything."

I growl into her ear, "Oh, don't say that. Way too many options for me."

Maeve turns around facing me again, my hands falling to her thighs, "What do you want to do to me James?"

I smile as I lean in close to her face, "So, so many wicked little things."

She gives me a little side smile as she puts a hand on my chest leaning forward, "Tell me."

I look her deep in the eyes, "I want to fuck you so hard that you forget that any other man exists in this entire fucking world. I want to bend you over this porch railing and ride you so hard that your screams scare the horses. I want to lick that perfect little pussy until I feel you cum all over my face.

"I want to take those pouty little lips and watch them fit perfectly around my dick. I want you to cum so fucking hard on my cock that it would physically be impossible for me to ever pull out of you. I want to lay you over my knee and spank your ass so god damn hard you know that you are fucking mine and no one elses'. Ever."

Her eyes are like huge crystal blue globes staring back at me, she lets out a soft moan as she leans into my lips. I kiss her hard and deep. She pulls back looking at my lips, "I want you to fucking break me James. I want you to fuck me so hard that I can't even walk after. I want to feel you everywhere. I want to give you everything."

I close my eyes, imagining all the things I want to do to this girl, "Fuck Maeve, do you know how fucking sexy you are?"

I open my eyes to see her smiling at me as she pulls the shirt up and off her body. She now sits in front of me, completely fucking naked. I sit back just taking her all in. She is fucking perfect.

107

Her tight little body fits perfectly into mine, like we were made for eachother. I take my hat off and throw it onto the porch then pull my shirt up, ripping it from my body. Maeve reaches down and unbuttons my pants while I start to pull them down at my hips.

I look down at the porch, "One of us is going to get splinters in our ass this way." She lets out a laugh then stands up in front of me. I follow the lines of her legs up to her hips, letting out a long sigh as my eyes travel up her body finally landing on that perfect smile on her face.

She turns and starts to strut her fine ass back into the house. I stand up, pants halfway down my hips following her inside. She turns to the right then climbs up to sit on the edge of the dining room table. I step up to her, placing my hand around her neck, pulling her into a deep kiss. Her hands move to my bare chest as she starts lowering them, letting her fingertips run across the ridges of my abs.

I reach down and slide my pants down my thighs before pulling her closer to me. She wraps her legs around my thighs then leans back onto the table. I lift her up as I gently slide into her. Her back arches off the table as I slam into her again.

I hold her up by the ass, slowly taking my time, enjoying every single moan as I slide in and out of her. Maeve takes her hands and starts to slide them down her own body. Her right hand lingering on her tit, rolling around her nipple. She opens her eyes, staring at me, no longer vacantly but with desire.

I push into her harder as a small gasp leaves her throat. I quickly pull out of her and drop to my knees. I pull her pussy closer to my face then lick her straight up her center, flicking my tongue on her clit, "Holy fuck, James!"

Her hands wrap up in my hair pulling me closer into her pussy. I flick her clit a few more times with my tongue before I pull down, sticking my tongue into her as deep as it will go. I can hear her panting as she uses my head like a joystick, directing it to the spots she wants teased next.

I lick up her center again then pull her clit into my teeth giving it a little nibble. I can hear her moaning from the table above me. I reach one hand up and start rolling her nipple between my fingers . Then I take my other hand, quickly starting to pump in and out of her with three fingers.

I see her hands wrap into her hair as she starts moaning louder. I pinch her nipple as she tries sitting up a bit. I look up to see her watching me devour her pussy.

She lets her chin fall to her chest a bit then moans, "Fuck James." I move back to her clit, circling it with my tongue then every few minutes nibbling on it again.

I reach down, removing my hand from her tit to start stroking my dick. I am raging hard and want to fuck her hard up against the wall but the noises she is making is too intoxicating for me to stop devouring her.

She is watching me lick her when she says, "Squeeze your dick harder." I do what she says then moan into her clit. She arches her back again as I stand up, still stroking my dick fiercely as she lays out in front of me with my fingers hooked inside her. She looks down at me again then smiles as she watches me claiming myself right in front of her.

Maeve sits up and slides down off the table. My fingers fall out of her but I can't stop stroking my dick. I am so fucking close. She drops to her knees then looks up at me, "Tell me if I do it wrong."

She wraps her little hand around the base of my dick then licks the vein on the bottom all the way to the tip. I put a hand on the table on either side of her head. She sucks my dick into her mouth then starts bobbing in and out on it.

I am panting, "Jesus fuck Maeve. Don't stop." I grab the back of her head as I start pulling her forward. She moves her hands and puts them both on my thighs as I stand back up and wrap both hands around the back of her head.

I feel her mouth hollow out around my dick and I start slamming into her lips. I am afraid for a second that I am hurting her but then I hear her moan in response to me as I slam into her mouth again.

Does she even know that she doesn't have a gag reflex?

I wrap my fingers around the hair on the back of her head as push her further down on my dick. I look down watching her taking all of my dick deep into her throat when my release hits me like a brick wall.

I quickly pull out of her mouth and try to shoot my load onto her chest. She smiles up at me with cum on her chin and neck, rolling down her tits. I growl as I pick her up. I lay her down flat on the table then put a thigh over each shoulder.

I smile down at her, "Hang on." Her eyes go wide as I stand up to my full height with my hands on her ass pushing her pussy straight into my mouth. I start licking her rapidly, flicking her clit with my tongue as she holds onto my hair with one hand, the other hand flat on the wall behind me to keep her balance.

I suck her clit deep into my mouth and I hear her scream above me. Her thighs tighten around my head as I continue to devour her throbbing cunt. She is thrusting into my face harder until she finally starts to slow down.

I feel her unclenching her thighs as her breathing tries to go back to normal. I pull back smiling up at her. Feeling her release running down my chin, onto my chest. I let her slide down me until my arms are back around her and she is wrapping her legs around my waist again. I kiss her hard, knowing she can taste herself on my lips.

She pulls back with a glow on her skin, "That was fucking amazing James."

I smile then sit her down on the table, "I am not done with you yet."

Her eyes are huge as she watches me pull my jeans and underwear off the rest of the way. She claims every single inch of my skin with her eyes.

I pick her back up then spin her to put her back to the wall. She looks into my eyes, nervous but excited, "We aren't done until you break my dick off in you baby." She smiles then slams into my lips again for another kiss.

Maeve locks her ankles behind me as I lean up into her core. I lower her down the wall just a bit then slam into her. She lets out a scream then I feel her running her nails down my back. I continue to slam into her with complete abandon.

I am not wearing a condom so I am trying to keep enough self control about me that I don't fucking fill her completely. I feel her sliding up and down the wall, meeting my hips thrust for thrust.

I look at her face, at her closed eyes, "Fucking look at me Maeve."

She opens her eyes looking deep into mine. I smile, "I wanna watch my dick fucking destroy you."

Her mouth falls into another O shape as she braces herself with my shoulders. I pummell into her with complete reckless abandon. I feel her start to flutter around my dick and I know she is going to explode soon.

I put both hands on the wall behind her then start thrusting into her harder, faster. I hear her scream my name and at the same time feel her clench down on my bare dick.

It is like fucking heaven. I am going to have to get this girl on some kind of birth control. This feels too fucking good. I want nothing more than to finish inside of her. She is still

III

squeezing me tight as I turn her back around, laying her back down on the table. I push down on her hips then start slamming into her so hard the table is trying to scoot across the hardwood floor. I feel my release starting in my spine.

Maeve is grasping for anything on the table to hold onto. Her pussy still pulsates around my dick as I pull out quickly and start slapping my dick onto her stomach with my hand. I watch the cum leave my cock in ropes, coating the underside of her tits and stomach.

I continue to finish on her as I close my eyes and tilt my head towards the ceiling. We are both breathing heavily, trying to catch our breath. I smile down at her as she lays there with her eyes closed, smiling into the nothing.

I pull away from her just long enough to go into the kitchen and grab a dishtowel out of the drawer. I walk back up to her quickly wiping the cum from her chin and neck, then her tits and her stomach. I look down at myself as I clean my dick up then throw the towel onto the table beside her.

She sits up wrapping her arms around my neck, "That was fucking everything James. I swear at one point I went to fucking heaven." I smile into her ear, then pick her up and start to head upstairs. I am just getting started.

10

Maeve

Heaven In Hiding - Halsey

James is carrying me upstairs with my legs wrapped around his center. I can barely hold myself up. I have never felt so unsteady before in my life. I never dreamed that sex would feel this good.

My body is quickly becoming addicted to his cock. He is so thick and full. Perfect. I am glad I have never wasted any of my orgasms on anyone else. His dick deserves them all.

James rounds the corner into his room then sits me down on the bed. He smiles down at me with this feral look in his eyes. I have seen that look in men before, but it was never something that I craved. Never something that brought out this need in me.

There is just something so different about him. Of all the horrible things that have happened to me in the last 3 years, this man has been able to help me try to forget them in just a few days. I have never felt this kind of connection to somebody before.

James kneels down in front of me and I lean in to kiss him. I wrap my hands around the back of his head pulling him in tight. When I run out of air, I finally pull back looking into his eyes.

Those amber orbs seem to be able to see straight through me. I want to tell him everything. About why I do what I do, what happened, what's still to come. I am afraid though. Afraid he will push me out, afraid I won't see whatever this is in his eyes anymore.

What if it changes everything? That is what I am trying to avoid at all costs. I blink heavily, trying to get the thoughts out of my head. I want to just focus on us. On now. I smile at him then scoot back on the bed. I have no clue what I am doing but apparently anything I do is just right for him.

I lean back on my elbows parting my knees, letting them fall wide. James stalks up in between them then starts kissing me at my belly button working his way north. I watch as he takes my left nipple completely into his mouth. I can feel his tongue circling it, then I feel him nip at it.

I moan softly letting my head fall back between my shoulders. I honestly feel like I could let this man do anything to my body and I would be absolutely okay with it. I have gone from never wanting to be touched ever, to craving his fingers running against my skin.

I feel his lips trace my collarbone then my neck. I tilt my head a bit to the right to give him more access. I turn my head to look at him, thinking of all the feral ideas running through my mind. Everything that has been done to me, everything I feared before, all of it feels like something I want him to do.

I want him to degrade me. I want him to just fucking destroy me. Because from him, it wouldn't be destructive like it was before, I honestly believe it could set me free. I turn my head and look him in the eyes. The golden warm honey of his iris' feels like it is drizzling down my face, straight into my veins. I want him closer than close.

James wraps one arm around me then rolls me on top of him. I part my knees and slide up his body to his hips. I sit there smiling down at him as I trace the lines of his muscles with my fingers. He is just staring at me. Like he can't believe that I am actually here, actually back in his bed.

"I am not experienced in this at all. Not because I never wanted to be, but because I am just not the type of woman that men really want. I was used, then tossed aside. It made me not want to be with anyone ever. But when I look at you, really look

14

at you. I feel wanted. That is new for me, it is almost like, empowering. I just want to be for you everything you want me to be."

James reaches up tucking my hair behind my ear then smiles, "Maeve, you are right. You are not like any other woman I have ever met before. You are rough and raw and fragile all at the same time. I want to fucking break you but at the same time I want to hold you so that you know I will always, ALWAYS, keep you safe. I don't understand it myself. I don't care that you are not experienced in any of this because to me, for me, everything you do is perfect. I don't care about the person you were, or the things you did. I only care about the girl in front of me, right now."

I feel myself letting go of a breath that was being held tightly in my chest. I have never felt safe with a man before. Not before the corps, definitely not during, but now, I feel safe.

James will never hurt me, he won't just toss me to the side when he is done with me. Because I don't actually believe he will ever be done with me. I lean down and kiss him, as powerfully as I can. I can feel him getting hard beneath me again. I smile into his mouth as I slide my tongue across his teeth.

He lets out a deep moan into my core. I sit back up then roll over to the night stand. I pull out a condom and toss it on his stomach, "Your turn." He smiles at me as he leans forward rolling the condom onto his ever largening cock.

I lay back again, letting my legs fall open, beckoning to him with my eyes. He settles between my thighs looking me in the eyes deeply as he slides into me. I don't dare breathe or even blink. I feel that if I do anything to break this connection that I may never be able to get it back. I am always afraid in a moment like this that I will have flashbacks, memories of what Lane has done but laying here with James I know it would never be like that with him.

He isn't just taking what he wants, he is giving me what he thinks I need. I arch my back a bit, moving my hips deeper into the bed to give him a different angle to work with and he finally sighs. I watch his eyes roll up into his head as he closes his eyes smiling while thrusting into me. I smile back, biting my bottom lip in the process. I can feel him everywhere at once. He is the air, the earth, my everything in this moment.

James grasps my hips tightly and starts to push harder, faster into me. I can feel it starting to build deep in the pit of my stomach. I can spend the rest of my life right here, just like this.

I let my fingers glide up his forearms onto his biceps then his shoulders. I hold on as he leans down, taking my nipple in his mouth again.

His hands are now wrapped around my ribs, he is savoring me with his mouth and hands. I reach down grabbing his right hand. James opens his eyes to watch me glide his hand up my chest. Then I let it settle on my neck. I look back at him, letting my hand fall back down to the mattress. I give him a quick little side smile then lift my neck up into his grasp. I feel his fingers tighten slightly around my throat as he starts thrusting harder into me.

I can feel my release building quicker now. I reach my hand up on his squeezing his hand tighter around my neck as I feel my pussy start to pulsate, teasing me with the moment that is about to arrive. James closes his eyes and is making a deep rutting noise in the back of his throat.

I watch him, "Look at me James." Those golden orbs land on mine and we both smile. He continues to push me past my boundaries until I feel myself clench around him, "Fuck me James! Harder baby, fuck me harder!"

He removes his hand from my neck balancing his arms on either side of my head as he destroys me. James roars with his release as he is fully seated inside of me. He continues to push inside of me until he feels my own orgasm start to die down. I lean up kissing his neck, then chest then mouth. He holds himself there, hovering over me, for I don't know how long before he rolls off of me and disposes of the used condom.

I feel him roll back over then prop himself up on an elbow as he traces the curves of my body with his pointer finger. I smile as I take a deep breath, content with lying in my own solitude.

I peek one eye open and see James just staring at me, "What?"

He smiles and starts twirling a piece of my hair in his fingers, "Why black?"

I roll onto my side and prop myself up so I am facing him, "Why black what? Hair or everything?"

He gives a slight grin, "Yes."

I laugh back at him, "Well, the clothes because I always wanted to be a ninja when I grew up. The hair because, well in all honesty, it was completely different from what my natural hair is. I needed something completely different. Don't worry, my soul regretted it the moment I did it. I don't know if it is something I will keep up with. I thought about just shaving my head completely and starting from scratch again."

James laughs out loud as we both start to shimmy up the bed then roll under the blankets. We lay on our pillows staring at each other, "So what now?"

I am nervous but I need to know. What is this? What are we?

James smiles back at me, "What do you want now?"

I raise a shoulder and give him my best I don't fucking know face. He gives me a soft laugh, "Maeve, I don't want to push you so far that you leave. I also don't want to rush you into anything and make you think you have to stay. I want you to be comfortable enough to make that decision on your own. Do I want you to stay? Fuck yeah I do, for as long as I can hold you. But will I force you to? Never. I would never force you into anything you aren't comfortable with.

"I am nervous, maybe a bit scared that the other side of you might come out. Not that you would hurt me, but you would do something erratic and hurt yourself. I won't begin to pretend that I understand what is fueling you. I just hope that someday, some time you might be able to let me into that part of your world as well."

I place a hand on his cheek, I don't want to lie to him but I am afraid of letting my real feelings out. What if I am feeling more than him? What if I think we are more than what we actually are? I don't think I could bear to hear him say it's not what I think it could be.

I take a deep breath and dip my toes into the shallow end, "I will not lie to you. Ever. I may not tell you the full story about some things but that isn't because I don't trust you, because I do, entirely. There are just some things about myself that are just not pretty. Things that I have to work out in my own head before I can let anyone else see them.

"But honestly, when it comes to you, I want to tell you everything. I want to be here. I want to be with you. You are not forcing me into anything, and I know you never would. I am just afraid that this will become something else that I will have to try to survive. And that scares the hell out of me."

James leans over kissing me softly on the lips. He pulls back and smiles slightly, "I am scared too. Probably for an entirely different set of reasons, but fear is fear. I just want you to understand, to believe me when I say, the feelings that I have for you are unlike anything I have ever felt for anyone else before. I feel this pull to you. I don't know why. I have only ever felt a slight tug at someone before but that was years and years ago.

"She was just some girl, I didn't even know her name. I never even spoke to her. I saw her when I was in basic and it was just a distant crush. But this, whatever this is between us, it is 1000 times stronger than that. I just want you near. However I can have you, whatever version of yourself you can give me, I will happily accept."

I push myself into him, nuzzling into his chest making him roll onto his back. I lay there with my head on his chest, feeling him run his fingers up and down the rough service of my spine. I know if I stay at some point I am going to have to tell him the whole story.

I also know that the longer I stay, when I do tell him the full truth, I am going to have to be afraid of something completely different. My fear is that he will try to burn down the world for my vengeance. I let out a sigh and close my eyes. I can feel myself drifting off to sleep. I squeeze him a bit tighter one last time before I let my dreams take me over.

Maeve

3 years ago

We got the drop on the group of enemies. Every last one of them is now laying in their own filth and pools of blood. I slide my night vision off and stare back towards the ditch that the woman had been laying in.

Would anyone ever know what really happened to her? Fuck even I don't know what had happened to her. I let out a heavy sigh when I hear the captain coming up behind me, "Reynolds. I am going

19

to do a final perimeter run. You are with me." I nod, "Sir yes sir." I slide the night vision back over my eyes and fall into his right flank.

We clear about 60% of the perimeter when I hear something snap behind us. Maybe a small twig, maybe it is an animal. I turn around just in time to see the butt of a rifle coming down on the side of my head.

I wake up in a muggy dirty ass room. I try to sit up but my head is screaming at me. I look down and see I have been stripped down to just my t-shirt and pants. I have no idea where the rest of my gear is. I try sitting up again but everything is fuzzy.

I feel like there is this haze around my peripheral that I can't shake away. I hear two voices behind me but can't tell if I know them or not. I feel my shoulders get pulled back down to the table from behind me. I look up and see Weathers holding me down, smiling towards the other end of the table. I try to push myself back up and he glares down at me, "Just lay there and take it like a good little bitch."

I feel myself being pulled towards the end of the table. I am able to look up just enough to see the captain taking a knife down the front of my pants, ripping the remaining pieces of fabric from my body. He looks up and sees me staring at him full of fear and he starts laughing as he drops his gear then unbuttons his own pants.

I start kicking with all the strength I can muster up but the captain grabs my hips and pins me to the table. He enters me violently. I scream as I feel myself tearing. I continue to try to kick him off, to sit up but they are overpowering me. Weathers is holding me down, watching the Captains every move, "Harder Cap, make her

120

really fucking feel it." The captain laughs as he grunts and then quickly finishes himself off inside me.

I try to get out from underneath Weathers but he keeps me pinned. I feel the captain grab my legs and they both flip me so I am face down on the table. I feel my shirt getting cut from my back and then I feel something being forced into my ass.

I scream from the searing burning pain of it all. I can feel blood running down my legs towards my feet. I scream louder and louder for anyone, anyone to help. The last thing I feel before passing out again is something sharp slicing into my back.

11

James

TV – Billie Eillish

I had fallen asleep holding Maeve. She is here. She is real. She wants me. It is still an unbelievable fantasy that I think I have just created in my head. We fell asleep wrapped up in eachothers arms.

I will never be able to look at that dining room table again without thinking of the things that conspired between us. I smile to myself, deciding it is okay to finally wake up. I can hear birds outside so it must be morning at least. I reach over to pull her close to me but I am met with empty cold sheets. I feel around a bit more before cracking an eye open to see the empty bed beside me.

I sit up and look around the room but no one is there. My heart flies into my throat. It is happening again. She is going to leave. Or she is already gone.

I move to throw the blankets off me when I see her duffle still laying on the floor in front of the dresser. I let out a heavy breath, trying to bring my heart rate back down. I can hear the water going in the shower. I smile as I stand up and walk to the dresser to grab some underwear and pants. I will take a shower later after taking care of the horses. I am gonna get filthy anyway.

I look around for my boots, quickly remembering they were removed in the dining room. I smile again thinking about last night as I turn to head out into the hallway. The bathroom door is cracked open so I peek inside.

I can see the steam flowing out around all sides of the plastic curtain. I laugh out loud, "I am going to have to buy a bigger water heater aren't I?" I hear a small laugh behind the curtain, "Yeah maybe."

I smile towards her, "I am gonna go down and make some coffee okay?"

She pulls the curtain back enough for me to see a head full of bubbles, "That would be fucking phenomenal." I laugh at her as I pull the door shut behind me and turn to head down the hallway.

What the fuck is that noise? Is that music?

I look around the hallway, then lean back towards the bathroom door thinking maybe she has a radio in there or something. The music seems to be coming from my bedroom. I take a few steps in realizing it is an Alanis Morrisette song.

I look to the floor recognizing that the music is coming from her duffle. I pick the bag up and set it on the bed then unzip it, digging to the bottom I pull out a phone. The screen is lit up with the word, MOM.

I stare at it, contemplating on answering it for her. Would it piss her off? I don't know, it might be an important call. I cut Alanis off mid sentence and pull the phone to my ear, "Hello?"

I hear a small voice on the other end of the line, "I am sorry. I must have called the wrong number. I was trying to reach my daughter."

I smile as I turn back towards the bathroom, "No, I am sorry. She is here, she is just in the shower. Do you want me to tell her you called or have her call you back?"

The woman on the other end of the line seems startled, "Yeah. I mean. Well. Are you sure this is the right number?"

I laugh again, "Well, the name Mom popped up on the screen so I am going to assume you are her mother?"

123

She lets out a small laugh, "Well, it looks like Carrie has a lot to tell me then. Yes, please if you could tell her I called. Have her call me back when she can."

I blink heavily. Carrie? She didn't even tell me her real name? I try to keep my voice cool and calm as the anger ripples through my veins, "Yeah, I can tell Carrie you called. My name is James by the way. Just in case you were wondering."

It sounds like the woman on the other end was pacing back and forth across a very creaky wooden floor, "James. Well that is definitely a name she has never mentioned before. Are you and Carrie close?"

I let out another heavy sigh, "I thought we were getting there yeah. I will tell her you called. Make sure she calls you back. You have a great day ma'am."

I hang the phone up before she can give me a reply. I stare at the phone in my hand. She lied to me. I don't even know her fucking real name. She laid in this very fucking bed last night and promised me that she would never lie to me. But it appears everything has been a lie from the beginning.

I slide the phone back into her bag, zipping it shut. I hear the water turn off so I turn and quickly hurry downstairs.

Everything she has said seemed so fucking real. Why doesn't she tell me her real name? Is she planning on leaving at any moment and she just doesn't want me to be able to find her? She knows if I ever try to look her up, I will never fucking find her.

She is playing with me. Was any of it real? I am fucking livid. More than that, I am fucking hurt. I quickly start the coffee then stare out across the field waiting for it to finish brewing. I hear her step up behind me.

I feel her go to wrap her arms around me and I quickly side step her to open a cabinet for two mugs. I slam them down on the counter and take a deep breath. I hear a meek voice behind me, "What's wrong James?"

I exhale loudly, unable to look her in the eyes, "Nothing."

I know I am lying.

She knows I am lying.

The coffee finishes running and I pour her a cup, scooting it down the counter away from me. I pour myself a cup then take a full step in the opposite direction. I stare out the window, trying to wrap my head around a fucking reasonable thought to the situation.

Maeve steps up beside me, touching my arm, her voice low and maybe even scared, "What happened?"

I move to take a drink of my coffee, quickly realizing I just need to get the fuck away from her for a minute. I don't want to say something I don't mean. I toss the coffee into the sink then slam the mug down before turning to her.

She is standing there in a pair of ripped shorts and my favorite Cardinals jersey, #12 Bonito. Her eyes are huge, concerned. I step around her, heading for the back door.

She screams at me from the kitchen counter, "What the fuck did I do James?"

I turn back to her, snarling as I say, "Nothing Carrie. You did nothing. Your mom called by the way." I hear the screen door slam behind me as I stalk out the door.

I barrell down the back steps and march straight to the barn.

She doesn't trust me enough, fuck even like me enough to tell me her real fucking name. I have never lied to her. Not fucking once. She has all these secrets, all this shit she is hiding.

I thought there for a minute that she really actually cared. Maybe all the shit she told me is lies as well. Maybe she is just a crazy ass narcissist. She is just using me.

I slam my fist into the barnwood. I let out a yell as I hit it three more times. I pick up a wooden stool tossing it across the barn like it weighs nothing. My chest feels tight, heavy. I ball my hands into fists and scream up into the rafters. I turn around to grab a bale of hay and toss it as well when I see her standing barefoot in the door of the barn.

She just stands there. She doesn't blink, she doesn't smile, she doesn't look like she feels anything. I heave out a breath, "What?"

She doesn't say a word. She just stands there, her arms at her sides. She doesn't seem like she is bothered by this at all. How is she so fucking calm right now? Why doesn't it even seem to bother her that I am this upset?

I point behind her, "Just fucking leave Maeve. Or Carrie, what ever the fuck your name is. Just go. We obviously both thought this was something completely different from what it is. There is your out. Just fucking leave. And don't come back."

My heart is fucking breaking. I didn't know how much I cared about her until this moment. My heart is clenched so tight I don't know what the fuck to do, what to say.

She doesn't say a word. She just stands there, staring at me, unblinking. Finally after a few moments, she slowly turns and walks back out into the sunlight. I punch the wall again, "FUCK!"

I turn around and take off out the door after her. She is leaning over the fence looking at the mares running around the field. I stop about 5 feet away from her.

Her voice sounds unfamiliar, distant, "I was never like this before. I was your typical barbie doll looking California girl. Blonde hair, blue eyes, loved to surf, loved the beach. Boys lined up around the block just waiting to ask me out. I went to basic not knowing that I was throwing my fucking life away."

126

Maeve takes a deep breath then turns to me, "I barely made it through training alive. I was beaten and pushed down at every fucking turn. Weathers, Lang, Sanders they all made my fucking life miserable. We went on our first mission, Brazil. There was a small cartel trading weapons. We were to take them down then meet back up at the mark. The captain told me to help him clear the perimeter before we left. I turned around to see Weathers bring the butt of his rifle down into my temple. I woke up on a table, Weathers holding me down, Capt cutting my clothes from my body, then. Then he." I take a step towards her but she takes 2 steps back.

She brings her hands up to stop me, "When he was done with me, he carved the cartel's logo into my back. Him and Weathers carried me out to the ditch where he stabbed me three times in the back. Weathers fired off two rounds into me, just to make sure. They threw me on top of the dead body of another woman the cartel had tossed aside."

She turns then starts walking back towards the porch. I take a few steps to try to catch up to her but she turns on me her eyes wild with fire, "They fucking threw me in a fucking ditch and left me to fucking die James! I laid there for 3 days before someone fucking found me. The only reason I survived is because I put that dead woman's rotting fucking corpse over mine to keep the elements off of me. I laid in a goddamn hospital for months. They had no idea who I was. I had no identification. I had nothing to prove what had happened."

Maeve marchs up to me, "Men, I was supposed to trust. Men that said they were on my fucking side, raped me, destroyed me and threw me in a ditch to die. Do you know what the fuck that does to a person? Can you imagine the shit I have had to live through?"

I take a small step towards her, "Maeve, I...I don't"

127

She pushes me hard in the shoulders, "No! No you don't know what the fuck that does to a person. Cause you are one of the fucking good guys. You would never fucking do that to someone. You will never ever understand." She turns and runs into the house, slamming the door behind her.

I pace around the backyard for a minute. I am trying to stomach, to understand everything she has just thrown at me. I feel nauseous. I want to find Chads' body and set it on fire.

She didn't lie to me about that, it was definitely deserved. I look towards the house. She is gonna fucking leave. She is going to leave and I am never going to see her again. I sprint for the door, running through the kitchen then through the dining room. I round the stairs to run up them to stop her. Maeve is sitting about 3 steps up just staring out the window, down the driveway.

I fall to my knees in front of her. Her eyes connect with mine,

"Maeve is my middle name. Carrie Maeve Reynolds, MIA since August 8th, 2021. She was never found. Assumed killed in combat with a drug cartel then left in the jungle to rot. I made it back to the states almost a year ago. Sanders was killed in Fallujah a year after our mission. Lang has been in a mental institution since 2022. Not entirely sure what happened to him.

"Weathers left the service not long after I died and bought a small piece of property in Montana. The Captain retired about 9 months ago, no idea where he is now. But I will fucking find him. I will fucking end this. Then maybe, just maybe I will get to have my life back. The only person that knows I am even alive is my mother. She doesn't know what I am doing, but she knows that I am not who I used to be."

I feel a tear run down my face. I close my eyes tight, "I am sorry Maeve. I thought you were lying to me the whole time. I

128

thought it was all just a front. For whatever reason. I just thought you were using me."

I am afraid to open my eyes. I don't deserve to look at her. I don't even fucking deserve to be in her presence.

"James, I haven't lied about anything. I may have withheld the truth about some things but I have never lied to you about anything. I am here because I want to be here. I want this to be over. I am tired of running. I am tired of being locked inside my own fucking nightmares. I am sorry that you thought I was lying. That was never my intention. But I think I was right about one thing, I told myself from the beginning that this, whatever this is between us, it's too good to be true." I open my eyes, looking up the stairs at her.

Maeve stands up and slowly walks back up stairs then into the bedroom. I fucked up. She is not leaving, I pushed her away. I did this.

I can't breathe. It feels like my lungs are collapsing in on themselves. I am just as bad as them. One little hint of something, anything and I am throwing a testosterone fueled temper tantrum.

I climb back to my feet and run upstairs. She has changed out of her shorts and into jeans. My shirt is laying on the end of the bed and she is standing there with her bare back facing me. I can see the carving, the marks, the stab wounds, the bullet holes. I can see it all. She slides her shirt over her shoulders then down her sides. She turns to me while tucking it in tight.

I take a step towards her, "I don't want you to leave."

She glances up at me but then moves over to her bag, pulling out her hoodie, "I shouldn't be here. This, whatever this is, this is not healthy. It's not good for either of us."

I pull the hoodie from her hands and throw it back down on the bed, "I was mad. I shouldn't have been but I was. I

129

thought you had lied to me about everything. I thought everything you had shared with me, everything you had said, was just shit you were saying to have a place to stay for a minute. I was fucking wrong Maeve. I am sorry." She doesn't even look at me as she reaches for the hoodie again.

I quickly step in her way, "Fucking look at me Maeve."

She shakes her head as she grabs her duffle. I turn around and shut the door, standing in front of it,

"At least look me in the eye and tell me goodbye this time."

She stops in front of me and looks me dead in the eyes, "I fucking trusted you more than I have ever trusted anybody in my entire life. I have told you things that I never would have.....I have done things to you, with you. Shit I have never done with anybody. You fucking made the pain stop.

"Okay? You made me believe that there was a chance for me, for us. But one notion of something not going the way you wanted and you fucking flew off the handle at me. You couldn't have just asked me? Like a fucking adult?"

I try to grab her hands but she pulls away from me again, "I am sorry Maeve. I didn't know what to do. You don't understand. I don't know what the fuck I am doing. I have never been like this with anyone before. I have never fucking cared about anyone before. I felt so fucking stupid because I thought..."

She looks up at me, "What? You thought what?"

I let out a sigh, "I thought someday maybe you would love me as much as I love you. But then I thought it was all a lie. I have never been close enough to someone to have my heart ripped out before. I am sorry."

She stands there before me. Not saying a word. I can't read anything on her face, on her stance. She is a brick wall. I nod my head, "It's okay. It's fine. I won't keep you. I hope you

130

get the peace that you are looking for Maeve. I hope you get your life back."

I turn and walk out the bedroom door. The tears are flowing down my face as I round the dining room table then slip out the screen door. I set out for the barn, prepared to sell the horses, sell the property and just fucking get as far away from Montana as I possibly can.

12

Maeve

I Guess I'm In Love – Clinton Kane

James said he loves me. That I broke his heart. Ripped it out of his chest. I have never been told that I am loved by anyone other than my parents before. He just apologizes again then just turns, walking away from me – from us.

Leaving me standing here completely alone, completely empty. I want to punch him in the fucking face. But instead I am left just standing here staring into the vacant doorway, crying. I didn't even know I still knew how to cry. Not really. I had just assumed that my tear ducts had dried up years ago.

What am I going to do? I don't want to fucking leave but this is just too fucking hard. I drop my bag squatting down in front of the dresser, holding my head in my hands. I pull the bag towards me and drag out my phone. I quickly punch my mothers number on the screen.

Her voice sounds so happy, so excited on the other end of the line, "Carrie?"

I smile at the sound of her voice, "Hey mom."

I can hear her walking the floors of the library, "Hey sweetie. I hadn't heard from you in a week or so. I was just calling to check in. Make sure you are still okay. That James guy, he seems really nice honey."

I sniff as I hiccup at the same time, "Mom, I think I really fucked it up this time."

I hear my mothers chair creaking as she sits down, "What do you mean baby. What happened?"

I let out a sigh as I run my hand through my still nearly wet hair, "He didn't know my first name. I go by Maeve when I introduce myself now. I didn't want anyone to know my real name. I didn't want anyone to put 2 and 2 together yet. He thought I was lying to him. About everything. I think I might have broken his heart mom. I think, I really think he might love me and I don't know what the fuck to do."

I now let the tears flow down my face. I am lost, I am confused. This topic is definitely out of my realm of expertise. I have never gone to my mother with man problems. Hell, I have never gone to my mother with any problems. My mom lets out a small sigh, "Do you love him?"

I shake my head back and forth, "I don't know! I have never loved somebody before, how am I supposed to know if I do or not?"

Mom laughs on the other end of the line, "When he is all that you can think about. When you can't even breathe right when he is near. Your heart races, your thoughts are confused, jumbled. You feel this pull, this tug towards them. Like your hearts are two pieces of puzzle just waiting to be connected. When it hurts you to hurt him. That's love baby."

I feel myself crying even harder. Well, at least that explains why I feel like I am dying right now. Why it feels as if every dream I have ever had just walked out the door, "Mom, what do I do?"

She chuckles at me, "You need to tell him how you feel. If you don't, you will regret it. Even if it doesn't work out, you need to tell him baby. He deserves to know."

I nod into the phone as I wipe my face. "I will....I mean, I can try. I really think I hurt him mom. I am scared."

Mom lets out another laugh, louder this time, "That is bullshit Carrie Maeve Reynolds. You have never been scared a goddamn day in your life. Now get your ass up and go find your man. I want you to call me in a few days and when you do, I want to hear about how you fucking grew a pair and faced this shit head on, okay?"

I laugh back into the phone. I miss her so much. I miss her fake sugar coating on issues. I miss just talking to her. I sniffle again as I wipe my nose on my shirt, "Aren't you supposed to be quiet in a library?"

She laughs loudly again, "Oh shut up. I love you sweetie. Follow your heart okay?"

I nod back, "Okay momma. I love you too." I end the call and let out another deep breath.

I tuck the phone back into my bag then stand up to shake out my shoulders. I look around the room. A thought quickly runs through my head as I smile to myself.

I empty the entire duffle bag out right there on his bed. I open his top dresser drawer, scooting everything over to one side, stacking my underwear and socks in there.

I do the same with the next two drawers until everything I own is now unpacked and put away. I open his closet, throwing my duffle into the top then grabbing a hanger to hang up my hoodie. I turn around smiling then head downstairs to go find him.

I step out onto the back porch but then quickly turn back inside. I root through the cabinets until I find two travel mugs then quickly fill them with coffee and turn off the machine.

I stroll down the back steps, letting the screen door slam behind me. I am trying to walk with purpose, some confidence. If anyone was to watch me, they would just see a strong woman marching her way towards work. But if they were to look any closer they would see a crumbling mess of nerves and trauma. I walk straight into the barn but James isn't there. The atv is gone too.

I sit the travel mugs down on a hay bale then get to work. I started scooping up horse shit with a pitchfork then put it into a wheelbarrow. I have no idea what to do with it next but this is a start.

I clean out the six stalls then grab a hay bale to start sprinkling fresh hay in them. I look out of the barn, it has been at least a few hours. Is he ever coming back? I hope he hasn't done anything stupid. At this point, I just want to know that he is safe.

I fill up the water troughs next. Then sit back on a hay bale to take a long drink of cold coffee. I sit the mug back down letting my forearms rest on my knees. It has been awhile since I did any kind of lifting at all.

My muscles are screaming at me but I kinda like it. I let out another breath when I hear him, "What are you doing?"

I look up at him as I wipe the sweat from my forehead then take his way too big gloves off, throwing them down on the hay bale beside me.

I stand up rolling my shoulders, pointing towards the horse stalls, "Your job apparently."

James stares back at me in shock. I point towards the horses in the pasture, "The horses aren't going to clean their own shit up. Someone had to do it. I figured I would give you some time to think so I just did it for you. I didn't know what to do with it though so it's just a barrow full of shit over there. Sorry."

James smiles widely at me then takes 3 quick steps towards me and kisses me hard. I pull his neck closer to me as I kiss him back.

He finally pulls away, putting his forehead to mine, "I thought you would have left by now."

I let out an exaggerated sigh, "I mean, I am all unpacked and settled in here. It would be alot of fucking work to pack everything back up and leave, don't you think?"

He smiles at me again while shaking his head at me, "What are you fucking talking about?"

I smile again pulling away from him. I turn to grab my mug to take another drink of my cold coffee, "You'll see."

He looks back towards the stalls then back to me. I quickly close the travel mug and sit it down, "Plus. I couldn't leave anyways. I love you too fucking much to walk away now."

James' eyes go feral as he grabs me and pulls me into his arms. He holds me tight then pulls back to give me another deep kiss. When he finally lets me come up for air he looks me in the eye, "Do you mean that?"

I smile as I nod, "You drive me fucking crazy, James. But I was already nuts so it wasn't a long trip. I didn't realize that this, what this is, that it's love. I have never felt this feeling, this pull towards someone before. I'm sorry it took all of this to happen for me to finally see it."

He smiles as he pushes a strand of hair behind my ear, "I love you too ya know. So fucking much." I smile and kiss him again.

He grins back at me then starts swaying with me in his arms, "Ya know. I had a dream last night."

I look up at him, "Oh God. What?"

He laughs again, "Well, I think it was more of a memory than a dream. The girl that I told you about from boot camp? She was never around anyone, ever. She would always do the obstacle course by herself. Over and over and over again.

"Like I would go to chow she would be doing it, I would go to the showers, she would be doing it. One day it was pouring down rain, but there she was, pushing herself through it. She fell off the rope at one point and her hat fell off, her long blonde hair fell out. She stood up and shoved her hair back into her hat just as I was walking by and said, "God Dammit Reynolds get your shit together.""

136

I remember that day. I was so fucking tired and that rope was so fucking slick from the rain.

I look amazed at him, "You remember me?"

He nods his head at me, "Even then, I was being pulled to you. I just didn't know who you were. I feel like this, us, that we are meant to be."

I grin as I put my hands on his shoulders and jump, wrapping my legs around his waist then pulling his lips to mine. I am never going to let this man go.

Never.

He spins me around giving me a deep kiss. I pull back, grinning from ear to ear, "So is it okay then if I stay for a bit?"

He grins back then rolls his eyes, "I mean, I guess. I will have to stop letting a different woman in the house every night but I think they will survive." I laugh as I smack him in the chest.

I slowly slide down off of him then walk back over to the hay bale to grab my coffee. James, still smiling, then walks over towards the wheelbarrow, "I will go dump this in the fertilizer box. You want to watch, just so you know. Then I can show you how to mix their feed."

I smile as I promptly chug down my coffee again, "Yeah that works."

I follow him around for the next few hours. I learn how to properly clean out everything, then feed them. I even help him groom them a bit. The horses are gorgeous.

I have never really felt comfortable with animals before. They were always too unpredictable for me. But these creatures, they just accept me for me.

We are finally done with everything by 2 that afternoon. James seems completely content with everything now. He has finally relaxed. I also have felt this kind of peace fall over me.

James and I are both covered in sweat, smelling all to high hell. I smile over at him, "I may have to go shopping soon. Find something not black to wear for a minute. I am fucking roasting in this shit."

James laughs loudly at me while he nods his head. I see him check his watch then he smiles, "Let's go get cleaned up then we can run in town. Maybe find something else to wear, maybe get some food too?"

The mention of food has me grinning at him, "Deal!"

We are slowly trudging our way up the stairs when James stops abruptly. I narrowly miss walking right into him from behind.

I laugh, leaning up against the wall, "What are you doing?"

He smiles then turns, opening one of the bedroom doors I haven't been in yet.

The room is so beautiful, it is like sunshine bottled. There is a beautiful white four post bed up against the far wall. The dresser and vanity match with the same white oak style. The bedspread has huge shasta daisies all over it. It makes me feel like I am back home.

I step in spinning around taking it all in then smile, "James? Whose room is this? It is beautiful!"

He smiles as he looks around the room, "This was my moms room."

My eyes automatically fall to his. He is still in so much pain from losing her. I look around the room again, my eyes falling to a few framed photos on her dresser. The rest of the room is spotless. Like he comes in here and dusts every few days or something.

I move around James, slowly stepping up to the dresser. The first photo is a younger James, probably around the age of 18.

He is smiling from ear to ear, hair almost down to his shoulders. His mom is standing right next to him.

She is beautiful. She has long dirty blonde hair and the same eyes as James. She has the kind of smile that will light up a fucking room. She has the kindest eyes I have ever seen in my life, other than James' of course.

I smile at him then step to the next photo. It is just a picture of her, sitting on the back steps staring out across the pasture. I can't see them but I know she is staring at the horses.

She has a scarf wrapped around her head, you can see she is a lot more frail in this picture. I feel my hand on my chest, feeling my heart beating a million miles a minute. I look back up at James but he seems to be lost in his own little world.

I step around him to see the last picture that is sitting on her nightstand. There are two children– a boy and girl. It must be James and his sister. They are wearing matching clothes, probably around Easter time.

There is a big stuffed bunny behind them. His sister is just as beautiful as his mom. I sit the photo back down and turn to him, "What was your sister's name?"

James lets out a heavy sigh, "Her name was Mallory."

I give him an apathetic grin before walking back over to him and wrapping my arms around his waist, "And your mom's?"

He looks back out the window as he smiles, "Janice. Her name was Janice."

It hits me like a ton of bricks at that moment. He is completely alone. His entire family is dead and gone. He was honestly planning on being here by himself for the rest of his life. I feel this sorrow run through my chest as I let out a shaky breath.

I feel James look down towards me, "Are you okay?"

I give a half smile to his chest, not letting my eyes go any higher than his collarbone, "Yeah. I am just realizing some stuff in my head."

He uses his hand to lift my chin, forcing me to look into those warm eyes, "What are you realizing?"

I blink heavily as I feel a tear run down my cheek, "Why you couldn't tell me goodbye when I was leaving."

He gently wipes the tear away and pulls me in close for a hug. We just stand there holding each other for what feels like hours. I finally pull back then turn to look at the picture of his mother again. I close my eyes and give the photo a smile.

I feel James turn towards me, "What are you thinking?"

I open my eyes, looking at Janice again, "I am just trying to figure out how to talk to angels. I want to find a way to thank her for bringing you into my life."

James' eyes snap open with a jolt and I think I am going to see a tear slip down his face. He takes the photo from my hand and sits it back down on the dresser. He picks me up, steps out into the hallway and closes the door behind him.

I look over his other shoulder, quickly realizing the other room must be his sisters. I take his hat off then slide it over my head. His dusty blond hair falls down to his ears as he smiles at me.

I feel him open the bathroom door as he sits me down on the counter. He undresses me slowly, methodically.

I jump down and turn to start the shower water when I hear him beg, "Please god let me use some cold water."

I bark out a laugh but turn the water to be just a bit more than lukewarm then pull the curtain back to step into the old clawfoot tub.

I just stand here, letting the water pelt into my side as I watch him undress. I have never really looked him over. Not

140

thoroughly, not without extremely sinful thoughts running through my brain.

I noticed the little tattoo over his heart. When I first saw it I thought that maybe it was a birthmark. But then last night, I saw that it was a heart. I can't tell what it says, but it seems to be some kind of cursive script. I back myself under the water some more as he steps into the tub in front of me.

I reach my wet hands up and run them over his chest. I lean in to see the tattoo is indeed a small heart seemingly broken in half. The ink itself isn't even an inch tall. One side curves with the word "Mother" the other side curving outward says "Sister".

I slowly trace it with my fingers. James is watching my finger drawing the shape onto his chest then he smiles, "I don't know how you are covered in them. I cried like a bitch on this little baby one." I burst into laughter at him then stand up on my tiptoes and kiss him.

I pull myself up, bracing my hands on his shoulders until my legs are wrapped around him. He turns around so the water is running over his shoulders and down between our bodies. I just smile at him, "Do you think your mom would have liked me?"

His returning grin lights up the entire room, "No. She would have loved you." I lean in to give him another kiss.

I unwrap my legs as I slide down his body then hand him a washrag to lather himself up. I do the same, also lathering my hair up with bubbles.

The cheap dye I had originally used on my hair over a month ago now is fading a bit more with every single wash. I am probably gonna have to dye it again but I am thinking I will go a bit closer to my natural color instead of black.

I turn around to set the shampoo down when I feel James' finger tracing the scars on my back. I instantly clench all my muscles.

No one has ever touched them before.

I feel my breathing pick up as he removes his hand. I smile over my shoulder then trade him spots under the water. I look nervously up at him, "It's okay. I don't mind. Just no one has ever touched them before. It was just unexpected is all."

James gives me a soft smile then slowly turns me around to face away from him. I tilt my head back letting the water pour over my face and head. I can feel the shampoo running down my back. Over all the ridges, bumps and valleys.

I pull my chin down and look towards the wall in front of me. I feel his fingers first touch the belt marks. He doesn't know that I have used a leather belt on my own back, just trying to cover up the carving Lane had left me with.

When I couldn't get the skin to break anymore, I had begged one of the nuns at the convent to do it for me. She knew what the carving was. She knew what I had been through. She cried for me everytime I begged her to hit me harder.

He slowly lets his fingers move to the knife scars, then the small circle bullet holes. He doesn't try to trace the red brocket deer carving that has been left. I know he can probably see it beneath the camouflage I tried to cover it with. I feel his hand fall from my back and I turn around to face him again. He looks like he wants to murder someone.

I reach my hand up and put it on his cheek, "It's okay. Lane is the last one. My last mission. Once he is gone, I will be free."

James pulls me in for another hug then just holds me there until the water starts to run cold.

142

13

James

Bloodsport - From the Room Below - Sleep Token

I stand there tracing the scars of her back. I have to find a way to help her. To help her move past all of this. I want to know her. Not just the person she has become but the person she was.

I want to travel the world with her and see it through her eyes, not just mine. I hold her close to me until the water starts to turn cold before I reach down to turn the shower off. We both dry ourselves quickly then get dressed, in silence.

She has sat down on the bed to slide her boots on and lace them up. I kneel down in front of her taking her hands in mine, "I hope you know that I will never do anything to hurt you. Not on purpose. Not like them."

Maeve smiles back as she reaches up cupping my cheek in her hand, running her thumb over the stubble on my face, "I know that. Truly, I know that."

I smile then kiss the top of her hands as I rise back up to my full height, grabbing my wallet then keys off the top of the dresser. Maeve finishes getting her boots on then grabs my hand as we walk down the hallway. I smile at her as she skips out the back door and down the porch steps.

She turns around smiling at me, her hair flying forward around her alabaster face, "So, where are we going?"

I smile back, "I don't know, there isn't really much around here. There is a local department store in town but I'm not really sure what they carry for women. We can try there, then maybe go to the tavern, get some food."

She smiles and nods, giving me a thumbs up, "Sounds like a plan!"

We jump into the truck and she immediately slides over on the bench seat so she is right up next to me. I wrap my arm around her as we take off towards town.

We finally make it to the small little mom and pop store. Maeve starts laughing as soon as we walk in. Her eyes are flying to everything at once. This is one of those rare times that she doesn't seem overwhelmed. Like everything isn't just sitting below the surface. I feel a sort of calmness wash over me as I watch her settle into a peaceful life.

She starts grabbing items left and right doing a little show for me. Luckily, she is able to find a few pairs of shorts and a couple of t-shirts.

She moves around to grab a few personal items then steps into a changing room to try them on. I peruse a few of the hats on the wall while she tries on her fashion montage to herself.

I pick up a hat, checking the back when I hear, "What do you think of this one?"

I turn to see her standing beside me, a vision in a soft yellow dress. The dress itself isn't anything special but the way it makes her face light up, the glow around her, it is angelic. It comes down to about mid shin and has buttons going up the front of it.

She looks down at it skeptically then up to me, "I don't know how I feel about it."

I step up close to her and wrap my arms around her, "I can show you how I feel about it." She giggles as she smacks my chest pulling back to go try on something else.

Maeve honestly has no idea how beautiful she is. I can watch her for hours, hell days and never grow tired of her expressions. She saunters her way back towards the dressing room as I turn to look around some more.

Not 2 minutes later I hear, "Well, hello there James. It's rare to see you in here."

I turn my head to see Sheriff Bob Winters walking up to me. I quickly glance over at the changing room doors then back to the sheriff.

I stick my hand out to shake his, "Hey Bob. How are you doing?" I am trying to keep my tone calm and level but on the inside I am literally freaking the fuck out.

He shakes my hand and then adjusts his belt, "Well so far so good I guess. Anything new going on? You out shopping for a new hat or something?"

I smile at him while looking over his shoulder at a smiling Maeve making her way back to me. The sheriff is dressed in his plain street clothes. She is going to freak right the fuck out when she figures out who he was.

I try to give her eye signals before she makes it to me but she is busy looking down, juggling all the items now in her hands. She smiles as she steps next to me then her face falls a little as she turns towards Bob.

He smiles at her, "Well hello there Ma'am. It's not everyday we see a new face in town."

He sticks out his hand for her to shake and she gives me a hesitant look then slowly shakes his hand, "Hello. Are you a friend of James?"

Bob nods towards me, smiling as he puts his hand back on his hip, "Well, I would like to think so. Name is Sheriff Bob Winters."

Her eyes jut back to mine quickly as I place my hand on her lower back to try to help keep her calm. She gives Bob a short smile, "Oh, well hello. My name is Maeve."

Bob smiles again, nodding his head at Maeve then turns to me. I pull Maeve in close to my side, "Maeve and I met while in basic training together. We just got reconnected about a month ago. She is staying with me out on the farm."

145

I can feel Maeve's arms twitching underneath all the clothes she is holding. She is thinking about bolting. I can't say as I blame her though. I just continue to rub my hand up and down her arm, keeping her calm.

Bob smiles back at me, "Well that makes sense why you kept our conversations so short. I would too if I had such a looker waiting for me inside."

I grin back then kiss her on the head quickly, "Yeah, she just came in from California oh what say almost a month now right baby?"

Maeve gives me a forced smile as she nods her head. I look back to Bob, "Yeah, she had already been with me a few weeks before you even showed up at the house. She has been helping me with the horses and such."

Bob nods his head again then looks back to Maeve, "Well, ma'am. Thank you for your service."

Maeve nods nervously again and gives another smile, "I wish I could have stayed in longer, helped more people. But I was wounded overseas in Fallujah. I was sent home after only a few years."

Bob smiles at her again, "Well just the fact that you even wanted to serve is something respected by me. Welp kids I am gonna head on back home, the misses will probably have dinner ready soon. I hope to see you around again Maeve." He tips his hat to us both then turns around to leave.

We both let out a collective sigh then look towards each other. I feel a full body tremor run through her as I smile, "I think the Sheriff loves you. He might invite us over to dinner soon or something."

She barks out a dying animal laugh, "Oh, I don't fucking think so!"

She quickly runs up to the counter and starts to pay for her things. She is constantly looking over her shoulder to make sure the sheriff is actually gone though.

I step up behind her as she turns around at me, trying to block me from seeing what she has laid on the counter, "Excuse me sir. I have this. You can just go wait out in the truck for me."

I raise an eyebrow at her, trying to see over her shoulder at what she is buying but the young girl behind the counter throws a plastic bag over all the items and smiles at me.

Fucking female solidarity.

I huff at them both then turn to head back to the truck. Smiling at the girl power moment I have just witnessed while I walk out the door. It isn't 5 minutes later and Maeve is climbing in with her two bags full of goodies.

I try to peek in one and she quickly smacks my hand, "Stay in your lane sir."

I smile up at her again as I start the truck. We are only a few minutes away from the tavern but as we pull up Maeve turns in her seat and looks at me, "What is your last name?"

I look at her in disbelief then laugh out loud.

How the fuck have I not told her my full name yet?

I throw the truck in park and turn it off. Turning myself towards her, "Well, now is a hell of a time to be worried about that don't ya think?"

She smiles, smacking me in the bicep. I smile back, "James Ryan Stuart."

She nods her head back at me as she turns to look out the windshield, "Alright. I can work with that."

I give her another confused smile, "Work with that how?" She just smiles out the window, "You'll see."

147

We both slide out of the truck then make our way into the tavern. It is the dinner rush, which around here means there are maybe 20-30 people inside. We quickly find a table and sit down.

Our waitress walks up, looking Maeve up and down then smiles at me, "Hiya James! How are you doing tonight?"

I smile back at her, "Hey there Loretta. I am good. I think tonight I will just have a beer, Maeve, what do you want to drink?"

Maeve gives me a side eye and smiles back at Loretta, who does not return the smile, "I will just have water. Thank you."

Loretta gives her another once over before smiling back at me then walking away. Maeve leans over the table, "She wants to fuck you six ways to Sunday."

I laugh out loud at her leaning back over the table, "I know."

She grins up at me then goes back to looking over the menu. Loretta takes our orders as we settle in just taking in the atmosphere. There are old men lining the bar and you can hear some kind of horrific singing going on in the next room. Maeve tilts her head towards the swinging door, "They always kill cats in that room or is it only reserved for special occasions?"

I laugh out loud at her again, then nod towards the swinging doors, "That is where they do like karaoke and dancing and stuff."

She smiles back knowingly as Loretta shows up with our food. Maeve leans back in her seat admiring the huge cheeseburger in front of her.

She then quickly pops up onto her elbows, "Hey Loretta?"

Loretta turns back to her with a bored expression on her face, "Yeah?"

Maeve smiles sweetly up at her, "I was just admiring your hair. It is like really, really pretty. Could you suggest a good salon

148

around here? I made a huge mistake dying my hair black. I was kinda hoping to get it all striped out. I would *love* for my hair to be able to look as nice as yours." I eye her, noting the fake tone in her voice. She is buttering Loretta up.

Loretta smiles back down at the compliment while running her hand over her hair, "Sure thing. I go to Donna's on Main street. I am sure James knows where it is. I can give you her number if you want. And thank you for the compliment. No one around here really has taste so...."

Maeve smiles back at me then at Loretta, "Well, I am from California and I can tell you in all honesty, you kinda look like you just stepped off a modeling shoot or something. It is absolutely gorgeous."

Loretta fake slaps Maeve's forearm and giggles, "Oh you are too much. I am sorry, what was your name again?" I am watching the conversation go back and forth while trying not to laugh out loud. How Loretta is buying all this bullshit I will never know.

Maeve smiles sweetly as she leans forward, "Maeve, my name is Maeve."

Loretta smiles back, "That is a unique and beautiful name. Maeve? I will definitely remember that, I will write down Donna's number and bring it by in a few. You guys enjoy your food."

Loretta walks away with a bit more of a pep in her step. I take a drink of my beer, eyeballing Maeve as she chews on a french fry, "What the hell was that about?"

Maeve smiles back, "I got tired of the stink eye. Plus, I do need to do something about my hair. I figured if I softened her up enough she would give me a good shoe in with someone."

I smile, "Oh, I thought you were trying to make a new best friend or something."

Maeve sits up laughing, looking towards the bar to make sure Loretta can't hear, "Oh yeah, I am sure she would want to put me at the top of her christmas card list." I chuckle at her again and start to devour my burger.

We are just starting to finish up when a song starts playing from the room next to us. Meave's head whips up, "Are you fucking kidding me?"

I laugh and look towards the doors with her, "What?"

She is grinning from ear to ear, "Do you know what song they're playing?"

I shake my head laughing back at her, "No? Should I?"

She groans out at me, "God, please don't tell me the only music you listen to is country."

I laugh, "No, I don't really listen to any music."

Her jaw nearly hits the table. Meave jumps up then grabs my hand to begin pulling me to the room next to us. There is some dude barely even old enough to be in here singing.

He is tall and scrawny but obviously from around here. The backwards ball cap and farmer's tan gives it away. He isn't horrible at karaoke but I have no idea what he is singing.

There is no one dancing but Maeve doesn't seem to care. She pulls me right out to the middle of the dance floor and wraps her hands around my neck. I stand there trying to sway to the music as the kid singing gives me a smile but then stares at Maeve for the rest of the song.

She keeps her hands around my neck and her eyes closed. At one point she starts singing along with the kid on stage. Her voice is angelic, but troubled. I can hear this rasp in the back of her throat like she is just trying to hold back a scream.

Maeve lets her head fall back between her shoulders as she starts belting out the words, "And somewhere, somewhere the atoms stopped fusing."

I watch her sway to the music and sing the words like they are pouring out of her own heart. Like the ink from the pen she is writing with is anchored with her own blood.

She leans her head into my chest as she softly continues, "I want to be forgiven. I want to choke up chunks of my own sins."

I kiss the top of her head then look back at the kid on stage. He is in it just as deep as her. The song continues to play as I sway to the music with her, not caring who sees us.

The song finally comes to an end as she turns to the kid on stage and smiles at him with her hand over her own heart. He nods back down to her then steps off the side of the stage. I am torn between the words of that song and her own heart wrenching version of it.

I place my hand on the back of her neck pulling her in tight. I kiss her with the passion and reverence of man drowning in his own sins.

Just hoping that she realizes that she is my lifeline.

Maeve

Death of Piece of Mind – Bad Omens

The drive home is quiet. I am kinda afraid I have scared him off a bit with that dance. But as soon as we get in the truck James reaches behind me and slides me closer to him in the seat.

He keeps one arm locked around me the entire time. I lean my head into his shoulder and just watch the stars as we speed down the road.

When we finally make it home, it is close to 10. Still early for me but the old man seems like he is a bit spent. I am worried that he is just being quiet because he is realizing the weight of what he is getting himself into.

I know I am a lot, that everything I have to offer right now isn't much but it is heavy all the same. A large part of me, even larger than I am ready to admit, is worried that every single thing I do and say is scaring him off. Pushing him away. The insecurity is screaming in my head from the moment my eyes open in the morning until they finally close every night.

I slowly walk up the stairs of the porch, with my bags in tow from the department store.

I smile up at James as he opens the door for me, "Thank you."

He smiles back down at me, "Your welcome."

I look down at the bags in my hands, "I am gonna go put this stuff away."

He nods his head at me and I hurry myself upstairs. I am glad I had made that room in his dresser earlier. I start unpacking clothes then removing tags when I hear the music coming up the stairwell.

I stop short, he is listening to Sleep Token. He must have had a computer in the office or something. I smile as he listens to Blood Sport again. I put away the majority of the clothes when I hear the music change to Bad Omens.

Oh, he is doing the reading rainbow lessons of music tonight it seems. I laugh to myself as I pull out the red lace, basically translucent nightie I had purchased earlier. I smile to myself as I slip out of all of my clothes then pull that negligee down over my body.

I walk over to the full length mirror looking at myself. I feel so fucking out of my element in this damn thing. I am standing here completely fucking naked except for a very small, very see through scrap of material covering my body.

I take a deep breath as still my nerves. I give myself a mental pep talk, 'You can do this Maeve. It's just James. You can do this.' I nod my head at the mirror to hype myself up a bit before I turn and walk down the hall.

I can hear the beginning of The Death of Peace of Mind playing as I smile to myself. That is the perfect intro song for me. I set my pace to the beat of the music and make my way downstairs.

James isn't in the living room, nor the dining room. I even poke my head into his office but he isn't there either. I slide the doors of the dining room open to look into the kitchen to find him sitting at the table with a laptop open in front of him.

His hat is laying on the table beside him. He has his eyes closed, head slowly bobbing to the beat of the music. He opens his eyes and they lock with mine when he hears the doors open. I slowly walk in, afraid to break the stare.

James eyes finally roam my body and he takes a deep shuttering breath, "I knew you would be fucking stunning in red."

153

I smile back and look down at myself sheepishly before looking back at him, "I take it you like this then."

He smiles as he scoots the chair back so he can face me fully. I can feel his eyes all over me at once. I instantly start to get nervous again. I put my right hand on my left elbow and stare past him towards the kitchen wall. I can feel myself biting into my lip from the nerves of the moment. He can say something anytime now, that would be super helpful.

He leans forward in the chair a bit and puts his forearms on his knees. His eyes are smoldering when he puts one finger in the air and twirls it, "Spin."

I give another sheepish smile as I do a slow, small twirl for him. My breathing becomes heavy, labored. As my body moves in a slow circle, I can feel the soft fabric rubbing against my skin. I have always known that I was pretty but at this moment, I feel like the most beautiful woman in the world. James has that effect on me. Just one look from him and all of my insecurities just disappear. I tilt my face back up to look at him. His breath catches in his throat, his eyes hooded as he stares at me, "Jesus Christ Maeve. You are going to be the fucking death of me."

I smile holding my palms up to him, "Not by these hands, no."

I grin as I turn towards the screen door and slowly walk through it. I turn to the left, taking a few steps before sitting down on the porch. I have positioned myself so when he walks out all he is going to see is me leaning back on my elbows with my legs up, knees bent. Inviting him in.

The anticipation of what is going to happen is heavy in the air around me. My heart feels like it is going to jump right out of my chest. I am trying to keep the smile on my face to a minimum but I know, whatever he does to me, it is going to take me to a higher level of contentment than I have ever been. That is what it is like with James. Each time is better than the last.

I watch him walk out the back door then look down at me. I can hear the crickets playing their nightly songs. Somewhere off in the distance, I can hear one of the horses rutting the ground with her hoof. I hear ya girl, me too.

James has taken his shirt and boots off at some point. He is just standing there in a tight pair of wranglers.

I can see the outline of his dick in his jeans and I quickly lick my lips. Everything about him draws me in. It is like he is the predator and I am welcoming the stockholm syndrome that I must be suffering from. The music is still wafting out to the porch from the laptop on the kitchen table. I lay my head back on the wooden porch smiling a bit.

James reaches down and unbuttons his jeans. He gives me a small grin as he turns his back to me then quickly falls down to the floor to his stomach. As soon as his hands hit the wooden floor, he is sliding his legs towards me. He slips his legs in between mine but under the bend in my knees.

I feel his feet lock tight around my hips and the next thing I know he has flipped me onto my stomach. My knees are still slightly bent so I am now on all fours. He has completely rolled over and contorted his own body to cover my own.

Who is this dude? A fucking ninja?

I can hear myself squeak in surprise then moan at the feeling of him holding me firmly. He has one hand splayed out in front of us, one holding me up by my abdomen. His fingers are spread wide but digging into the wood of the porch. I can feel his dick pressing into my ass as he wraps his other hand around my neck burying his face into my hair. I feel a moan escape as I see him pull his hand back from the porch. The next thing I hear is the zipper of his jeans go down.

He enters me roughly from behind. I belt out a scream but push myself back into him so he knows that I am okay. He has one hand on my hip and the other is tightly gripping the hair at the base of my neck.

He gently tugs and I arch my back for him, letting him in deeper. I am flat against the floor of the porch now with my hips and ass up in the air. He grips my hair harder as he starts to slam into me from behind. I looked around for anything to grab onto but there is nothing here.

All I can do is scream out in pleasure. He is going so deep at this angle I can feel him hitting the walls inside me. Before I can even warn him, I feel myself clamp down on him. I have never cum so fast or hard. In all the times we have been together, this one is different. I don't know if it is from his surprise ninja moves or the realization that we are really together but something has heightened my emotions tonight. He continues to thrust into me as I scream his name into the night, "JAMES! GOD DAMMIT!"

He grunts but says nothing. He puts both of his hands on my hips and pulls them up higher to him, closer to him. I am still pulsing around his dick when I feel him smack my right ass cheek hard. I feel myself clench down even harder as he screams my name, "Fuck MAEVE. Fuck!"

His thrusts become erratic as he leans over me completely and slams himself into me. I feel his dick pulsating inside of me then he abruptly leaves my body. I lay down flat on my stomach trying to catch my breath.

I look over my shoulder and see him quickly jerking his dick as ropes of cum fly out over the railing of the porch. I roll onto my back to watch him finish himself off. It is the sexiest fucking thing I have ever seen in my life.

I kinda wish he would have just shot his load all over me. Let him just spread his seed all over my chest. The thoughts I am

156

having are just down right fucking vile. I lay there, just watching him until his eyes come back and meet mine. He is still stroking his dick slowly as I lick my lips. He pulls his jeans back up on his hips then bends down to pick me up.

James literally throws me over his shoulder, my ass bare to the world. He has one hand wrapped around on my asscheek as the other roughly pulls the screen door open.

He passes the table going straight into the living room. I can still hear the sounds of Carnal Decay coming from the laptop as he rounds the corner to the stairs and takes them two at a time. I feel myself giggle as he hops up the stairs while all I can do is stare at his ass in his wranglers. He reaches up and pinches a cheek which leaves me only able to use both hands smacking his ass relentlessly.

I can hear him laughing as he moves us quickly into the bedroom. He stands me up in front of the mirror then reaches down to the bottom of the negligee then quickly pulls it up over my head. I watch his hands reach around my body, one going to my tit the other sliding down in between my thighs.

I growl out a small moan as I let my head fall back into him as I spread my legs apart a bit further. I hear him whisper in my ear, "Look in the fucking mirror Maeve. Watch my hands."

I do as I am told and look back down at the mirror. God his fingers feel so fucking good. He gives my nipple a pinch as I let another deep moan leave my body. I watch myself in the mirror as I grind my pussy down into his rough hand. I should be embarrassed or at least feel some kind of shame right? Then why am I reveling in the expression on his face when he watches me rubbing myself on his palm.

James eyes meet mine in the mirror as he smiles wickedly, "You would do anything to please me wouldn't you? You would let me defile you in the most wicked ways you can think of wouldn't you? Look at you, right now, riding my fucking hand. You want to cum so bad don't you?"

I stare back at him, unable to even get a word out. He is right though, the things I would let this man do to me scare the fuck right out of me. If I thought it would bring him one ounce of pleasure at all, I would let him butcher me alive.

I feel it start to build in my core again. I quickly turn around and start pulling his pants down his hips. He smiles at me as he helps me tug them down then he steps out of the jeans standing before me completely naked.

I push him back until the bed is behind his knees and he sits down. I quickly climb up on top of him grabbing his dick with one hand while I position myself to slide down onto him. I instantly wrap my arms around his neck, pushing my knees out as flat as they will go so I can feel him as deep as possible.

I squeeze his neck tight as I continue to throw myself into him. I feel his hands go around and grip my ass tighter. I hold onto him, feeling myself start to crest again. I can feel myself gnash down into him and then my pussy grips him tight. As tight as a fucking vise. "Fuck James. Yes. I would let you do anything. Fucking anything."

I can't even bring myself to move. I am frozen in ecstasy. I can't even control my movements. My hips start slamming into his completely on their own. He brings his hands around to my back and sits up close to me. I hear James roar into my neck, "Baby, I'm gonna cum. You have to move. I am gonna cum."

I hold on slamming myself into him harder, "I don't fucking care. I can't stop."

I feel myself pulsating around him as he slams himself into me deeper and I scream his name, "James! Fuck Yes!"

My hips start slamming into his again and I feel his dick swell inside me then he goes completely still. I continue to ride him until the waves in my muscles start to slow down.

I am finally able to pull back from him and look in his eyes. He smiles at me then grabs my face on either side and pulls me in for a deafening kiss. The reality of what just fucking happened starts to creep into my brain, but in all honesty I don't even care.

If we have just made a baby, so be it. There was no fucking way I was letting his dick out of my body at that moment. I physically couldn't bring myself to do it.

James pushes some of my hair back behind my ear and I can feel him pulse inside of me again. I let out a little yelp and let my head fall onto his shoulder.

He smiles as he lays back across the bed and moves inside of me again. I put my hands on his abdomen and pull my chin down tight to my chest. Everytime he pulses inside of me it sends a shockwave to my core.

I have never felt so fucking satisfied in my life. I look up at him and he is smiling from ear to ear. I smile back then drape myself over him. I can't bring myself to let him leave my pussy yet. Even though I can feel his seed seeping out of me.

I still feel so fucking full. I sit back up and trace the small heart on his chest and then let out a deep sigh. James sits up on his elbows, "What's wrong baby?"

I smile back at him, "Literally nothing. I just want to stay like this forever. Just us here like this, your dick buried inside me. Forever." He smiles and kisses me again.

James continues to just sit there and hold me tight. After a while, I feel him kissing my neck then my jawline. I look down at him and he gives me a half smile, "That was the hottest thing I have ever seen."

I give him a grin back, "What?"

He gives me a quick kiss, "When your pussy was clenched around me and you couldn't even force yourself away. I have never felt so wanted in my entire life."

159

I smile down at him then kiss him again. I pull back, "Yeah I may have to find a morning after pill tomorrow." He nods his head, "Yeah, that's fine. But just to let you know, we are going to have to get you on some form of birth control because now that you have let me cum in that tight little pussy, that is all I want to do."

I laugh, sitting up straighter to look at him. His eyes curl with his smile as I feel him thickening inside of me. I look down at where we are joined then back at him, "Again? Really?"

James smiles as he wrap his hands around my ass and starts moving me back and forth on top of him, "I can't fucking help it. This is what you do to me."

I smile as I lean in and kiss him again, rolling my hips into his. James kisses me back fiercely then rolls us over.

He has one of my legs pulled up under his armpit and the other pushed open as far as it can go. He starts pushing himself into me harder. I let my hands roam his chest and upper arms as he starts slamming himself into me.

I tilt my head back, smiling to the ceiling. Nothing matters when he is inside of me. Not tomorrow and what it holds. Not Lane and what he did. Not even air being in my lungs. This is the only time it is just us, no outside anything getting in the way. I hear his rasp, "Touch yourself baby."

I open my eyes, staring directly into his as I slowly move my fingers towards my center. I start circling my clit and bring my other hand down to make my fingers into scissors so I can feel his dick as he thrusts in and out of me.

James' breathing becomes heavier above me. I look up to see he is watching himself slam into me. I look down to where his gaze is watching his dick sliding in and out of me. Watching him lose himself in me, does something to me. Just knowing this is when he is feeling the most at home, when he is buried deep inside me.

I can feel my release building up quickly again. I cum on his dick again as he continues to slam into me, screaming my name as he finishes inside of me.

We are both covered in sweat but I don't care. I pray to any god that will listen that this is what my future holds for me for the rest of my life.

If this is heaven I don't know how I was allowed in, but I am completely content with it.

15

James

Ascensionism – Sleep Token

I wake up way earlier than intended this morning. I had been completely out of it but something jarred me awake with a jolt.

I look over beside me and Maeve is still curled up, legs scissored, ass pointed at me. I smile down at her as I pull the sheet back up over her body then stand up. I quietly find a pair of sweatpants and slide them on then make my way downstairs.

The clock on the wall says 5:30. I stretch out my shoulders and clean up the mess I left in the kitchen from the night before. I start a pot of coffee then take my laptop back to the office to charge again.

I step out on the back porch with a hot mug of coffee just as the sun is starting to peek up over the horizon. I smile as I watch the horses start grazing out of the barn one by one.

It won't be much longer and I will be taking them to the auction. Just to turn around and get some more to start raising them all over again. I turn to the side leaning against the railing, staring into the house through the screen door.

I think about last night and I can't stop the smile that spreads over my face. I look down at the porch and I can see little lines in the paint where her fingernails had gripped the wood tight as I slammed into her from behind.

I know as soon as she wakes up we are gonna have to go a few towns over to find a morning after pill but I am completely fine with that. It was well worth it.

My mind starts roaming off into dangerous territory again. I want her to stay, forever. I want us to fill this house with little versions of us. I want her to say my last name when she introduces herself to new people.

I think about it a bit longer as I sip my coffee, staring off into the pasture. There is no way she is going to be able to let herself be completely happy until Captain Lane Masters is dead and gone. By her hands.

I let out a heavy sigh, knowing damn good and well what I am going to have to do. I have sworn to myself that I am out. That I will not let anything drag me back in, no matter what it is. But I know to get the information I need I am going to have to reach out to people that will require a favor in return for their silence.

I slowly walk into the house quickly grabbing my cell phone off the table. I step back out onto the back porch and pad over to the porch swing. I sit there just holding the phone for a minute but inevitably scroll through my contacts until I see the word Bleu. I let out another heavy sigh and hit the call button.

He answers on the the 3rd ring, "What the fuck Stuart? Has hell finally froze over? Why the fuck are you calling me?"

I can hear the laughter in his voice. I smile and turn toward the pasture, "You still have me saved cause you miss me you little bitch?"

Bleu lets his laughter ring out at that, "Yeah, you bet baby. No one is as good as you. No seriously, what is going on my man? It's been years."

I smile as I look down at my feet, "Yeah, I know. Honestly, I never had any intention of ever calling but something has happened."

I hear a chair rake across the floor on the other side of the phone, "Who surfaced?"

I shake my head, "No, nothing like that. I haven't heard a peep from any of them. It's something else."

Bleu lets out a grateful breath, "Okay. What is it?"

I lean back in the swing, glancing towards the screen door, praying Maeve is still asleep, "I need you to find someone for me. I need you to keep it quiet though."

Bleu lets himself chuckle a bit, "What? Some girl leave you heart broken? Need me to track her down for you?"

I laugh again, "No. No, nothing like that but,"

I hear something inside, knowing damn good and well it is just the coffee maker but I still whisper into the phone, "Hold on, let me go to the barn real quick."

I stand up leaving my mug on the railing. I glance in the back door seeing the kitchen is still empty but turn and trot down the steps anyways. I pick up my pace a bit as I get closer to the barn then slide the door open, giving one more look towards the house before moving inside. "Okay, so I need you to find the location of an ex marine captain."

Bleu lets out another loud laugh, "Um okay. That shouldn't be too hard. Why?"

I shake my head, "I can't tell you why. I just need you to do this for me and I will owe you one."

Bleu lets out another sigh followed by a raspy, "You know that is not how it works. I do not go into shit not knowing what the fuck is going on. That is how you get made, or killed."

I pace the dirt floor, "I know Bleu but this is different. It's not my story to tell."

Bleu curses under his breath, "Stuart, man we are close. We are brothers. But I can't just run out half cocked not knowing what the fuck is going on. You know this. You know how the game is played man."

I rack my brain for some kind of story to tell him that will appease him. Get him to help me. But there is nothing, I am coming up blank. I know what I have to do. I just hope she either

164

never asks me about it or if she does, she is feeling forgiving at that moment.

I look back towards the house and say a silent apology, "Okay, fuck, fine I will tell you but this is strictly confidential. If you can't pull it off then just tell me that. Don't go spreading this shit to everyone, copy?"

I can almost see Bleu nodding his head, "Yeah, I copy."

I take another deep breath, "There is someone in my life. Someone really fucking important to me. She served the same time as us. She was special ops. Some shit went down when she was on assignment. This captain did some shit. He uh, did some shit to her. There were some others involved but they have already been dealt with. The captain is the last one left. We have no clue where he is, he basically dropped off the face of the planet when he retired."

I can hear Bleu taking notes on the other end of the phone. He clears his throat, "Okay names? I need names."

I look out the doors again, "Okay whose, his? The other guys?"

I can hear a pen clicking rapidly through the line, "All of it. His, hers, theirs, all of them."

I let another hesitant sigh leave my chest, "You swear man, you can't fucking say a word to anyone."

I can hear Bleu getting frustrated with me, "James. This is not my first fucking job man. I know what the fuck I am doing. I have kept all your secrets this fucking far haven't I?"

I nod and start pacing again, "Yeah, but that is different. That is my shit. If it gets out then it's just me that has to deal with it. This is someone elses' fucking trauma man. She would fucking leave me if she knew I was even talking to you about this."

Bleu stops clicking the pen and I hear him chuckle under his breath, "Your in fucking love aren't you?"

I straighten up a bit, "Yeah, I am."

Bleu starts laughing again, "Okay so what, this dude was a prick to her in basics then what her captain was an even bigger dick? What? She wants to try to push charges on him or something?"

I run back to the door, expecting to see a pistol pointed at my forehead but instead just see emptiness leading up to the house.

"I wish it was that fucking small man. Okay, so, she was special ops. Got her ass tortured all the way through basics by the guys in her reg. She went on assignment and shit went bad. Like one of the guys knocking her out with a rifle and then holding her down while the captain fucking raped her. Then he stabbed her 3 fucking times and threw her in a ditch, left for dead. The guy that had held her down, shot her two or three times for good measure by the way. She is currently listed as MIA even though she is very much alive and laying in my bed right fucking now."

You could hear a pin drop. It is so silent on the other end of the line I think the call must have dropped, "You there Bleu?"

I hear him clear his throat, his tone a bit deeper now, "Give me the fucking names Stuart. I will take care of them."

I shake my head, letting a nervous laugh out, "Really no fucking need for that Bleu because the other side of that coin, she has been hunting them down and killing them all off one by one. Also any other fucking pedo's or women beaters she comes across. But she is done. She just wants to finish off the captain, once that is done she is done. She will be free of all this shit. I will get her the help she needs and I will keep her safe until my last fucking breath. On christ."

I can hear the pen running across paper again, "What is her name? What is the captain's name?"

I let out another sigh, checking the doors one last time. This is it, this is my last chance to walk away from this. I roll my neck to look at the rafters. If this brings us closer to Lane I know she will forgive me. I close my eyes, imagining the life we could have. The freedom she would have from herself. I reserve my emotions, stating plainly, "Carrie Maeve Reynolds and Captain Lane Masters."

I feel a weight lift off my chest. Like what I am doing is the right thing after all. Bleu speaks somberly again, "And the others?"

I shake my head, "I don't have names for all of them but I know for sure of Chad Weathers. She has a list of names, one of them died in combat, another is in a psych ward. She doesn't seem too bothered by them. She is just working her way through the list to get to Lane. He is all that is left."

I hear the pen clicking on the other end of the phone again, "Give me 2 days. I will text first with a number. Call it within 10 minutes. I will update you when I know more. And James, this ones on me."

I smile into the phone, instantly feeling more grateful than I should, "Thanks Bleu, but we both know if you want me you know where to find me."

I hear him chuckle one last time before he hangs up the phone. I pull the phone away and check the porch again. It is still empty.

Now I just have to play dumb until I hear more from Bleu. I stroll back up to the porch and sit down to finish my coffee. I haven't been sitting here 5 minutes when Maeve comes walking out with a mug of her own.

She is wearing a light blue tank top and grey sweatpants, just like me. She comes over sitting down beside me, stretching her legs out on the swing while leaning her back into my chest. I

67

swiftly kiss the top of her head and watch the horses grazing in the pasture with her. I feel so guilty. I know I have betrayed her trust. But there was no other way around it. This is what had to be done to find Lane. I try to keep my breathing calm but it is really fucking hard.

She lifts her face up to mine, smiling, "Good Morning." I smile back down at her, hating this feeling sitting in my chest. Knowing I have just spilled all her secrets then just sitting here chatting over coffee, "Good Morning Maeve."

She turns leaning forward a bit, "How did you sleep?"

I give her a devious smile as I lean in to kiss her neck then whisper in her ear, "Like I had a siren laying next to me naked all night."

She laughs at me again as she turns her gaze back towards the horses. She grins towards the pasture, "I will never get tired of watching them running free out there."

I keep my eyes on her the entire time. I wonder what she is going to look like when she is finally free. Just imagining a lighter, happier version of her convinces me that I am doing the right thing. No matter how wrong it may feel right now.

I let out a small cough, "I gotta take care of the horses before we head into town." She nods at me as she stands up, "Yeah I will go get dressed then we can get to it."

I follow her into the house, depositing my mug right next to hers in the sink. I know I am being more quiet than normal. I am scared shitless that she is going to turn around and see right through me. I am not a good liar. I know I am not a good liar. But she doesn't know that. I just have to keep this curtain pulled for a little bit longer.

Once we have found the captain, she will be able to be free. I just have to keep my eyes on the prize. This is our future I am thinking about.

16

Maeve

Feel Me Now – If Not For Me

After taking care of the horses in the morning, we spend the rest of the day driving all over god's green earth to find a morning after pill. We end up buying as many as they will allow. Mainly because we both know we have zero self control. I then stop by Donna's and get myself set up with an appointment to get the black stripped from my hair.

Maybe I will go blue next time. Or even green, I like green.

James has seemed a bit distant this morning but when I ask him if he was okay he just says something about the horses. He says it was almost time for them to go to auction. I hate that, I have grown to love seeing them every morning. But I am sure there will be more horses in my future.

James is cleaning out their stalls again as I decide to work on getting some new hay laid. I had begged him to buy a radio today so we can have some kind of background noise while we work in the barn but in his brain fog he has completely forgotten.

He must have remembered as I was moving bales because I turn around and the truck is pulled up to the barn doors with radio blaring. I laugh at him and go back to chucking the hay bales to the other side of the barn.

I find a machete and get to work cutting the baling twine off the haystack. I whack at it a few times, watching the twine spring back.

It is almost cathartic doing that. I have always been one of those people that loves instant gratification. Like the people that watch lawn mowing videos or power washers.

I kinda wish we had more bales that require being cut. But at least I will get to do this once a day. I let my thoughts race as I stick the machete down in the neighboring hay bale then start sprinkling the hay through the open stalls. I really can't believe I am staying. I am so fucking happy, it feels foreign to me though.

I think about all the things we can do with our future when I have a flash of Lane's face in my head. I instantly feel the anger roll through my veins. I can not let him get away with this. I will not be safe or sane until he is dealt with. I instantly start to feel that pull on my soul. The pull to keep moving, keep searching.

I am a little pissed at myself that I have let my guard down enough that I actually forgot about him for a minute. I know that James will understand when I finally get word on Lane.

I know he will get that it isn't about him or us and that I will be back. At some point. I am lost enough in my thoughts that I don't even notice when James walks up behind me and starts to wrap his gloved hands around my waist.

I smile up over my shoulder, "What's up big man?"

James smiles down at me as he kisses my temple, watching me spread out the hay. I feel him inhale deeply, "I could really get used to this."

I smile again, "What? Me doing all your work over here?"

He laughs as he grabs my waist tighter. I let another chuckle roll from my chest as I turn and wrap my arms around him. I smile up at his face, "I know what you mean. I really do love it here. I feel like I am serving a purpose somehow. I know I am not, but I just feel like I belong."

James smiles again then leans down and kisses me gently. I smile into his lips as I kiss him back.   I turn around leaning back into him, wrapping his arms all the way around me.

I let out a sigh, "So what are tonight's plans?"

James rests his chin on top of my head, "Oh I can think of a few things."

I promptly smack his forearm which makes him chuckle. I smile out into the nothing again as he starts rubbing my arms with his gloved hands. I lean over to pick up some more hay to sprinkle and his hands grip my hips tightly.

I stand up and give him a little side eye smirk as I walk away to finish with the last stall. I turn back around in time to see him looking me up and down then taking his gloves off, throwing them onto a hay bale.

I raise one eyebrow at him, "What are you thinking?"

He gives me a wicked grin as he walks over to me, "I am thinking I haven't had you in the barn yet."

I laugh looking around at the dirt and hay everywhere, "That doesn't seem very hygienic at all."

His eyes turn darker as he looks down at me, "You don't like it dirty?" I feel my pulse quicken immediately. Jesus god, this man. He knows he can see right through me. He knows exactly which buttons to push and how hard to push them. I try to keep my heart from beating out my chest.

I look back up to him, "Depends on what you have in mind."

James smiles wickedly as he pulls the collar of my shirt down, planting a kiss on my pulse, "Do you trust me?"

I let out a small moan, leaning away to give him better access. My eyes shut, "Of course."

James leans in closer and whispers into my neck, "How much do you trust me?"

I pull back looking into his eyes, "With my life." His lips slam into mine as I wrap my arms around his neck. I do trust him with my life. If we were dangling off a cliff and he said the only way to live was to take his hand and let go, I would. Happily.

His hands are roaming my bare skin in a matter of seconds. He quickly removes my shirt, sucking a nipple into his mouth and nibbling. I reach down quickly unbuttoning his jeans then slide the zipper down. I reach in and start stroking him as he removes my jeans from me as well. He stops then just standing in front of me staring into my eyes while I massage his dick with my hand.

I grip him tighter as he picks me up then walks over past the stalls. He lays me down in a pile of hay and quickly removes my underwear. I watch his face as I part my bent knees, opening myself to him.

He stares down at me then falls to his knees. He places a hand on each knee, "God you are fucking beautiful."

I smile at him as he leans in between my thighs and starts to kiss my abdomen. He looks back up towards me as he licks straight up my center. I feel his tongue flick against my clit and my entire body jerks forward.

I wrap his hair up in my hands as he continues to devour me. I try to keep my legs open but they keep attempting to tighten around the sides of his head on their own.

I open my eyes again as he starts to pull back from me. His eyes are locked with mine as he sticks two fingers into me then starts pumping them in and out. I hold his gaze, afraid to look away.

He slides another finger in and I feel my jaw drop as I continue to hold his gaze. His eyes glance to the right then another wicked grin comes over him. I watch him reach over and grab the machete.

My pulse instantly starts racing again, "James....what are you doing?"

He smiles at me again, his eyes almost glazed over, "You still trust me right?"

I nod my head while looking at the machete, "I do but what are you doing?"

James pulls his fingers from me and grips the blade of the machete down towards the hilt. I watch his face as he turns the handle towards me then places his other hand low on my abdomen.

I instantly start to clench as he rubs a soft circle with his finger, "It's okay baby. I promise it won't hurt. Just keep your eyes on me okay?"

My eyes fly from his to the machete and back. This is fucking insane. He is not going to stick that fucking thing inside me!

I squirm a little then I feel him gently push the handle into me. I instantly feel myself grip the strange object. The handle itself is smooth but the pommel has a slight curve to it as it gets wider at the base.

James keeps his eyes on mine as he continues to slowly move the handle in and out of my pussy. It feels weird, foreign. I am not really for sure if I am liking this kind of play. I am about to say as much when I look down to see his hand pushing the handle into me.

He has a small stream of blood running out of his palm. I sit up to say something but the sight of the blood seems to have me in a trance. I watch that now maroon hand moving the wooden handle and I feel myself start to build.

My brain wants me to tell him to let it go but my pussy is saying don't fucking stop. I can't for the life of me understand why this is giving me such a rush. I lay back down but keep my eyes on him, on his hand as he continues to pleasure me with more than he intended.

As it starts to build higher, I raise up to my elbows and look James in the eyes, "I want you baby." James smiles as he pulls the handle out of me.

I watch him drop the blade then move his hands to his jeans. His right hand is leaving a trail of blood everywhere he moves it. He pushes his jeans down his hips then starts to lean towards me.

I put a hand out to stop him then nod towards his hand with my chin, "Touch yourself."

He looks down at his hand then back to me, with one brow raised he lifts his cut hand to his dick. I start panting as I watch him coat himself in his own blood.

This is by far the scariest and hottest thing I have ever seen in my life. He continues to stroke himself as his head falls back between his shoulders and he lets out a deep guttural moan. I move my fingers to my clit and start working myself while watching him run his bloody hand up and down his dick.

James brings his eyes back down to me and then sees my fingers rolling over my clit. He watches as he starts pulling on himself harder. His hand glides across his veins leaving a blood smear each time.

James uses his other hand to push me flat down into the hay then leans over me shoving himself inside. I grip the hay on the ground around me as I scream out his name.

He reaches his hands underneath me and grabs my ass as he starts pummeling me with his dick. His hips are hitting mine so hard I know they are going to leave bruises.

I feel my orgasm start to grow again deep in my core as I look down and see his bloody dick spearing into me. I cry out again as I feel myself clamp down around him.

He screams my name and starts thrusting into me harder, deeper than before. I wrap my arms and legs around him. I can feel his dick getting thicker inside me then he screams, "Maeve, fuck me Maeve!"

I start pushing my hips back to meet his at every thrust. Throwing myself into him just as hard as he is pushing his dick into me. I feel myself start to flutter around him and he screams my name again.

The force that he is throwing himself into me is sending me spiraling. I arch my chest towards him as I let out another guttural moan. As if he knows what is about to happen, he violently slams into me, jarring my entire body back a few inches. I scream into the air around us as he grunts and slams into me again.

I feel myself clench down tight on him, sending pulsating waves down his dick. He quickly slams into me repeatedly until I feel him swell inside me then his release is slapping him in the face. He screams my name before finally starting to slow down. He lays there on top of me for a few minutes before pulling his face back and smiling at me.

I let my arms and legs fly out around me, "Well, that was unexpected."

He smiles as he pulls out of me and leans back onto his haunches. I sit up pulling his hand towards me. There is a thin line cut straight across his palm.

I look up at him, "That is definitely going to get infected."

He smiles as he looks down at his hand, "I don't even fucking care."

I grin again as I look back at his hand, "I don't know what the fuck came over me. I saw the blood and I just...don't know. I kinda just zoned out, lost it."

James smiles back at me, "It didn't bother me at all baby. I saw that look in your eye. The one you give me when I know you are about to go all feral on me. It was fucking hot. Primal even."

I bark a laugh out at him, "Jesus Fuck James!"

He laughs back at me as he stands up and pulls his jeans back up then buttons them. He reaches his good hand down for me and I take it as I stand up, quickly gathering my clothes so I can get dressed.

I pull my jeans up, smiling towards him, "Good thing we bought stock in plan B huh?"

He laughs back at me as he watches me sliding my shirt back on. Knowing my luck, if I was to step out of the barn bloody and naked then the fucking sheriff would be standing there or something.

We gather ourselves up as best as possible then head inside. We both take showers then make sure that his hand is completely cleaned up and wrapped. The cut isn't nearly as bad as the blood made it look. It might leave a small scar but at least it isn't deep enough that he needs stitches.

I know from this day forward whenever he sees that mark on his hand he is going to think of me, of us. It makes a smile stay on my face for hours.

After that day in the barn, we kinda fall into a new normal for us. We will take care of the horses in the morning, sometimes going for a ride in the afternoons. Sometimes taking the ATV out. Sometimes we just lose ourselves in each other.

I finally have my hair stripped of the black, it still doesn't look as blonde as my natural color but anything is better than that horrible box job I have been rocking. I have even reached out to Sarah a few times.

James invites her over to dinner once we have the horses sold. I am really starting to like the little life I am making here.

Maeve
2 years ago

176

This fucking hospital is not any better than the jungle. I will probably die from an infection I get from here instead of what I would have caught in that ditch. Nobody, not one fucking soul seems to speak a word of English either.

I have been here 3 weeks and I haven't been able to speak to one person coherently. But that gives me plenty of time to think about my next steps. I need to reach out to my mom but I have no phone, no id, no money.

After I have been here for about a month, I am visited by a nun from a local convent. The Sisters of Peace. I laugh out loud when she introduces herself but then I realize rather quickly that she speaks english. She is from the East Coast, New England area, she says. She also tells me that I will always have a place welcome for me at the convent. She never asks me my name and I never tell her.

The convent is a lot nicer than my brain has convinced me it is going to be. I decide to stay here until I am healed. Until I am able to get back home. Then I will have my revenge. I am going to hunt down every last fucking one of them and end them. Lane will be my last.

I promise myself that I will never give up, never back down. I live with the sisters for over a year. In that time, I have learned quite a bit about what working with my hands means. I do a shit ton of gardening and cleaning floors.

But that has bought me a lot of alone time as well. The sisters never know that I am using the belt from the clothes they give me to try to cover up the scars on my back. I never tell them, they never ask, even when they see the fresh stripes of blood through my clothes.

Only once does Sister Marie ask me about it. I tell her the truth. She cries when I show her my back but she has insisted on seeing it. I confess to her that I am upset that I can't cover the carving completely. I just can't reach it on my own. She cries again when I convince her to hit me with the belt, to cover what I can't.

It is a sunny summer day when I leave the sisters. As I wave goodbye, I see Sister Marie smile. She is the one who has saved me, the one who welcomed me in. She doesn't wave, she just gives me a smile and nods her head. I take that as confirmation that I will be forgiven for what I am about to do.

Whether that is what it actually means or not.

17

James
I'll Be Good – Jaymes Young

Bleu contacts me just a few days after our barn rendezvous with a message to call him. It is almost impossible to find a private place to hide that I am not afraid she is going to overhear me on the phone. I hated lying to her but I told her I was going to check the fenceline real quick. I took the ATV halfway down the drive, out of sight of the barn and called him back. The plan started to craft itself from that point on. The day she drives into town to get her hair done is the day I am really able to get everything nailed down.

Bleu has dug up a lot more than I thought he would be able too. I had never anticipated needing his help again but now I am glad to have kept his number.

"Lane has been holed up in a condo down in Miami for several months now. On the front, it looks like he retired but unofficially he was booted man. He has allegedly done some fucked up shit to some female recruits.

"I am guessing nothing was able to really be proven but there were enough fingers pointed his way they made him leave. Everytime something else pops up on this dude I would think about what you told me about your girl. I 100% believe she has given you the entire truth. This motherfucker is sick."

Bleu is never one to sugarcoat anything. Not that I need my hand held through this but it would have been nice if maybe some of it had been brought on by stress and was all in her head. But I have seen her back. I have watched the anger and fear and resentment on her face when she wakes from a nightmare. I knew it was all true. I didn't need him to confirm that part of it.

It is just easier to stomach if you think it might be exaggerated to some extent.

I let out a sigh, writing down any pertinent information he happens to relay, "So do you have an address for him?"

I can hear Bleu typing on a keyboard, "Yeah. I can forward it to you. Now you should know he mainly hangs out at a military bar. Vets fucking everywhere. I looked it up and talked with a few buddies stationed down there. It is one of the rougher ones. It won't be easy to get him alone there. Also, I don't think she should go in alone. I don't know how that would play out."

I nod my head along with him, "Yeah, I am still trying to work out how I will get him alone. Honestly, the first plan to run through my head is to grab him somehow and sedate him. Then bring him back here as a little present for her. I think out here it will be easier to dispose of any leftovers if you catch my drift." I smile to myself, knowing damn good and well that Bleu knows what I mean.

Bleu lets out a heavy sigh, "Fuck James. That's a lot, man. You have been out for a minute. I mean fuck we haven't even worked together in what 3 years? You think you are gonna be able to swing this one on your own?"

I lean back in my chair, sighing again, "Yeah, I think I should be fine. And I have to do this on my own. There is no way I am taking her to Miami. What if he recognizes her before we get the drop on him? I can't risk her being found before. She will only let the truth out if he is gone. She has made that abundantly clear.

"Also, I don't know how she would react just seeing him out and about. I like to think she would be smart enough to keep her cool until the timing was right. But man, you haven't seen the amount of vengeance this woman has running through her veins. I could honestly see her walking up to him and slicing his throat in the middle of DisneyWorld if she could. I don't want her getting caught.

"I just have to figure this all out before I get there. I can handle it though. For her, I could handle anything. I just need to be smart, safe. And listen to my fucking gut this time."

I can almost hear the wheels turning in Bleu's head, "So why not just wait it out with her? Let her find him on her own?"

I understand what he means but he doesn't see what I see, "Bleu, if you could see her you would understand. She has started to become better, I guess is the right word. When she first got here she was just so fucking lost. She just had this darkness in her eyes at all times.

"She has lightened up some but when she gets lost in her memories, she just completely shuts off. Then she will talk for days about what she is going to do to him if she ever finds him. If he ever comes up for air. I have never seen someone living purely for revenge before. It was pretty fucking intimidating at first."

I hear Bleu chuckle on the other end of the line, "Honestly dude, she sounds more like my type than yours. She got a sister?"

I bark out a laugh, "No, Bleu she is an only child. And if you even think about I will fucking castrate you."

Bleu laughs back at me, "Okay so, she can't be seen and you have been out of the game for years. Jesus dude..."

He lets out a heavy sigh, "Fuck alright. Count me in."

I sit up straighter in my seat, "What do you mean count you in?"

Bleu starts typing again, "You get here and we will go do this together. We will get him and then take him back to your place. Let her deal with him her own way. You just gotta find a good fucking cover if you don't want her hunting your ass down as well."

I lean up onto the desk, running a hand down my face, "Bleu you don't have to do that. I am not looking to get back in full time. This is a one and done situation."

Bleu stops typing and becomes real silent, "James, what you did for me in Fallujah needs to be paid back. I am not asking if you want my help, I am repaying a debt. Maybe after this is done I will be able to sleep at night as well. I am not expecting you to get back in the game by any means. I just want my debts to be paid. Neither of us will owe the other anything after all this. Deal?"

I grin into the phone, "The only thing I will expect after this then is friendship. I cleaned up your mess so I will let you help clean up mine. Send me the timeline. I will figure the rest out."

I hang up with Bleu very fucking grateful that he has jumped in last minute. He is right, I have been out of the game for too long to try to handle this alone. Hopefully, once all this is over I will be able to let Maeve know everything. The full story.

I mean hell she has shared enough of her secrets, maybe it is time to let my demons out for a breather too. I shake my head fiercely, NO. Not now.

I do not have time to let that shit out now. I have locked it down for almost 2 years now. I have shit to do. I need to come up with a good cover for this.

For the next week, I make sure to slip in a comment a few times a day about needing to head out soon to get everything prepared for the auction. I am not about to tell her the truth. That I have cancelled the sale and plan on letting her decide which ones to keep and which ones to sell to neighboring ranches.

Bleu has sent me the timeline. I have 4 days left before I need to meet up with him in Kansas City. From there, we will haul ass to Miami. Hopefully, be back here with a present for her in less than 2 weeks time max.

I have already buttered up Sarah as well. I talked her into coming and either staying with Maeve or at least finding a way to keep her occupied while I am gone. Sarah was happy to help thankfully. I think if it came to Maeve she would do just about anything. Sarah may be small and meek but when it comes to her friendship with Maeve, she would probably walk through the fires of hell if asked.

Maeve has taken to brushing down all the horses in the afternoons. I will just sit up on the porch swing and watch her go from mare to mare. She looks so in her element out here. She is just as wild as the creatures she is grooming.

I sit back in the swing just watching her. I have been checking my phone incessantly for the last week. Just making sure that nothing comes through while she is around. I am scared shitless that she is going to find out.

I haven't felt this kind of fear in a long fucking time. I can't actually remember the last time it has gripped me like this.

James

3 year ago

"Bleu, I don't know what fucking happened." I am pacing around the room, covered in blood. I am supposed to be here for fucking medical help if needed. Instead, I am standing over the body of a teenage fucking boy. His throat sliced clean open from one ear to the other. I feel fucking sick. I did that. Granted he was coming at me with an AK but still.

Bleu comes up beside me and clutches my shoulder, stilling me. "Stuart, you need to fucking calm down. With you losing your shit right now, I cannot focus on the fucking job. I need to go upstairs and take care of Ahmed. That is the fucking mission. Now get your shit together and cover me god dammit."

I nod my head at him, looking back at the boy briefly. I slide my knife back into its holster and throw my bag back around to my back. I reach down and take the kids' gun, checking the ammo supply.

60 seconds later we are quietly going up a flight of stairs. There is an open door to the left, Bleu does a quick sweep of it, motioning for 2 hostiles to the left, 1 to the right. I take a deep breath and motion me to the right. Bleu nods and runs into the room on the left. I take another deep breath and pull the AK up into my shoulder to aim it. I swing tight to my right, seeing a woman standing before me with her own AK raised. I don't even have time to beg for forgiveness before I pull the trigger.

I turn to check on Bleu and he is standing over a man that is holding a young woman. The woman in turn is holding an infant.

None of them are armed.

Bleu starts hyperventilating. I grab him by the shoulders and force him to sit back then look away. I quickly lift my hand and make him pucker up his lips like he is trying to whistle, "Breathe Bleu, slow in, slow out."

I put one hand on his chest and another on his belly, "In through the nose, out through the mouth. You got this. You're gonna be fine." His eyes move back to the civilians he has just dropped. The man has a bullet hole in the back of his head, the woman through her back then it unknowingly went through the head of the infant. I look

184

back to Bleu as the tears ran down his face leaving trails in the dirt and mud caked there.

I know what I have to do. I run back downstairs and grab the body of the teenage boy. I carry him up and place him halfway between the family and the woman I have shot. I put the kids gun back down in his hand then repositioned the woman so it looks like she has shot the family then possibly got into a gun battle with the kid.

Bleu is still shaking and punching himself in the head. I give him a hard slap to get his attention. When his eyes finally fall on me his pupils are dilated, "Come Bleu, we gotta go. We gotta go now!"

Bleu watches me walk over and take the dead woman's gun and shoot the teenager in the chest once. Hopefully it will look like a gun fight that ended with somebody slicing his throat then taking off. Bleu gives me one quick nod before we bolt down the stairs and from the building.

Bleu is finally able to breathe normally as well as we continue to skulk through the shadows, making our way to safety. I tap him on the shoulder with a canteen and he stops to take a deep drink.

He hands it back to me shaking his head, "The mark was supposed to be Ahmed. Why the fuck was it a woman? I don't understand what fucking happened."

I shake my head back at him, "We know nothing. We were not there. We didn't even make it to the building, we were under too much fire."

185

Bleu's eyes connect with mine as he nods his head slightly. I pat him on the shoulder again as I walk around him to check to see if we are clear, "We were never fucking here."

I am laid out on the porch floor. I wake up and all I can see is Maeve above me, freaking the fuck out. I blink hard 3 times before pulling myself up.

"James? Baby, are you okay? What the fuck happened?" I scoot myself back to lean up against the house. I close my eyes but all I can see is the woman standing there. Holding a gun, covered in blood, smiling at me. I open my eyes again to Maeve back in front of me.

I can feel her hands on my face, trying to pull me out of it but I just can't be touched right now. I can't fucking do it. I jump up running inside the house quickly trying to outrun the memories, the visions. I hear the porch door slam behind me as I barrell through the living room and up the stairs.

I run into the first door on the right, shutting it behind me. I step over between the dresser and the closet door, grabbing the stuffed bunny off the dresser then slide my back down the wall until I land on my ass.

I stare up to the ceiling, "Mallory, if you can hear me, I need you. I need to know how I can be saved from this. What do I have to do to be forgiven?"

I feel my chest getting tight again. I can not let myself slip again. I sit here staring at her bunny until I feel the muscles start to let themselves loosen a bit. I can feel my breathing coming back to normal. I let out a small cry into the empty room and start weeping. I sit there for a fucking long time, just wishing my sins will stop haunting me.

I step out of the room a few hours later. Maeve is sitting in the hallway, asleep against my mom's bedroom door. I know I

186

scared her earlier. But I am pretty certain she had figured out what was going on.

She opens her eyes when she hears the door shut behind me. She stares up at me, then gives me a soft smile, "Are you better now?"

I smile back at her and nod, "I'm sorry. I just couldn't. I just needed a minute alone."

She nods her head back at me, "I totally fucking get it baby. It's not a problem at all. I just hadn't really seen you like that before so it scared me at first. I figured it out pretty quickly though."

I nod back at her as I slide down the door to sit facing her. I let out a heavy sigh, "We both have our shit I guess."

Maeve nods at me, "Everyone does."

I smile at her as she tilts her head to the side and raises an eyebrow, "You know if you need to you can talk to me about anything. It won't make me see you any differently. I will accept you and your past just as you have accepted me and mine."

I smile back at her, "I know baby. One day I will. I will fucking tell you everything. But just not today, okay?"

Maeve smiles at me then leans across onto her hands and knees to give me a kiss. She smiles again as she pulls back, "I will love you regardless. Whether you tell me today or in 50 years I don't care. It's your timeline."

I grin as I give her another kiss.

18

Maeve

Wish You Were Here – Incubus

James has been gone for 3 days. That's all, 3 damn days and I already feel like I am going out of my mind. I didn't realize how dependent I had become to just his presence. I have spent my mornings taking care of the horses then the stalls but then by mid afternoon when everything is taken care of I find myself just sitting and thinking.

Which is a dangerous pastime for me. I will just sit thinking about what I still have left to do. What I should be working on right fucking now. I do pull out my phone a few times to do some searches but I don't find any new information on Lane or his whereabouts.

Day 4 starts the same as all the others but I just feel like hammered shit. I can barely even bring myself to roll out of bed. If James was here he would be pulling shit duty all by his little self. But instead I roll out of bed and get dressed.

I go downstairs to start some coffee but the thought of it just makes me nauseous. By noon, I am finally starting to finish up with the horses and Sarah has shown up. She follows me around the barn asking me every 3 seconds if I am okay.

I smile at her, "Yeah I am okay. It's probably just a stomach bug or something. Maybe I caught it from the horses? Can that even happen? Do horses get the stomach flu?"

Sarah laughs at me, "I have no fucking clue. I haven't even ever had a goldfish let alone a horse."

I laugh back at her as I finally finish up with the horse feed. We make our way back up to the house, slowly. I collapse on the porch swing when Sarah asks, "Do you want me to get you some water or milk or something?"

I scrunch up my face at her, "God no. That all sounds awful."

Sarah stands there with her hands on her hips just looking me up and down. I glance over at her just as she stands up stock straight, "You don't think you might be pregnant do you?"

I laugh at her, "No. I don't think so. The only time we didn't use protection I got a morning after pill, so I don't think that is what's up."

She starts pacing across the porch, "But, I mean if all you have used is condoms since, you can still get pregnant. I mean the odds are low but they still exist."

I roll my eyes at her, "I really don't think that is what is going on Sarah."

She shakes her head adamantly at me, "I am running in town and buying a test." I laugh at her as she books ass into the house.

I sit here staring at the horses as I hear her speed off down the driveway. I really don't think I am pregnant. But what if I am? What will James do? What will I do?

I am in no position to bring a child into this world. Not while I still have so much shit possibly going down at any time. It's not like I can hunt Lane down while 6 months pregnant.

James would fucking kill me if Lane didn't first.

I shake my head at the nothing, No that can't be it anyways. I go inside and make myself a grilled cheese sandwich. Just as I sit down to eat it, Sarah comes running back in the house. She is smiling from ear to ear as she sits the bag down on the table.

I take a quick peek in, quickly realizing she has bought 3 different tests. I laugh at her as I take a bite, "I think it only takes one test to say yeah or nah."

She makes a face at me then starts pulling the tests out of the bag. "I didn't know which kind to get. I panicked. I got one that is early detection, then another that is like electronic or something, like words show up on the screen. Then the last one is just your one line two line situation."

I smile at her again, quickly finishing the last of my sandwich. Sarah looks down at the empty plate then scrunches up her face again, "Did you have mustard on your grilled cheese?"

I look at the plate then at her, "Yeah?"

She grabs the early detection test shoving it into my face, "Go piss on this right fucking now!"

I laugh at her but grab the test then head to the bathroom. I follow the directions carefully then open the bathroom door to sit on the stairs watching Sarah wear a hole in the carpet by walking back and forth in a 3 foot area about a thousand times.

I laugh at her when my alarm goes off on my phone. She jumps and starts shifting from foot to foot, "You good?"

She flips me off and smiles, "I might be an aunt in 9 months. I am kinda trippin balls right now."

I laugh at her again then walk into the bathroom.

I pick up the test and stop breathing as I stand there staring at a plus sign. I look from the test to Sarah then back at the test again, "Go get the electronic one."

Sarah screams at the top of her lungs, "OH MY FUCKING GOD!!!!!"

She throws her hands in the air as she takes off running through the living room, tripping over the edge of the couch then cussing her way into the kitchen to grab the other test.

I stare at the plus sign in my hand, there is no fucking way this is happening right now. Sarah comes running back a few seconds later, hands shaking as she opens the box and takes the test out. 5 minutes later we are sitting side by side on the stairs, staring at the positive tests in our hands. I feel myself start crying.

Sarah quickly wraps her arm around my shoulders, "Is this a good cry or a bad cry?"

I can feel the streams of tears rolling down my face, "This is a scared shitless cry." I lay my head on her shoulder, still just staring at the tests. This can not be fucking real. James is going to lose his shit. And most definitely not in the same way I am losing mine. He is going to be over the fucking moon excited. I just want to vomit.

Like he knew what the actual fuck is going on, 2 minutes later my phone starts to ring. I look down and see the name I have set for him, "Dumbass McGee".

I let out a heavy sigh as I stare at the screen, having no fucking clue what I am going to say. Sarah reaches out and snatches the phone from my hands, "Hey James, Maeve is in the bathroom."

She nods at me as I continue to sit there in shock. "Yeah, no, everything is going great here. The horses are fine, we are fine. Everything is great."

She continues to pace the floor in front of me. I hold my hand out for the phone, "Oh, here she comes now James. See ya soon!"

She hands me back the phone and I slowly raise it to my ear, "Hey baby."

I can hear him smiling on the other end, "Fuck Maeve, I miss you. I missed your voice."

I smile into the phone as I stand up to go pace the hallway upstairs, "You just talked to me this morning."

He lets out a sigh, "I know but it still feels like it has been weeks not hours."

I laugh at his ridiculousness, "How are all the preparations going?"

He lets out a small breath, "Really good actually. I am gonna be home a lot sooner than I anticipated. Prolly in the next few days actually."

I smile as I let out a breath I didn't know I was holding, "That's awesome! I can't wait for you to be home. I miss you."

I can hear him smile again, "I miss you too baby. I actually met up with an old friend of mine out here, he is gonna come back with me. Help me get the horses prepped for travel."

I nod into the phone again, "Yeah that sounds great babe."

I lean up against the hallway wall, trying not to pass out or throw up. I hear him shuffling around on his side of the phone, "Maeve, are you alright? You sound like something is wrong."

I shake my head, there is no way I am telling him this news over the phone. "No, I am okay. I think I might be coming down with a cold or something. I am just gonna drink some hot tea and take some meds then go to bed. Call me tomorrow okay, let me know where you are at that point."

I hear him let out a little noise, "Are you sure that's all it is?"

I smile down the hallway, "Yes baby I promise that is all it is. I love you James"

I hear him let out a little chuckle, "I love you too Maeve. I will talk to you in the morning. Bye."

I hang up the phone and slide down the wall. I drop the phone on the floor between my legs and put my head in my hands.

What that fuck am I going to do?

This fucking changes everything. I feel a tear slide down my face, knowing now it is going to be nearly impossible to get the revenge that I have vowed for myself. I want to hunt him down now and finish this for good so I can move on, start this family.

But I don't want to jeopardize anything happening to the baby. I cradle my abdomen as I realize this is the only blood relative that James has left. This is his child. I can't be reckless.

Sarah slowly comes up the stairs and sits against the wall opposite of me. I lift my head and see her big brown eyes staring back at me, "I don't know what to do Sarah."

She immediately moves across the hall and pulls me into her arms. I can feel her smiling into my temple, "You are going to be an awesome mom you know that?"

I pull back and look at her like she is insane, "Dude, you don't understand. You don't know the whole story. Sarah, no one even knows that I am alive. Everyone thinks I went MIA 3 years ago. It's not like I can just pop into a doctor's office for a visit or something. I mean, I am going to have to come up with some kind of story. I can't tell the truth, if I do.....Lane will never come out of hiding. And I have to finish this. I have to finish him. I will not allow my baby to come into a world that he exists in. I just can't."

Sarah just nods at me again and pulls me back into a hug. She lets out a heavy sigh, "Here is what we are going to do. We are going to talk to James when he gets home. We are going to figure this out step by step as a family. Because that is what we are now. No matter if we don't share blood, you are my sister. We will get through this together."

I smile into her shoulder, it feels really fucking nice to have someone on my side.

In the next few days it takes for James to get home, my emotions have been a fucking rollercoaster. I am happy then I am sad. I am worried then ecstatic. I am sick then I am fine. I am all over the fucking place.

But at one point I do go and look at paint colors. I even pick up a cheap put it together yourself crib. Sarah helps me set it up in my old bedroom. I don't want to disturb Janices' or Mallorys' rooms. We just set up the crib, put the paint color schemes on the dresser and shut the door.

I am sitting on the porch swing when I see the truck pull up to the barn. I jump up and immediately start running to James.

He meets me halfway picking me up and swinging me around as I laugh at him. He finally puts me down and pulls me into a deep passionate kiss. I pull back, smiling at him. I have never been this fucking happy before. Never.

I stare into those honey glaze eyes as they search my face. I smile again and wrap my arms around his middle, "I am so fucking glad you are home. Next time I am going with you. I can't handle being away from you that long ever again, okay?" I feel him smile into the top of my head.

I pull back and see somebody approaching from behind him. I know the stance right away. I know the distant look in his eyes all too fucking well.

This guy is either military or ex military, and he has seen some shit. Probably caused a lot of it.

His hair is jet black, eyes a sparkling green. He is about the same height as James but is somehow thicker, more built. He

194

is wearing a pair of brown khaki cargo pants and a very tight t-shirt.

He smiles as he gets closer, "This must be Maeve."

I give him another once over, no longer smiling and look to James, "Who the fuck is he?" I point towards the new guy.

James smiles down at me and then points to his companion, "This is Bleu. Or at least that's what I call him."

I turn back to Bleu and he has stuck his hand out towards me, "Heya Maeve. My name is Chris Bleuth, but like James says, everyone just calls me Bleu."

I grip his hand tight and shake it back with all the strength I can muster up. I look back to James quickly before staring down Bleu again, something about this guy just screams danger.

I pull my hand back and take a step back by James. Bleu smiles up at me, "Hey, I get it. You don't know me. I don't blame the hesitance. But you should know, me and James, we go way back. We served together. We are brothers in every sense of the word that matters."

I nod again, giving myself an inner high five for calling it ahead of time. I look at James, "He cool?"

James just laughs at me, "Yes, he is cool. And if you are super nice to him, he might just give you all the dirt on me. Get all those deep lingering questions answered."

I smile at James then look towards Bleu. Bleu lets out a laugh and looks at me, "Fuck, you don't even have to be nice. I will spill his shit for free." I let a grin cover my face, I might just like this guy after all.

I push myself into James' side as we hear the porch door slam. We all look up to see Sarah standing at the top of the steps. She comes barrelling down them then quickly leans into James for a hug. She turns her head towards me, giving me a little wink.

I feel my cheeks start to turn red as she pulls back smiling. It is then that she seems to realize there is another male in our presence. She takes a full step towards me lowering her gaze to the ground. This is how she gets around all men that are not James. Like she is just waiting for the other shoe to drop. For someone so in love with dick, she sure is scared to death of men.

Bleu seems to be in some kind of trance. He looks from Sarah to James then to me finally settling back on Sarah. He lightly clears his throat taking a step towards her with his hand stretched out, "Hello ma'am. My name is Bleu. It's nice to meet you."

Sarah looks at me and I give her a small nod. She turns towards Bleu putting her hand delicately into his. She doesn't even look him in the eyes, "Hi. My name is Sarah."

Bleu can sense her hesitation. We all can. But he doesn't seem offended. I give him a long thankful blink as he pulls his hand back then glances at me.

He smiles back at Sarah, "That is a beautiful name Sarah. That was my grandmother's name actually."

Sarah looks up at him quickly then back down to the ground, "Oh. Well. That is nice."

I lean over towards her, turning my head to whisper into her ear, "What the fuck is wrong with you?"

Sarah gives me a quick glance as she turns her back towards the guys then whispers, "That dude is fucking massive. And gorgeous. I panicked."

I allow a chuckle to leave my chest as I smile towards Bleu. He looks at me in confusion until I give him a quick wink, then he lets a smile cover his face.

196

James lets out a laugh then chimes in, "Well, Bleu and I have a few things to unload into the barn. How about you go inside, we will be right behind ya. Maybe 5 minutes tops."

I step up to him, "I can help you unload. I don't mind."

James gives me another smile as he leans into my ear, "I think Sarah might need a little girl talk before she has to face Bleu again."

I smile into his shoulder then give him a quick kiss. "We will be inside then. I will make everyone some sweet tea."

James and Bleu both nod at me then turn heading towards the truck. Sarah reaches over then links her arm in mine as we turn towards the house.

When she knows they are out of hearing distance she lets out a soft moan, "After Bleu shook my hand, I could have sworn I needed a pregnancy test too. Jesus fuck that guy is hot."

I bark out a deep laugh, another one of my duck call laughs. I try to get to the porch quickly when I hear Bleu, "What the fuck was that?" Then there is nothing but James' laughter rolling out the barn doors.

No more than 10 minutes later, James and Bleu are walking in the back door. I am sitting on the counter, letting my feet dangle over the side. Sarah is sitting at the kitchen table, trying to not let Bleu catch her staring at him.

When we had come inside, it didn't take her more than 30 seconds to profess her undying love for the man. I tell her that is completely fueled by her vagina, she does not disagree.

James walks over to me standing between my knees, leaning into my body. He wraps me up in another hug, "God, it feels like I was gone for a year."

I smile back at him, "Yes it fucking does."

He gives a quick glance to Bleu then back to me, "I uh, got you a present."

I perk up, smiling at him then at Bleu, "Really?"

James lets out another hesitant smile, "Yeah. I really think you are going to like it."

I start squirming on the counter, "Where is it?"

James looks over at Bleu, who now has a different kind of shadow in his eyes, "It's in the barn."

I smile jumping off the counter. James quickly wraps me up in a hug, "Not yet. Not yet. In a little bit. I need to just hold you for a minute first."

I smile again as I lean into him. My eyes lock with Sarahs as she gives me a small nod. I let out a long breath, feeling my nerves tick up a notch.

I lean back just enough to look up into James' eyes, "I have a surprise for you too." He leans back a bit further giving me a confused look. I smile over at Sarah then lean off the counter.

"Follow me." I grab his hand and start leading him towards the living room. I can hear Sarah behind us, explaining to Bleu that we just need a few minutes alone. I continue to pull him through the living room then up the stairs.

We make it to the end of the hall and I turn to him. I let out another huge sigh squeezing both his hands, "I don't know how you are going to react to this. It has taken it a few days for it really to grow on me but I am really happy about it now. It kinda changes everything but I think it is what we both want. Hopefully."

James continues to search my face for some kind of clue. I square my shoulders then take another deep breath as I turn the door knob to the spare bedroom then walk in.

198

James follows me in and then his eyes land on the crib. His jaw drops and I swear he becomes almost as pale as me.

His eyes turn to me, "Are you fucking kidding me?"

I shake my head no and give him a small smile. His face then lights up. I have never seen a person grin that big in my life. His entire face lights up like a christmas tree.

He picks me up, spinning me around before sitting me back down then kissing me deeply. I laugh at him as I pull away, "Best I can guess is I am maybe a month along. I am not sure yet. I wanted to wait for you to get back before I reached out for a doctor."

He continues to hold me, unable to stop smiling. I take a few steps back to lean against the dresser. I close my eyes and tilt my face towards the floor in front of me.

James is to me in an instant, "What's wrong baby? This is good right?"

I smile back up at him, "No, yeah this is good. It just, well it really fucking changes everything. I feel like everything I have been working up to has been for nothing. I will never find Lane. I will never get some kind of closure. How am I supposed to be a good mom when I am in fucking hiding? I guess.....I guess I am just going to have to let it go. Come forward about being alive, forget about my plans. It's just hard to kinda accept."

James pulls me into another hug then kisses me on the top of my head. He grabs my hand gently pulling me towards the door, "Come with me."

I follow him out reluctantly, giving one more smile to the crib before closing the door behind me. He leads me across the hall then turns me and sits me down on the bed. He kneels down in front of me, "I have to tell you something."

I feel the nerves run down my spine. I don't like his tone. Something has happened, something has changed.

I pull my hands back out of his, "What did you do?"

James gives me a soft smile, "Nothing bad, I promise. I just want to prepare you for your present."

I lean back a bit further on the bed, "Okay?"

James quickly stands up walking to the door. He turns to face me as he leans against it, running his fingers through his hair, "So, I didn't just go to Kansas City for the horses."

I stare up at him, "Okay, then why else did you go to Kansas City?"

James gives me a soft smile again, "That is where Bleu lives. I went there to pick him up before I drove through to Miami."

I feel my eyes go wide as I stand up, "What the fuck do you mean Miami? Like Miami, Florida?"

James looks back at me, a little more concerned than before, "Yeah, Miami. That is where your present was. I had to go pick it up. I took Bleu to help me with it."

I turn around walking further into the room, before turning back to him, "What kind of fucking present did you have to go get in Miami? Why the fuck would it take two grown men to pick up?"

James has a serious look on his face now, "I didn't want to attempt it alone. I didn't want the whole thing to go sideways on me, and Bleu offered to help. He owed me one."

I start pacing the room again, what the actual fuck is going on? I stop turning back towards him, "So what the fuck was in Miami then? What was so important that you had to lie to me about where you were?"

James lets another small smile onto his face as his eyes turn darker, "Lane Masters."

19

James

Chemicals - Normandie

It takes us less than two days to make it to Miami. We take turns driving through the night. We park on the street not a block away from Lane's condo, deciding to keep an eye on his place for almost another full day before he finally makes his way out. At least it isn't a horrible neighborhood. I mean I have seen worse, but I have definitely seen better as well.

He even looks like a piece of shit. He steps out onto the street with his shoulders squared and chin held high. His steps are purposeful and confident, like he owns the fucking world. But his dark eyes show the devil that is lying beneath the surface.

We quickly follow him on foot a few blocks to his favorite watering hole. I can see through the window that Bleu had been right, this place is crawling with military, both active and retired. There are big ass dudes wall to wall in here. This is one of those bars where one wrong look will land you in the hospital. I am starting to become more grateful that Bleu is riding shotgun on this mission.

We are going to have to be careful how we step around in here. Lane keeps a smirk on his face as he strolls through the door. I want to rip his fucking head off. The misogynistic sway of his walk makes me want to vomit. We make our way inside just a few minutes behind him.

He is already sitting at the far end of the bar with what looks like a glass of whiskey in his hand. Bleu and I both sit a few stools down from him. I keep my eyes trained on everything but him.

The bartender steps up and Bleu casually orders us both a draft. I let my gaze wander over to Masters again, noting he still has that smug fucking grin on his face but there is more to it.

He is fucking tired. You can see it in his face, in the lines. It is as if the brimstone and evil he has been seeping out into the world has finally caught up with him. That is the only pleasure I get out of seeing this guy. That he is miserable to his core.

Then, as if tasting the danger in the air, his gaze quickly meets mine. I give him a slight nod then turn my attention back to Bleu. Bleu is standing with his back to Lane, taking in the surroundings more than anything. There are alot of big fucking dudes in this room. Whatever we are going to try to do, it isn't going to be here. We sit there at the bar for a few hours, watching as Lane orders drink after drink. We have an unspoken agreement to just wait until he is wasted and then figure out our next move then.

It has been a few hours, when we hear Lane, slurring his words, telling the bartender he's done for the night. That he is going to hit the head then walk home. Bleu and I give each other a quick nod then pay our tab and head out the door.

About a half a block from his house, there is an especially dark alley. We both flank it, just waiting on our prey to walk by. Now we just have to hope that luck is on our side. Not 5 minutes later we hear him shuffling his way down the sidewalk. I give a quick nod to Bleu as I step out of the alley and turn towards Lane. I square my shoulders, "Captain Lane Masters?"

Lane looks up at me surprised then squints his eyes towards me, "Do I know you boy?"

I let out a soft chuckle, "No Sir. But I know you."

He flicks his hand towards me like he is dismissing me and moves to step around me. I quickly step in front of him, blocking his way. He is unable to see Bleu step up behind him, blocking his retreat as well.

Lane looks back up at me again, this time with anger in his eyes, "What the fuck do you want soldier?"

I smile over his shoulder at Bleu then look back down at the shriveled old excuse of a man, "Me? I want nothing more than to rip your fucking head off and leave you here to bleed out." Lane stands a bit taller, trying to intimidate me or something. He lets out a short huff, "Yeah, I would like to see you try."

I smile again as I take a small step back, trying to get out of the way of his whiskey breath. I look down at the ground before catching his eyes again, with a wicked smile over my face, "The thing is, I can't do that. No matter how much I want to. Because your death, your end cannot be in my hands. It belongs to someone else."

Lane sways to the left a bit before straightening back up, "Oh yeah. And who the fuck would that be?"

I look over his shoulder at Bleu and smile as he leans into the old man's ear and whispers, "Private First Class Carrie Maeve Reynolds."

The smile falls from his face as he whips his head around towards Bleu. Lane starts shaking his head back and forth, "No fucking way, she is dead."

Bleu gives him another smile as he leans in a bit closer, "You sure about that old man? When you left her in that ditch, did you check for a pulse or just walk away?"

I see the panic slide over his face in an instant. He rears back to punch Bleu but is met with a punch to the gut instead. He doubles over and turns back towards me. The last thing he sees before he blacks out is me smiling as I pull my knee up into his nose.

I stay with his unconscious body while Bleu runs to get the truck. We have to "Weekend at Bernies" him into the truck then promptly zip tie his hands and feet. Thankfully the truck is a club cab so we just duct tape his mouth shut and throw a blanket over him.

We drive as quick as we feel is safe enough to get the fuck out of Miami. We don't stop for anything other than gas until we are crossing into Georgia. We pull into a rest area and I check Lane's pulse just to make sure I haven't killed him in the process of knocking him out.

Luckily, his pulse is still strong. I slip out of the truck and quickly make a call to Maeve. I want to warn her that we will be back a lot sooner than I anticipated. I hate lying to her but I honestly believe when I am able to deliver her gift she will love me even more than she already does.

The phone rings 4 times before it is finally answered, "Hey James, Maeve is in the bathroom."

I smile into the phone, grateful that Sarah has kept her word and is keeping Maeve company. "Ah, okay. How is everything going there?"

I can hear Sarah pacing back and forth, "Yeah, no, everything is going great here. The horses are fine, we are fine. Everything is great."

I make a face towards the truck, something is wrong. She has just said the words great and fine a few too many times. I open my mouth to reply and she quickly adds, "Oh, here she comes now James. See ya soon!"

I hear her hand the phone over to Maeve then a little voice says sweetly, "Hey baby."

I instantly stand still and smile into nothingness. I feel a warmth come over my chest, "Fuck Maeve, I miss you. I missed your voice."

I let out a heavy sigh and hear a little giggle from her end of the line, "You just talked to me this morning."

I let out another sigh, "I know, but it still feels like it has been weeks not hours."

I hear Maeve let out a little laugh, which has me smiling again, "How are all the preparations going?"

I smile and let out another sigh, "Really fucking good actually. I am gonna be home a lot sooner than I anticipated. Prolly in the next few days actually."

I can hear the excitement in Maeve's voice, "That's awesome! I can't wait for you to be home. I miss you."

I smile into the phone, staring at my feet shuffling back and forth, "I miss you too baby. I actually met up with an old friend of mine out here, he is gonna come back with me. Help me get the horses ready for travel."

I fucking hate lying to her, but if I was to tell her now she will have had way too much time to sit and let it stew before we get there. I look up at Bleu now leaned against the side of the truck.

I hear Maeve sound a little distant, like something is on her mind, "Yeah that sounds great babe."

I stand a little straighter, looking towards Bleu again, "Maeve, are you alright? You sound like something is wrong."

I see Bleus' eyebrows raise on his forehead. He tilts his head towards me a bit and I shrug my shoulders. I hear Maeve let out another low sigh, "No, I am okay. I think I might be coming down with a cold or something. I am just gonna drink some hot tea and take some meds, then go to bed. Call me tomorrow okay, let me know where you are at that point."

I let out a heavy sigh while giving Bleu a skeptical look, "Are you sure that's all it is?"

She is lying to me, I can hear it in her voice. I hear her voice change like she is smiling and my guard starts to go back down, "Yes, baby, I promise that is all it is. I love you James."

I smile back into the phone, looking to my feet again, "I love you too Maeve. I will talk to you in the morning. Bye."

I hang up the phone, still staring at it in my hand.

Bleu walks up in front of me with his arms crossed over his chest, "What was that about?"

I shake my head at the phone again then look up at Bleu, "I am not sure. She said she might be coming down with a cold but she didn't sound sick. There is definitely something wrong. She lied to me. I can tell. I just don't know why."

Bleu nods his head at me, "Well, let's just book ass and get back. That way you can see for yourself. Plus, that guy reeks, I don't wanna be stuck in that truck with him forever."

I nod my head pulling my keys out of my pocket. I stop halfway to the truck, "If we take turns driving we can probably be back in Montana by this time tomorrow. But that's really pushing it."

Bleu smiles back at me and puts his hands up to catch the keys, "I will take the first shift then. The sooner we get back, the sooner this shit is over."

I laugh and toss him the keys before jumping into the truck. I look at my watch, it is a little after noon. With any luck, I will be holding Maeve this time tomorrow. Bleu starts the truck and pulls out onto the highway.

I sit there just zoning out trying to figure out in my head what is going on. My biggest fear is that she has done something that got herself hurt. She won't fucking tell me if she did. She is too stubborn for that. I lean into the door and slip off to a fitful sleep.

I wake up about 10 hours later, as we are pulling into a gas station somewhere between Omaha and Sioux City. I sit forward, noticing it is dark outside now. I stretch my shoulders then look into the back seat. I see two beady eyes staring back at me.

I smile broadly, "Oh lookie there, you decided to join us."

He grumbles something back, but with his mouth taped I can't understand a word he says. I look around, noticing no one near us but still cover his head back up anyways. You never know, there could be cameras on us.

Bleu fills up the tank as I jump out and stretch my legs. He nods to the cab of the truck, "He came too a few hours ago. Been rolling around and making noises ever since."

I nod my head then crack my neck. "I will take over driving for a bit. That way you can get some sleep."

Bleu agrees and puts the gas pump back in its arm. I circle the front of the truck while he moves around to the passenger side. We both hop back in and start making our way down the road again.

At some point, Lane must have fallen asleep or passed out again. I haven't heard anything from him for awhile. Bleu on the other hand is snoring as loud as fucking freight train beside me.

I drive straight through the night, only stopping for gas once. It is almost 8 in the morning when I pull into another station somewhere just south of Billings. Lane is awake again, making all kinds of racket in the back seat. Bleu had woken up about an hour before that.

I fill up the tank again then check my watch, "If you don't care to drive, I will sleep until we make it to Great Falls, then I will take over."

Bleu gives me another smile as I toss the keys to him. He nods towards the truck, "Go ahead and hop in or call your lady. I am gonna run inside and grab a drink."

I nod my head back at him and turn around to lean my back against the truck. Maeve answers on the second ring this time. "Hey baby, how are you this morning?"

I hear the screen door closing behind her, "Hey, me and Sarah just got back from town. I got up early and took care of the horses."

I smile into the phone, "Well, you will be happy to know we should be home in about 5 or 6 hours."

I hear Maeve drop something heavy on the other end of the line, "Are you okay Maeve?"

My heart starts thudding in my chest. Maeve lets out a little giggle, "Yeah I am good. I just scared the shit outta Sarah and she fell on her ass."

I let out a laugh along with her, "You sound like you are feeling better at least."

I hear her let out another soft sigh, "I am. I am doing much better now."

I smile at the ground again before seeing Bleu approach the truck, "Well Bleu is back at the truck now. I am gonna hop back in and get on the road, but I love you baby. I will see you soon."

I hear another small noise then Maeve, "I love you too baby, Be careful."

I hang up the phone just staring at it again. Something is off, not necessarily wrong but just off. She sounded fine, but she sounded tired. Like her brain is running on fumes or something.

I slide into the truck and take off my coat to use it as a pillow. Bleu heads back out onto the highway and we are on our way again. Lane won't shut the fuck up.

After a few hours of restless sleep, because of his moaning and groaning, I promptly turn around then pull down the blanket. His eyes go wild looking around the cab of the truck.

I glare down at him, "If you don't shut the fuck up I am going to fucking stab you right here and let you bleed out in the back of my truck. I don't give a fuck, I will torch the bitch. You hear me?"

Lane's eyes glare at me angrily as he tries to say something else. I quickly pull the bowie knife out of the glove box and hold it up to the side of his face, "I am not fucking around old man. You get me?"

His eyes wide, trying to stare at the blade then back to me he slowly nods his head yes. I nod my head back, swiping the knife across his cheek, slicing into him about two inches long.

Lane lets out a scream as I smile and pull the knife back, "Whoops."

I throw the blanket back over his head and wipe the knife off on a napkin from the console, then throw the knife back in the glove compartment. Bleu has an all knowing smile on his face as he turns to me chuckling, "Whoops." I let out a laugh then settle in to get a few hours of sleep.

Bleu wakes me up about a half hour from home. I quickly trade places with him then start towards the farm. The closer we get the faster I drive. I can't fucking wait to see Maeve. It is going to take all of my fucking restraint not to run through her like a train as soon as I see her.

How have I survived without her until now?

My every fucking thought, every fucking breath is for her. I drive the old country roads as fast as I will allow myself, without risking getting pulled over. I finally see the house and quickly pull into the drive. I drive up to the barn, angling the truck so the passenger side is facing the doors.

209

I look out the driver's side window and see Maeve running out the screen door. She is fucking beautiful. She is wearing the yellow dress we bought at the store. She is barefoot, running down the back steps, skin a soft tan, short blonde hair whipping in the wind as she runs towards me.

I quickly jump out of the truck and run to meet her halfway. I pick her up holding her tight as I spin us both in a circle. I can hear her giggling until I sit her back down. She wraps her arms around me and pulls me in tight.

I put my face into her hair as I hear her say, "I am so fucking glad you are home. Next time I am going with you. I can't handle being away from you that long ever again, okay?" I let out a laugh into her hair, finally letting myself smile.

I pull back from her, just taking her in. She looks over my shoulder and the smile starts to fade from her face.

I hear Bleu approaching from behind me, "This must be Maeve."

I look back down at Maeve as she continues to eye him. She is taking him in. I can tell by the way her eyes scan him from head to toe. She nudges her chin towards him, "Who the fuck is he?"

I can hear the hesitance in her voice as she points towards Bleu. I smile as I move to the side a bit, "This is Bleu, or at least that's what I call him."

Bleu sticks his hand out for Maeve to shake and she gives me another side look as she hesitantly raises her hand to his. Bleu gives her a smile, "Heya Maeve. My name is Chris Bleuth, but like James says, everyone just calls me Bleu."

I watch Maeve as she assesses him, then she steps back into my side and wraps her arm around me. Bleu puts his hands up in a form of surrender, "Hey, I get it. You don't know me. I don't blame the hesitance. But you should know, me and James, we go way back. We served together. We are brothers in every sense of the word that matters."

I stare at Bleu, I have never heard him be so sentimental before. He gives me a small nod and I smile back at him.

I turn to look at Maeve as she leans into my ear, "He cool?"

I let out a loud laugh and look back down at her, "Yes, he is cool. And if you are super nice to him, he might just give you all the dirt on me. Get all of those deep lingering questions answered."

I tap her on the temple and smile at her. Bleu lets out a loud laugh then steps up to Maeve a bit more, "Fuck, you don't even have to be nice. I will spill his shit for free." I let my jaw drop at his admission as Maeve lets a smile cover her face.

It isn't two minutes later and Sarah is wrapping her arms around me too. She is looking so much better than the last time I saw her. She is even putting some fucking weight on which is great considering she was barely even 100 lbs when Alan died.

I watch her face go tense when she sees Bleu beside me. Her eyes blow wide as she looks him over quickly then points her gaze towards the ground. I look over at Bleu and I can see the astonishment roll over his face.

I stare at him as he starts blinking rapidly and I can see the vein in his neck pumping faster. He can't take his eyes off Sarah.

I smile at Maeve, knowing the feeling all too well and pull her closer to me. They introduced themselves to each other awkwardly and I can't help but let out a laugh, "Well, Bleu and I have a few things to unload into the barn. How about you go inside, we will be right behind ya. Maybe 5 minutes tops?"

Maeve quickly turns towards me then looks towards the truck, "I can help you unload. I don't mind."

I look at Bleu, who is still staring at Sarah while she looks anywhere but at him. I smile again then lean into Maeve's ear, "I think Sarah might need a little girl talk before she has to face Bleu again."

Maeve smiles back at me and gives me a quick kiss on the cheek, "We will be inside then. I will make everyone some sweet tea."

She turns and links elbows with Sarah before walking away, whispering to each other in hushed voices all the way up the steps towards the back door.

I turn to walk towards the barn, quickly opening the doors then stepping inside. Bleu is right beside me when I hear Maeve laugh from the back porch. I let out another chuckle because it is her deep, guttural duck laugh.

Bleu's eyes fly open and he runs to the doors to look back out, "What the fuck was that?"

I laugh out loud again, "That was Maeve. That is how you know it's a real laugh."

Bleu turns around giving me an incredulous look, "You mean that was fucking normal?"

I beam back at him, "Yes. Yes it is."

Bleu lets out another laugh as he shakes his head back and forth. He quickly steps up beside me and crosses his arms over his chest, "So, what's the story with Sarah?"

I give him a quick side eye before finding some more rope and throwing it on the ground in front of the main support pole in the middle of the barn. I stop turning to look back at him, "What do you want to know?"

He shrugs his shoulders, "Whatever you can tell me I guess." I let out a sigh then look towards the truck then back at Bleu, "Well, her and Maeve met a while back. Maeve was leaving town and Sarah picked her up hitching. Sarah had been beat up pretty bad by her boyfriend and Maeve took care of the issue. They have been friends ever since."

Bleu looks like he wants to fucking kill somebody, "Who is the fucker? I will fucking end him."

I let out another chuckle and pat him on the shoulder, "Whoa there big guy. No need, he has already been dealt with."

Bleu shakes his head back and forth, "Not enough."

I cross my arms over my chest as I turn to look back at him, no longer smiling, "Maeve put a bullet in the back of his head and Sarah lied for her saying some dude broke in to rob them and she fought back. Alan is dead and gone, my friend."

Bleu's eyes sparkle wider as that sinister smile I have seen one too many times comes back over his face, "I really, really like your woman James."

I let my arms fall as I nod at him, "Help me get this bitch tied to the pole."

5 minutes later we are walking to the house. Lane had woken up when we were moving him into the barn. He has shit and pissed himself at some point but I don't care. He isn't gonna be around much longer anyways.

Bleu and I tie him tightly to the pole, a rope around the neck, a rope around his waist, then another across his shins. Hands tied firmly in front of him but pinned down by the rope going around his waist. He isn't going anywhere. I pull the barn doors closed as I watch his eyes scan the entirety of the barn, probably trying to see a way out.

There isn't one.

I walk into the kitchen off the back porch to see Maeve sitting on the counter swinging her legs. Sarah is sitting at the table so Bleu immediately walks over and sits down across from her. I walk over to Maeve, stepping in between her knees, wrapping her in another hug, "God, it feels like I was gone for a year."

I can feel her smile into my chest, "Yes it fucking does."

I pull back and see Maeve turn her gaze back to me. I smile over my shoulder at Bleu then meet her eyes again, "I uh, got you a present."

She sits up straighter, smiling widely, "Really?"

I nod and smile at her again, "Yeah. I really think you are going to like it."

I hear Bleu chuckle behind me. I took a step back from Maeve as she starts fidgeting on the counter, "Where is it?"

I smile again, then look back at Bleu. His eyes have that look again, the one he gives when he is ready for shit to go sideways. I turn back to Maeve, "It's in the barn."

Maeve lets out a little squeal and jumps off the counter to run around me then out the door. I quickly grab her, wrapping her up in a little hug, "Not yet. Not yet. In a little bit. I need to just hold you for a minute first."

I feel Maeve smile into my chest then pull back and look up at me, "I have a surprise for you too."

I pull back a bit more and look her over. She is nervous. She lets out a deep breath before nodding at Sarah then grabs my hand, "Follow me." She leads me out of the kitchen slowly as I hear Sarah whisper something to Bleu.

She takes me through the living room and up the stairs that lead down the hallway. She stops me right outside our bedroom door then grabs both my hands squeezing them tight, "I don't know how you are going to react to this. It has taken it a few days for it really to grow on me but I am really happy about it now. It kinda changes everything but I think it is what we both want. Hopefully."

I stand there staring at her dumbfounded. I have not one fucking clue what she can be talking about. She lets out another

214

deep breath then slowly turns the doorknob to the spare room and steps in.

I walk in right behind her and see a baby crib sitting in the middle of the room. I feel my heart drop out of my stomach. I am in complete and utter shock. We had used protection. We had even got her a morning after pill at one point. This can not be happening. She can not be pregnant with my child while I just tied up a man in the barn for her to butcher.

I turn my eyes towards her, "Are you fucking kidding me?"

Maeve shakes her head no and gives me a soft smile. I feel this rush of pure adrenaline run through my veins. I have never felt so fucking happy, so fucking complete in my entire life. I pick her up and spin her around again before sitting her down and kissing her hard.

Maeve is laughing at me as she pulls away, "Best I can guess is I am maybe a month along. I am not sure yet. I wanted to wait for you to get back before I reached out for a doctor."

I continue to hold her, unable to not smile at any of it. Maeve gently pulls away and walks over to the dresser then turns to lean against it. She seemed happy a minute ago but now, she just seems lost.

I step up to her quickly. I put my hand on her stomach as I stare deep into her eyes, "What's wrong baby? This is good right?" Does she not want the baby? Why would she put a crib together if she doesn't want to keep the child?

I am confused but then she smiles back up at me, "No, yeah this is good. It just, well it really fucking changes everything. I feel like everything I have been working up to has been for nothing. I will never find Lane. I will never get some kind of closure. How am I supposed to be a good mom when I am in fucking hiding? I guess, I guess I am just going to have to let it go. Come forward about being alive, forget about my plans. It's just hard to kinda accept."

I look down at her, I feel her pain. I know what she has been through to get to where she is. She is at the finish line and thinks she isn't going to be able to complete the race.

I tug her back in for another hug before taking her hand and leading her to the hallway, "Come with me."

I lead her from the room, softly shutting the door then walk into our bedroom and sit her on the bed in front of me. I kneel down in front of her and let out a heavy sigh, here goes nothing, "I have to tell you something."

I see a kaleidoscope of emotions run over her face as she yanks her hands from mine, "What did you do?" Her mind obviously goes to the worst possible scenario.

I smile again, "Nothing bad, I promise. I just want to prepare you for your present."

She leans back a bit further from me, "Okay?"

I stand up and walk to the door, shutting it so she can't just take off on me halfway through my confession. She needs to hear the whole thing.

I turn back around and lean against the door, nervously running my hands through my hair, scared of what her reaction might be, "So, I didn't just go to Kansas City for the horses. That is where Bleu lives. I went there to pick him up before I drove through to Miami."

I watch Maeve as she jumps to her feet, nearly screaming at me, "What the fuck do you mean Miami? Like Miami Florida?"

She is making me nervous. I have never seen her flip like this before. Normally she is silent and brooding. This new Maeve kinda scares the shit out of me.

216

I nod slowly, "Yeah, Miami. That is where your present was. I had to go pick it up. I took Bleu to help me with it."

She starts pacing in front of me before stopping mid room and turns back towards me, "What kind of fucking present did you have to go get in Miami? Why the fuck would it take two grown ass men to pick it up?"

I stare her down, hoping to god she doesn't lose her shit on me with the rest of my confession. I have never been so fucking scared in my life.

I nod slightly again, "I didn't want to attempt it alone. I didn't want the whole thing to go sideways on me, and Bleu offered to help. He owed me one."

I try to keep my voice as calm and level as I can as she starts pacing the room again. Her face is turning red, "So, what the fuck was in Miami then? What was so important that you had to LIE to me about where you fucking were?"

I feel a small smile come over my face, thinking about all the things she is going to do to that piece of shit. Knowing she is going to be free from this prison she keeps herself in. We are going to be done with it all, and can be free to be ourselves, all the time, anywhere. I let out a small, devious chuckle as I state, "Lane Masters."

20

Maeve

Who's Afraid of Little Old Me? - Taylor Swift

I shake my head, I could not have just heard him right. I take a step closer to James, "Did you just say Lane Masters?"

James has a stoney smile on his face as he nods his head at me. I hold my breath, "Where is he?"

James takes another step towards me and smiles down into my eyes, "He is tied to a pole in the barn, covered in his own shit and piss from being knocked out for a few days. We jumped him outside of his local watering hole. He was walking back to his condo. In Miami."

I feel that familiar burn roll through my veins. I take a step back, "So you are telling me you found Lane, then went and fucking kidnapped him then brought him back here for me?"

James' smile drops a bit, he thinks I am mad. That couldn't be further from the truth. He nervously nods his head at me again as I launch myself into his arms. I wrap my legs tightly around his waist and kiss him harder than I ever have before. James has one hand on my ass and the other wrapped up in the hair at the nape of my neck.

I hold him close as I shove my tongue into his mouth. He lets out a deep moan as I pull back to kiss his neck, then pull his earlobe into my mouth. He quickly turns us and puts me up against the wall.

I reach down to unbutton his jeans quickly as he pulls them down his hips. I feel him bundle my dress around my hips then rip my underwear from my body. I let out a shudder at the forcefulness.

His eyes meet mine as he roughly shoves his dick into me. My arms fall from his body and try gripping the wall around me. He has me pinned to the wall, one hand around my throat, the other on the wall behind me as he forcefully grunts his way into me.

I smile into the air above his head. This man has gone to the other side of the fucking country to bring me back the one last name on my list. He knows what I am going to do to this man and he offers him up to me on a silver fucking platter.

I wrap my arms around him, running my nails deep down his back as he pushes himself deeper into me. I feel myself start to quiver around him and he spins me around again then lays me back down on the bed. He doesn't leave my pussy the entire way.

I reach my hands up, tightly gripping the far side of the mattress. He pushes my thighs open until they are flat against the bed around me then starts pummeling me with his dick again.

I look down to see him watching us where we are joined. I look down as well watching his dick thrust in and out of me. I let a smile come over my face as I reach down and start rubbing my clit furiously.

He lets out another growl as he forces himself into me harder, faster. I feel myself clench down on him and I let out a scream, "Fuck James! Fucking break me!"

I feel his dick thicken inside of me then he lets out a scream as he finishes inside of me. He continues to thrust into me for a few more minutes as I ride out the waves of my orgasm. I smile up at him, him down at me then kiss him hard.

I pull back smiling, "I think I forgot to tell you that I like the present." James lets out a laugh as he pulls out of me and stands up to pull his jeans back on, "Yeah, I think I got the message loud and clear though." I smile at him as I try to sit up and gain some composure.

I sit there for a few more minutes before I stand and walk to the closet. I pull out my black hoodie then the duffle from the top of the closet. I pull the bag open, taking out my two leg knife holsters.

I walk to the dresser, opening the drawers, pulling out a black tank top, then black jeans. I smile as I open the top drawer, pushing my underwear to the side then pull out my two knives and gun.

I sit them all on top of the dresser then pull the dress up over my head and throw it in the hamper. I rip the remaining remnants of my underwear from my body and toss them in the trash can beside the dresser.

I slowly walk back to the bed to grab my jeans. I am so lost in my own thoughts, in my own fantasies that I don't even notice that James is watching my every fucking move.

I quickly dress then attach both knives to my legs. I pick up my gun ensuring it is loaded and that the safety is on. I slip it into the back of my jeans then turn to James.

He has a complete look of satisfaction on his face. I give him a small nod of the chin as he pushes off the door then turns and opens it for me.

I slowly walk down the hall, then the stairs. I round into the kitchen and see Bleu and Sarah through the window, sitting on the back porch swing. I take a sturdy step outside and turn to them.

I look straight at Sarah, "I don't care what happens. It doesn't matter how long I am out there. I don't care what you hear or what either of these guys say. You do NOT come into that barn for any fucking reason. You get me?"

Sarah looks completely terrified. She stands up quickly, her eyes darting to James walking out the door and onto the porch behind me.

She turns her head back to me, "Maeve you have to be careful. Remember the baby."

I see Bleus' eyes go wide as he looks to James for confirmation. I smile back at Sarah and place my hand softly on her cheek, "Sarah, do not worry. He is tied up. He can't hurt me anymore. It is finally time for me to get some fucking payback. I promise I will not let myself get put in harm's way okay. I won't risk the baby."

Sarah smiles softly at me then pulls me into a deep hug. I pull back, smiling at her. This little auntie is being overprotective and somehow, it doesn't even bother me. I am still just surprised that she has become more like a sister than a friend. I have never had that before. Ever.

I turn to James and Bleu, "Are you two alright with being my fallbacks? My help if I need it?"

James and Bleu look at eachother then back at me. Bleu lets a devious grin come over his face before he leans into Sarah's ear, "I won't let her get hurt. I promise."

Sarah jumps a bit at his mouth so close to her ear but then slowly nods her head. She then quickly grips Bleu's bicep and he turns to face her as she whispers, "Please be careful."

Bleu looks like he is going to melt into a puddle before her feet. He smiles back down at her, "Always baby, always."

I feel James put his hand on my lower back. I look up to him and smile, "I fucking love you."

He smiles back as he kisses me on top of the head before I turn and slowly make my way down the porch steps. I watch the horses following my movements as I stride towards the barn.

I am flanked by the guys. My hands tremble with anticipation, my knuckles white from clenching them so tightly. The adrenaline is now coursing through my veins making me lightheaded with anticipation.

My tongue feels dry and heavy, the taste of what is about to happen sitting squarely in my mouth. My heart races in my ears, each beat sounding louder and faster.

My breathing grows heavy with excitement for what is about to happen with every step I take. I have waited for what feels like a lifetime for this moment, and I am going to enjoy every fucking second of it. My eyes narrow with determination as I round on the barn doors.

James and Bleu slowly pull the doors open so I can step inside. They close the doors quickly behind me. After letting my eyes adjust, I see the back of a man tied to the main support post in the middle of the barn.

James moves to the left of me, Bleu to the right as they both circle around staring at the man the entire time. They are both smiling at him like the Cheshire cat.

I pull the machete out of a bale of hay as I take a few slow steps towards the man while skillfully swinging the machete through the air, making slashing noises.

"So, Lane. You have been a hard man to find. I have looked for you for months and months now." I am slowly running the edge of the machete down the stall doors, occasionally letting it clang onto the metal of the hinges. I can see Lane's head moving in different directions trying to get a look at me. He probably thinks he is hearing the voice of a fucking ghost.

James looks over at me then takes a step back as I smile at him and turn to face Lane. The old man's face has aged a lot in the 3 years since I have last seen him.

Deep wrinkles etch his face, carving lines around his eyes. His once salt and pepper hair is now completely white and is thinning on top, receding at the temples.

His eyes though, are still as dull and evil as they had been the last time I looked into them. Begging him to let me go, not to hurt me. There is a faint scent of shit and fear.

I smile as it registers across his face who is standing in front of him. I reach up and rip the duct tape from his mouth making him inhale deeply. With each breath, a soft wheeze escapes bringing a smile to my face.

His eyes wild, he looks around the barn before settling back on me as he asks, "Who are you?"

I feel the smile fall from my face, he doesn't even fucking remember me? How? How can he not remember what he has done? Who I am? My heartrate kicks up a notch as my mind races a million miles a minute.

James steps up beside me, "Don't let him fool you. He knows exactly who you are. He is fucking with you."

I turn my face back to Lane and bring the machete up, resting it on my shoulder. I take a few steps around him, "You know. It took alot for me to track you down. I mean, I myself was completely unsuccessful. But these two gentlemen here, it didn't take them what? 2 weeks? And here you are, trussed up like a Thanksgiving day turkey."

I turn to Bleu and smile, "And it's not even my birthday."

Bleu smiles devilishly back at me. I step up to Lane and then around the pole. I bring the machete down hard on the rope around his neck. He jumps, screaming, but then starts turning his head back and forth as he realizes I have cut his neck free.

James and Bleu move further behind me as I stand there staring at Lane, trussed up and scared shitless. I tilt my head to one side smiling, "Awe...are you scared? Don't worry....I am not going to kill you. Yet. I will give you a chance to save yourself, redeem yourself of your sins."

Lanes' eyes move from Bleu to me as that recognizable evil snarl comes back over his face, "I have nothing to be redeemed of. I have done nothing wrong."

I nod my head as I turn my back to him. Bleu and James are leaned up against the far wall. I walk over between them picking up the hoof pick laying on an old wooden table.

I smirk as I touch the tip of it to my fingertip, seeing a small bead of blood forming under the sharp edge. I smile briefly at James then turn back to Lane. "So you say, you have done nothing wrong? What would you call South America then?"

Lane's eyes quickly scour the room again before landing on James. He quickly looks from James to me and gives that same disgusting grin, "Cleaning up a mess."

I step forward slowly, "You know, you really should have made sure I was dead when you left me in that ditch."

Lane smiles again, "I don't know what you are talking about."

I wave my hands around in the air, so that he can now see the hoof pick in my right hand. His eyes follow the movement of the instrument before settling back on my face, "Well, let me give you a little reminder. You had Weathers hold me down on a steel table while you and your pitiful excuse for a dick raped me."

Lane's eyes never leave mine, even when he hears Bleu and James both snickering behind me. I take another step forward, "Then when you couldn't even force me to come on it, you flipped me over and shoved something up my ass. I still

224

don't know what it was. There was no way it was your dick though."

I hold up my pinky finger as I smile at him, "It wouldn't have hurt so bad."

Lane glares at me as he spits towards my feet. I look down towards the floor then slowly bring my eyes back to him, smiling, "Then you both stripped me naked and you decided that was the time to stab me, what 3 times was it?"

I slowly lift one finger, then another, then finally a third as I give him a maniacal smile. I turn around and see that James is no longer smiling. Bleu looks like he is just waiting for me to snap my fingers letting him jump into action.

I slowly turn back around, smiling at Lane again, taking in the image of the weak old man in front of me. If he wasn't such a fucking monster I would feel bad about seeing his feeble ass tied to the pole. But since he is the devil incarnate, it doesn't really bother me at all.

I lean against the wooden table behind me, "So, I had been beaten, raped, sodomized, stabbed then you have someone carry me out to the ditch. Just throwing me in with the other dead bodies. Then, just for good measure, you have Weathers put a couple rounds in me. Is this ringing any bells yet?"

Lane looks from James to Bleu, "No, none of it. I think you have me mistaken for someone else."

Smiling, I leaned forward a bit, "No, I know for certain it was you. You know for certain it was you. I am not going to kill you right now either. I laid in that ditch for 3 days, slowly dying from blood loss and infection. I wonder how long you will last tied up to this pole?"

I glance at James smiling again, "Wanna place bets how long it takes him to crack?"

I hear Bleu snicker behind me, "I got 20 bucks on a day."

225

I laugh at that, "Oh we should at least give him a credit of 48 hours."

Bleu shakes his head back and forth, "Nah, cowards never last that long."

I smile back at James, "I really do like your friends."

James smiles, nodding back at me. He looks over my shoulder towards Lane. He pushes off the wall and takes a few steps towards Lane before smiling, "Lane, we are going to give you 3 days. You have 3 full days to come clean. Admit what you did. If you do not, I don't think you are going to like what is unleashed on you."

Lane chuckles, "You children aren't going to do anything. You don't have the balls."

I grin as I step around James, "Oh, I can honestly say his balls are much much bigger than yours. But James is right, we should at least give you the chance to own up to your mistakes. I mean I am fine either way."

I smile as I twirl the hoof pick in my hand again. Lane's eyes move to it as I turn my head towards Bleu, "You still got that duct tape?"

Bleu steps up beside me smiling towards Lane, "Sure do."

I grin wickedly turning back to Lane, "Tape his mouth shut again. Don't want the neighbors to hear."

Bleu nods as he steps around the pole to the other side of the barn.

I let out a worried gasp, "Oh No! There are no neighbors. I already killed him."

James lets out another chuckle as he steps up beside me and wraps his arm around my waist. Lane's eyes follow James' hand as it wraps around my side. Bleu dutifully steps up and puts another wide strip of duct tape over Lane's mouth.

I smile as I take a step forward, bringing the hoof pick to Lane's chest. I lower the pick down swiftly, popping all of the buttons off his shirt. It falls open and away from him as I nod my chin towards Lane, "You boys wanna hold this shirt open so I can focus on my work?"

James looks confused but steps up beside me and grabs one side of the shirt. Bleu looks inspired but does the same as James. I smile into the eyes of my attacker again, "Don't worry, it won't hurt that bad. Maybe."

I bring the pick down on his chest and quickly carve my initials in large lettering across his chest. His thin skin shredding like paper under a pair of dull scissors. He is screaming into the duct tape but it is muffled enough no one outside of this barn is going to hear him.

After I carve my initials, I move a bit lower and carve that same animal symbol into his soft belly skin. He screams, his begging is like a drug. I watch the thin red lines appear as I continue to draw my masterpiece.

I want to keep going but I don't want him to give up too soon. I finally take a step back and stared at my work. Small trickles of blood are pouring from different spots in my handiwork.

I smile up at James, "Do we still have that radio out here?"

James looks confused but nods, "Yeah, why?"

I smile widely as he walks with me over to the side where the sleek MS3 is sitting. I quickly click onto my spotify and find the song I am looking for.

I turn back to Bleu, "Go ahead and cover his head. I think we are done for the night."

Bleu nods with a smile, grabbing a burlap sack then pulling down over the muffled screaming coming from Lane. I turn back to the MS3 quickly turning on Taylor Swift, Who's Afraid of Little Old Me? on repeat.

James lets out another laugh as Bleu walks over towards us. He smiles at the radio then to James, "I get it now man."

James shakes his head, "Get what?"

Bleu smiles towards me before looking back at James, "Why you love her so much." I wrap an arm around James, smiling towards Bleu.

After a few minutes of standing there in silence, listening to Lanes' muffled cries from across the room we decide to go inside. We slowly slip up the porch steps and into the back door.

Sarah instantly jumps up from the table, "Is it done? Did you kill him?" I smile watching her search my body for injuries, "No Sarah he is not dead. Not yet. I am going to give him some time to decide if he wants to own up to his actions or not. Don't get me wrong, either way he will die. It's just up to him if he dies with a guilty conscience or not."

Sarah nods her head at me, looking slightly to her right to see Bleu leaned up against the sink, staring directly at her. Her eyes quickly come back to mine, "I am going to fix dinner."

She turns on her heels and pulls the pantry door open scanning the shelves. She pulls out a few items then hurries over to the freezer. Her head is still half in the freezer as she calls out, "How does everyone feel about tacos?" James and I both watch as Bleu silently steps up behind her, "I could destroy a taco right now. Want some help?"

You can see Sarah's shoulders instantly tighten and rise just a bit. She slowly turns her eyes landing on mine. Her cheeks are the brightest shade of red I have ever seen. I smile and grab James' hand, "Come on. Let's go chat while they start supper." James chuckles and follows me out of the kitchen into the living room.

We sit on the couch, facing each other. I smile as I grab his hand, "So you really aren't freaked out about the baby?"

228

James smiles wider at me, "Freaked? No. Excited? Yes!"

I smile as I look down at his hand, drawing small circles over the top of his protruding veins. He lets out a heavy sigh and I look back up at him, "What's wrong?"

James turns his eyes back to me, "I am kinda nervous about having him out in the barn. I mean, what if the sheriff stops by again randomly or something?"

I nod back at him, "Yeah, no I get that. I honestly just want him to think that I am going to leave him out there tied to a post all day. When, in all reality, I am going to take care of him later tonight. I just want him to fear the future a bit."

James nods his head a bit, letting out a relieved breath, "Okay, that's good. I mean it doesn't matter what you do, Bleu and I will take care of the rest. So don't worry about that part. We already have a disposal plan in place."

I give him a crooked grin, "I don't want to know, do I?"

James smiles widely back at me, "No, It's probably safer if you don't know." I nod and lean in to give James another kiss.

229

21

James

Left Behind - The Plot in You

Maeve seems to be lost in her thoughts as we sit on the couch, holding each other. I don't want to think about the stress she is putting on herself with this situation. There is nothing I can do anyways.

I mean if I was to step in and finish this for her, she will never forgive me. This is her story to finish. Her demons that need to be defeated. I can't take that away from her, no matter how loud my brain is screaming at me to just end it.

I can hear Bleu and Sarah in the kitchen. Sarah's voice has never sounded as nervous as it does right now. I turn my head to try to hear a bit better as Maeve looks at me.

She smiles, "What are you doing?"

I grin back, not taking my gaze off the open doorway leading to the kitchen, "I am trying to hear if that is fear in Sarah's voice or just nervousness."

Maeve smiles wider and squeezes my hand, "That is the sound of a woman trying not to cum all over herself while in the presence of a man she finds extremely hot. Like H A W T kind of hot."

I quickly whip my eyes back to Maeve, "Are you fucking kidding me right now?"

Maeve smiles, letting out a little giggle as she nods her head, "Uh no. I am not joking. She told me earlier her ovaries almost exploded when he simply said, Hello."

I let out a laugh again, "Well fuck me. I did not catch that vibe at all."

Maeve smiles, turning her head towards the door, "You might not have but Bleu did. He has been eye fucking with her ever since you guys showed back up. I think he might actually be into her."

Maeve turns her face towards me, a little more serious of an expression on her face, "You don't think he would hurt her do you?"

I let out another heavy sigh, "I have never seen him in any type of relationship. I mean, sure, I have seen him with women but they were always like one night stands or just fuck buddy situationships. I honestly don't know if he knows what the word monogamy means."

Maeve nods as she looks across the room and out the window, "We should probably put some feelers out, just in case. I would really hate to have to kill him for hurting my girl."

I laugh, not only at her seriousness but at the fact that she thinks she can take him. Then I stare at her a bit harder, in that type of situation, maybe she could. She has this darkness that flows through her veins and I am pretty certain I have not seen even half of it yet.

I wrap my arm around her and pull her close to my chest. Sighing, I kiss the top of her head, "So, once this is all over what do you want to do? How do you want to approach the future?"

I can feel her smile into my chest, "I would really like to see my parents. Maybe not necessarily go to California, but maybe they could come here?"

I am rubbing small circles on her lower back, smiling into the nothing, "I would love for them to come here. I would really like to get to know them."

Maeve pulls her face back and looks deep into my eyes. She leans forward giving me a soft, slow kiss. I smile back down at her as we hear Sarah announce that supper is ready.

231

We pull ourselves away from the couch and make our way back into the kitchen. Bleu is slicing an avocado while Sarah sits at the table. It is fucking weird seeing him all domesticated and shit.

I shake my head at him as I pull a seat out for Maeve. We all load our plates and dig in. I know me and Bleu are starving but it is still pretty fucking impressive how much food the girls are able to throw back as well. Stomachs completely full, we are all leaned back in our chairs.

Sarah has gotten a beer for me and Bleu while her and Maeve have sodas. I smile towards Maeve, "So you wanna fill them in on the plan or should I?"

Maeve smiles back and turns towards Sarah, "I am not going to wait the full 3 days we said we would let Lane suffer. I don't want to risk this somehow going sidewinder on us. I want to just get it over with and get him out of here. I don't want to press my luck on the situation."

Bleu nods his head towards Maeve, "Do you need anything from me?"

Maeve smiles but shakes her head, "No, I think James and I have it covered. He said something about you helping with the aftermath though, that would be greatly appreciated."

Bleu nods his head then turns back to me for some sort of confirmation. I give him a slight nod with my chin and he starts to clear plates off the table.

Sarah reaches over and grabs Maeve's hands, "Are you still feeling okay?"

Maeve grins at Sarah then starts to pat her hand, "Yes worry wart. I am fine. I promise. If I didn't think I could handle this then I wouldn't even attempt it."

Sarah shyly smiles again, nodding back towards Maeve, "I know, I just worry."

232

Maeve kisses the top of Sarah's hand, "I promise you. I am fine. I will be fine. The baby will be fine. We will all be fine. Well not Lane but the people that matter will be fine."

Sarah laughs out loud, nodding her head at Maeve. She raises her hands in defeat, "Okay, Okay, I get it."

Maeve and I move from the table, both exhaling loudly. Sarah and Bleu both turn their attention to us. Maeve gives a smile before her eyes turn dark, "It's time to finally finish this bastard."

I am rubbing small circles into her shoulder but she doesn't even seem to notice me. She steps around Bleu, grabbing the dirty cheese grater off the counter then opens the drawer and pulls out a metal set of tongs.

I tilt my head slightly to the right, "What the fuck are you doing now?"

Maeve turns her gaze towards me, her eyes still dark, "About to have some fun."

Bleu makes a noise deep in his throat and Sarah's jaw drops almost totally to the floor.

She looks at me with worried eyes, "I don't want to know, do I?" I nod back at her while still staring at the crazed smile on Maeves' face, "I don't think any of us do."

I try to pry my eyebrows off my hairline as I follow Maeve out the back door and down the steps towards the barn.

I flick the lights on and slowly shut the doors behind us, catching a glimmer of Bleu in the kitchen window staring back out towards us. I turn around to see Maeve laying her torture instruments out on the table.

She turns to me slightly, "Do we have like a gas lantern or maybe like one of those long lighters you use for lighting a grill?"

I think to myself for a minute, "Yeah I think I have a gas torch light inside."

She nods back at me, "Can you grab that and maybe a sponge and some bleach?"

Again, my eyebrows are at my hairline. I can hear my voice shaking, "Remind me never to piss you off."

She laughs back at me beautifully as I turn and head back out the door.

It doesn't take me more than a few minutes to grab her supplies and head back to the barn. I am hoping she hasn't done anything crazy in the short time I have left her alone with Lane.

As I walk in, I see Maeve is sitting on the ground about 25 feet in front of Lane. The music is no longer playing as she just sits there staring at him. He is still bound to the pole with the sack over his head.

I let out a relieved sigh then slide the doors shut again. Maeve grins at me as she walks over, "Can you work the lantern for me?"

I nod back at her, not really sure of what words to say. She hands me the metal tongs, "Heat up the grabber part of the ends for me."

I slowly remove the tongs from her hand, nervously looking towards her, "Why?"

Maeve snickers under her breath, "Do you really want me to answer that?"

Nope she is right, I don't.

I quickly shake my head no and start to heat up the bottom of the tongs.

Maeve slowly makes her way over towards Lane. I watch the shadow that falls over her face as she removes the burlap sack from his head. He is still alive. He looks pissed too. She grabs both his cheeks with one hand like she is trying to force him to smile, "Did you miss me?"

234

Lane mumbles something but with the tape over his mouth we have no clue what message he is trying to convey. Maeve rears her hand back and slaps him right across the face, hard enough his head flies to the left.

She leans closer to his face, "No one said you could talk bitch."

I can see the glare that Lane is sending towards Maeve's face. She just smiles back at him as she reaches down to start unbuckling his pants.

His eyes go wide, looking from her to me, pleading for help. I continue to keep one eye on the tongs, the other on Maeve. She grabs the waist of his pants and underwear, quickly yanking them both down.

She smiles at his crotch then over to me, "Just as tiny as I remember."

I let a small chuckle leave my mouth while Lane still tries to yell something again. He is moving his head, wiggling his entire body trying to get free. Maeve walks around the pole and starts to loosen the ropes around his waist.

I step up quickly, "What are you doing?"

I don't want her to be caught off guard by him. She smiles up at me, "Don't worry I am not taking it off completely just loosening it up."

I go to ask her why once again but then remember, I really don't want to know why. I just nod my head as she loosens the ropes just enough that he can move his hips to one side of the pole or the other.

She walks back around to the front, studying him up and down, "It's not even cold out tonight and there it is….looking like a little shriveled raisin."

I can't hold back the full out laugh this time.

Maeve looks in my direction, smiling brightly. She makes her way over to me and untwists the cap off the bottle of bleach. She sits the jug down, picking up the sponge, turning it over in her hand.

She walks back over to the other side of the room, quickly grabbing the machete. I literally have no clue what she is doing. At this point, the ends of the metal tongs are now glowing red.

I watch her use the machete to cut the sponge in half then grab the open jug of bleach and douse the sponge. She makes sure every millimeter of surface area of the sponge is saturated with bleach then grabs the tongs.

She looks over her shoulder at Lane then back to me, "Did you really mean it when you said you would help with whatever I need?"

I nervously nod my head back towards her. She smiles wildly again, motioning with her chin towards Lane, "I need you to spread his ass open for me."

A small cough leaves my body and Lane starts pulling even harder against the ropes, screaming into the duct tape covering his mouth.

I blink rapidly looking from Lane to Maeve, "Do you want me in front of him or behind him?"

Maeve smiles at me, "In front, I won't make you watch."

I give her another short nod and start over to Lane. He is begging into the tape, pleading with me to not let it happen. He has sweat and tears running down his face, onto his chest.

I shrug my shoulders at him, "Sorry dude. You brought this on yourself."

I move his hips to the left of the pole then reach around the sides of his waist and downwards to pull his ass cheeks apart. I watch Maeve as she walks up with red hot tongs in one hand and a sponge soaked in bleach in the other.

236

She looks happy.

She looks like she is enjoying every last little second of this. What catches my attention the most though, is that I am not even the littlest bit afraid of her right now. If anything, I love her more than ever.

I am not even afraid of her when she sticks the crimson red ends of the tongs into his backdoor and maneuvers his asshole open with them. The smell of burnt skin and hair permeating around the barn.

Lane is screaming into the thick duct tape. His chest is convulsing like he is trying not to vomit. Maeve smiles as she pushes and nuzzles that small half of sponge into the open wound that is now his asshole.

Lane is screaming bloody murder in my ear. I am super grateful though that I can't see this from her angle. My taco's may not have stayed down at that sight.

She grins widely as she stands up. She tosses the tongs out onto the dirt floor far enough away from anything to let them cool off on their own.

I am definitely throwing those away as soon as we are done here. Lane is still screaming in my ears as I let go of his cheeks and step back. He is crying, snot is running down the tape covering his mouth. He is sweating and cussing up a storm that we luckily don't have to listen to.

Maeve moves back over towards her instruments and picks up the cheese grater. She looked from the back of Lane's head to my face, "Hey babe. Can you come over here and douse the other half of this sponge?"

I slowly move towards her. When I am closer and she knows Lane can't hear she leans in close to me, "Are you okay?"

237

I look at her wide eyed, "Yeah. That was a bit more fucked up then I thought it was going to be. Other than that I am fucking fine but are you okay?"

She gives me that all knowing grin again, "I'm great. I think he is finally understanding me, five by five baby."

She smiles again as she walks around in front of Lane. I quickly douse the rest of the sponge in bleach and move up beside her.

She tilts her head to the left, looking Lane up and down, "My first thought was to use this on his dick, but it's so small I am afraid I will nick my own finger trying to get ahold of the little guy."

I chuckle again, looking Lane in the eyes, "I could go grab some tweezers."

Lane lets out another curse as I smile back at him, "What's that? You say something?"

Lane looks like he is trying to summon lasers with his eyes. Maeve steps up to him, "I wonder?"

She lays one side of the grater flat on his chest, tightly gripping it on both ends. She smiles into Lane's face as she pushes in and down, raking it down the side of his chest. She grins again, "Look babe. I took a nipple off!"

I look around her smiling, "Nice babe. That's a pretty awesome accomplishment."

She smiles back at me, "I know right?"

Lane is crying again and I can't help but wonder, what is hurting more right now, his ass or his nipple? Or what's left of either of them?

I hand the remaining half of the sponge over to Maeve and she starts ringing it out on the open wounds on Lane's chest. His screams are coming out louder now from behind the duct

238

tape. Out of the corner of my eye, I see the barn doors start to slide open.

Before I even know what is happening, Maeve has her gun drawn and trained on the head poking through.

Bleu smiles at Maeve, "Calm down kitten, it's just me."

She lets out a breath as she slides the safety back on then puts the gun back down the waist of her jeans. "What's up Bleu?" He looks to me then Maeve then quickly notices that Lane's pants are around the ropes at his ankles. He turns his head to the left, pointing at Lane's ass then looks back at me, "Is that a kitchen sponge sticking out of his ass?"

I remain stone faced, "Actually, yes, yes it is. And I am sure you would probably love the story. Don't worry I am sure Maeve will tell you later."

Bleu nods again then looks back towards Maeve, "You need any help?"

She gives him a soft smile and shakes her head, "Nope we are all good here. We are almost done anyways. I already burned his asshole open and grated off a nipple. We are in the home stretch now."

Bleu's eyes go as wide as mine had at the time. He turns to me again, grinning wildly, "Dude, seriously....I love this bitch."

I let out another laugh, "Me too."

He gives me another quick nod, "Alright, we will be in the house waiting for you guys then."

Maeve gives a short wave to Bleu as he looks at Lane's ass again making a pained face, then pulls the door shut behind him.

Maeve glances back towards me. She puts her hands on her hips, popping one out to the side, "I guess it's time to really get down to business. Playtime is over."

I smile back at her, "That's completely up to you baby. This is your night."

She walks over and gives me a deep kiss, "Thank you." I smile back at her, "Anything for you baby."

22

Maeve

Medicate Me - Rain City Drive, Dayseeker

I pick up the machete before I walk back over to face Lane. He has beads of sweat running down his temples. There is snot, blood and tears all mingling on his chest.

I am wondering how many times he has had to swallow down his own vomit so he didn't choke to death while I was shoving that bleached sponge into his burning hot asshole.

I look down at his chest and frown, "James! Dammit! I messed up my initials."

James walks around to look at Lane's chest as well. He put his hand on my back, "You want me to grab the hoof pick?"

I shake my head, "Nah, the canvas isn't blank anymore." James nods at me then takes a few steps back to sit on a hay bale.

I slither up towards the old man struggling to get free in front of me, "There are so many dreams that I have had about this exact moment right here. What I would do to you when you were face to face with me again. You know, I laid in that ditch for 3 days. With a rotting corpse of a pregnant woman on top of me. Can you imagine the smell?

"Can you imagine what happens when a body swells from the heat of the jungle around it? Her stomach actually split open and spilled out around me on the 2nd day. What do you think that does to a person? I had an unborn dead fetus and the bloated remains of its mother soaking into my skin for 2 full days."

I turn back to James, "I can't even eat pulled pork anymore. I used to love it."

James widens his eyes at me, like he is telepathically telling me he will never eat it again either. I smile and wink at him before turning back to Lane.

Lane is again trying to say something through the tape. I roll my eyes, "Jesus, fine."

I reach up and rip the tape from his mouth. He instantly spits at my feet, "I am going to fucking finish you all."

I laugh and look towards James, "Awe, isn't it adorable? He thinks he is walking out of here."

Lane's eyes come back to mine and he lets an evil smile come over his face, "You kill me and they will be here for you in 24 hours, flat."

I smile, nodding at him, "I don't think so Lane. You know, you have been missing for days now. And it didn't even make the news. Who exactly is going to come and "get" me? Huh?"

Lane looks around again and starts laughing, "Weathers will be here. So will Lang."

I let out another deep laugh, "Oh Lane, Lane, Lane. Lang is in a psych ward. He isn't going anywhere. And Weathers, well, I paid him a visit not long ago. He isn't going anywhere. He was shipped back to his family in a pine box. So who exactly do you think is going to save you?"

I take a step closer to him, bringing the machete down on the rope that has his hands bound. Lane leans forward and spits right onto my cheek. I turn my head, reaching my hand up to wipe the phlegm from my face.

James steps around me and clocks Lane hard in the jaw. I put my hand on his chest and smile, "It's okay baby. I am okay."

He nods back to me and Lane lifts his bleeding face back up to meet mine, "Should have known this little slut would have fucking thugs working for her. She pay you with her pussy like she did everyone else?"

242

He lets out a deep laugh and I bring the machete up to his cheek, "The only man that has ever demanded that kind of payment from me is standing right in fucking front of me."

I lean in closer to him, "And it was quite an unfulfilling payment indeed."

Lane laughs again, "It didn't seem so unfulfilling when I shoved that maglite up your ass."

He turns his head towards James, "You should have heard that little bitch scream. It was glorious."

James tries to barrel past me again but I put out my hand and stop him. He is shaking with anger. I smile at him as I give him a quick kiss on the cheek, "It's almost over baby. I am okay."

He stares deep into my eyes and gives me another quick nod before taking another step back. I turn around and Lane has brought his hands up wrapping his fingers around my neck.

I laugh out loud, "What? Are you trying to dance with me?" I slam my left elbow down hard on his forearms. He is so weak from being tied up non stop for 4 days that he doesn't have the strength to hold his grip.

He leans back against the pole, rubbing his raw wrists as I nod towards the doors, "Can you make sure those are shut baby?" James nods and runs towards the doors, ensuring they were indeed closed tight.

James walks back up to me, "They are good babe." I smile and swing the machete hard into the pole at Lane's hips, cutting through the rope holding him there.

Lane glances quickly between us then bends to reach down to pull up his pants. He quickly stops and lets out a guttural scream. My best guess is that the bleached out sponge just found a fresh part of the burn out asshole to mold into.

Lane halts his movement and slowly stands back up, leaning on the pole again. I walk a bit over towards the side of the pole and bring the machete down hard on the last set of ropes holding him against his will to that pole.

James' eyes keep jumping back over to me as he watches what I am doing. I smile at Lane, reassuringly, "I think it is only fair that you have a chance to fight back. I will at least give you more respect than you gave me."

I look up at James' eyes, "Maeve?"

I nod my chin towards him, "It's okay James. It's okay."

I walk around the pole facing a now completely cut free Lane. The only restraints left on his body are his wrists in front of him. He lunges for me and I move swiftly to the left as he falls onto the ground in front of me.

James turns smiling at the old man laying in the dirt. He is twitching as he gets up and swings his hands at James like a battering ram. James dodges the incoming blow then drives his knee into Lane's guts.

I let out a laugh, "Good move babe!"

James smiles over at me while he bows like a gentleman then spits on Lane as he rolls across the dirt floor in pain.

I shrug my shoulders and look at James, "I guess we probably shouldn't play with him too long. He has come here to serve a purpose so we might as well get to it."

Lane is up on his knees now, knelt in front of us, his eyes jumping from my face to James', "What kind of purpose? I thought you were giving me 3 days."

He spits blood at my feet and I snarl at him, "You are the last name on my list Captain. Once you are gone, then I am done. I can quit killing random fucking woman beaters and rapists. I can stop carving a fucking knive through this country one fucking pedo at a time. I will be free from you, you sick motherfucker."

Lane lets out a laugh, "You will never be free from me. I am in here."

He taps his temple forcefully with his pointer finger. I laugh back, "Not anymore you're not. Look at you. Look at how pathetic you are."

I look to James, "It's almost inhumane to put an end to him when he is just so fucking weak."

James smiles back at me but we both see movement out of the corner of our eyes. Lane lunges for my leg, pulling one of my knives free. James instantly steps out in front of me and throws his arm out to stop Lane from stabbing me with my own knife. James yells and recoils. He turns and I see my knife sticking out of his forearm.

The world goes red around me. I let out an animalistic scream as I bring the machete down on Lane's shoulder. It cuts all the way down to his collarbone.

He screams as he throws himself back down on the floor. I look at James but he just nods that he is fine.

I point my chin towards Lane's arms, "Hold him down."

James quickly runs over, knife still protruding from his forearm as he pins Lane's arms down up over his head. I quickly climb over and sit on Lane's thighs, holding his legs down. I reach down, grabbing my other knife with my right hand.

I smile as Lane's eyes go wide, "Just lay there and take it, like a good little bitch."

I smile as I cut his dick and balls clean from his body. He lets out an earth shattering scream until I reach up then shove both dick and balls into his mouth. He is trying to spit them out when I grab the machete and shove it through the underside of his chin and up into his brain. I can see the light fading from his eyes as I look back down into them, "Who's the bitch now?"

Lane fades quickly. Quicker than I had wanted him to, but James has already been hurt. I am not going to risk our safety anymore than I already have.

One punch to my stomach and I could have lost the baby. James stands up walking around beside me and wraps his arm around my shoulders, "Seriously. Remind me not to piss you off."

I let out a chuckle and look to his left arm, seeing my knife still protruding from it.

I reach for it, "We need to get that cleaned."

He shrugs, "It's just a flesh wound. I am okay."

I shake my head at him, "No, we are getting it cleaned up. Then we need to figure out what to do with him."

I have this surge of energy running through me. Like I can run a fucking marathon. I have to do something, anything. I feel like I am going to explode if I don't.

I watch as James reaches up and pulls the knife out of his arm. Blood starts to run down towards his hand and I feel myself get pulled into the colors of it. It is a deep maroon but it has swirls of rust colors in it. I watch it as it drips from his fingers onto the floor near Lane's feet.

James lets out a sigh, "You okay Maeve?"

I feel this pull tug at me again. Like the last time when he cut himself on the machete.

What the fuck is wrong with me?

Why is this turning me on?

There is a dead fucking body at my feet and all I can think about is James bending me over a fucking hay bale and slamming into me. I feel my breath catch in my throat and I try to shake the images from my head.

James steps up to me smiling, he pushes a strand of hair behind my ear with his good hand, "You like the blood don't you?"

246

I nod my head, my eyes never leaving his arm, "I don't know why though. And it's only yours. I don't know why this happens to me."

I feel disgusted with myself. James leans into my ear and whispers, "Everything I am belongs to you. My blood, my life, my cum. It's all yours baby."

I look into his eyes as he pulls back and I wrap my arms around his neck kissing him hard. He kisses me back but I suck his bottom lip into my teeth and bite down.

Tasting the copper of his now bleeding lip. I reach down and unbutton his pants quickly as he pulls them down around his thighs. I turn around, pulling my jeans down as I bend over the hay bale, just like my imagination had me doing a few moments ago.

I reach across the bale and hold tight as James grips my hips, using his good hand to guide himself into me. I smile over my shoulder at him as he slams into me.

I moan loudly at the intrusion. I look back again and he is watching us where we were joined.

God, I love how much this man likes to watch himself fuck me. It is like some weird form of voyeurism or something. I lay my forehead onto the hay bale and moan again as he starts hitting deeper inside me.

I am panting hard into the night air when I feel his hand come down hard on my right ass cheek. I scream into the night and feel myself begin to pulsate around him.

I am so fucking close. I look over my shoulder again, "Harder James, fuck me harder." I can hear my gravelled voice begging him.

He looks up towards my face and slaps my ass hard again. He immediately starts slamming himself into me, harder and deeper than before. I can feel him thicken inside of me as I scream my release.

James continues to slam into me but reaches around in front of me and starts vibrating his finger over my clit in tight circles. I feel like the air is being ripped from my body as he whispers, "Give me one more baby."

I grip the bale tighter and shove my ass higher into his stomach. He grabs my waist one more time with his free hand and continues to destroy my pussy. I feel another orgasm building in the base of my spine, "Baby I am close."

I sound so needy. James grunts as he picks up his pace and continues to swipe his fingertip quickly back and forth across my engorged clit. It hits me again harder than the last time and I feel myself clamp down hard on his dick.

He lets out a louder moan and puts both hands on my hips as he slams harder into me. I hear him roar his own release a few thrusts later. I can feel that I still have his dick clenched inside of me. He continues to pump into me until the waves start to subside.

James slowly slides out of me with a hiss. I reach down and grab the waist of my jeans to slide them back up. I turn to see him doing the same thing. His arm and jeans both now coated in blood. Mine probably are too but I am wearing all black so there is no way to really tell.

I look from him down to the corpse lying in the ground behind us, "We probably shouldn't tell Sarah about this part."

James lets out a cackle as he turns to follow my gaze, "Yeah probably not. But Bleu will probably put it on his bucket list."

I let out another laugh as I start to collect my torture items from the floor. I quickly walk over to a trash can and throw them away. We can easily get a new hoof pick, grater and a set of tongs.

248

James smiles as he grabs the MS3 and the gas lantern, he quickly nods to the tongs in the trash can, "Yeah, I was thinking the same thing."

I smile back at him as I turn to him. I look past him to the body laying on the ground in the middle of the barn. I let out a breath I don't even know I have been holding.

I feel this insane feeling of relief flood my body. I am actually done. I have finished what I started all those years ago. I will be able to sleep at night without being scared that I am going to wake up and see one of them standing over my bed.

I feel myself almost start to tear up. James is by my side in an instant, "Are you okay baby?"

I smile up at him, feeling a single solitary tear roll down my cheek, "I am fucking great. It's over. I am finally fucking free."

James pulls me in closer to him and we just hold each other.

I finally pull back from him many moments later, "What are we going to do with his body?"

James smiles and looks back towards Lane, "Don't you worry about that. Bleu and I already have a plan worked out. We are going to go inside, get cleaned up, maybe stitch up my arm if needed, then you are going to chill and rest with Sarah while Bleu and I dispose of the trash."

I smile at him, "I can help clean up my own mess."

James gives me a quick kiss on the forehead then turns his face to rest his cheek where he has just kissed, "You have already cleaned up a mess tonight. Let me take over from here."

I let out another sigh and giggle, "Yes sir."

James pulls back and looks at me with his eyes hooded. He stares at my lips, his voice deep and breathy, "You are going to have to call me that again...and soon."

I laugh as I pull the barn door open behind me before stepping out into the cool Montana breeze. I stare up above the pasture as James closes up the doors behind me. The stars seem to all be dancing.

Like they are finally free too.

Bleu and Sarah must have heard us leaving the barn because they are quickly running out the back door. Sarah barrells down the steps and makes a bee line for me.

She grabs my hands, seeing them coated in blood "Oh my god Maeve! Where are you hurt?"

I smile back at her, pulling my hands away, "It's not my blood. I am fine. He didn't hurt me at all."

Sarah's eyes are wide, "So it's his blood then?"

James steps around us, handing the radio and lantern to Bleu, "It could be mine too. Not quite sure."

Sarah turns on James then. She grabs his arm and starts to drag him towards the back steps. Bleu let out a small laugh, "Best not to fight her man. Just let her help you." James laughs back but continues to let Sarah pull him up the back steps and into the house.

Bleu smiles as he turns back to me, tilting his head to the side, "You sure you are okay?"

I give him another honest grin, "Truly, I am great."

I step around him and take a seat on the back steps, watching the dark shadows that are the horses move around the meadow. Bleu sits down beside me, "So, you're knocked up?"

I let out another loud laugh, "Yeah, seems so."

Bleu nods his head again, looking out towards the horses as well, "James is going to be an amazing dad. He has always had that nurturing side to him. But he also doesn't take any shit either. I think it's a healthy dose of both. Just the thing to make a perfect parent."

I smile as I turn my head towards him, resting my cheek on my propped fist, "You guys really have known each other a long time huh?" The smile falls from Bleu's face, "Since Fallujah." I nod and sit back again, "Good. I am glad he has you."

I can feel Bleu staring at me. He stands back up as he looks back down at me, "I am glad he has you too." I smiled towards the horses as I listen to Bleu shuffle inside, letting the screen door slam behind him.

23

James

Obsessed – Jutes

Sarah stitches me up pretty nicely once she finally lets me get inside. I thought she was going to do it under moonlight there for a minute. She just stood there staring out at Maeve for what felt like an hour.

I grin down at her, "She is fine Sarah. I promise. He didn't even get to touch her."

Sarah frowns at me as she drags me inside to the dining room table and starts to clean then stitch me up. When she is done she is still frowning as she looks up into my eyes, "It was too reckless of her. She could have been hurt."

I shake my head at her, placing my hand on top of hers, "I would not have let that happen. I didn't let that happen."

She gives me an exhausted sigh as she points towards my arm, "You got fucking stabbed James. What if that had been her? What if he would have hurt the baby?"

I understand her fears. I felt all the same ones in that moment in the barn. I give her another small smile, "Sarah, she wasn't hurt. He got the drop on her and took one of her knives. Before he could do anything with it I was there. That is how this happened. Also, it's all over now. She is done. She is ready to just leave the past where it belongs, in the past."

Sarah nods unconvinced towards me, "Yeah until she hears of the next asshole on the news or through the grapevine. Do you really think she will just be able to stop?"

I lean back in the chair and let out a deep breath, "Yes, yes I do. This whole situation has been a means to an end. She didn't know where Lane was. She couldn't kill him so she was killing anyone that reminded her of him. Did she ever tell you what happened to her?"

Sarah looks towards the back door then back to me, slowly shaking her head back and forth, "No, but I kinda figured it out on my own I think."

I nod at her, "Whatever you are thinking, multiply it by about a thousand. He did more than just use her, he tried to destroy her. But our girl is a fighter. She was not giving up at any cost. She needed this closure. She can move on now. She can sleep at night without worrying about him standing over her when she wakes up. She will be able to raise our child with me without worry that her past is going to show up at any time and take her away. She is finally free, Sarah. Let her have this okay?"

Sarah looks down at the table then back up to me, letting a single tear fall, "She is the closest thing to a sister that I have ever had. She saved my life James. I can't help but worry about her."

I nod as I pull her into a soft hug, "I know sweetie. She loves you too. More than you know. Before you, she had not entrusted anyone with her secrets. Not even me. I kinda figured it all out on my own way before she ever told me the truth. You are her sister in every sense of the word. She needs you to be strong for her now, just like she was for you. Can you do that for me?"

Sarah is smiling as she pulls back from me, wiping the tears from her face, "Yeah, I can do that."

I give her another wide smile back as Bleu and Maeve come walking inside.

Bleu steps up to Sarah, placing a hand on her shoulder and looking down at my arm, "You get him all stitched up Doc?"

I look at Sarah immediately, understanding what Maeve had said earlier. Sarah looks like she is going to melt into a puddle at his feet.

She lets out a shaky laugh, "Yeah, No. Yeah he is good. All stitched up."

She quickly jumps to her feet then runs into the living room. I watch the dust trail she leaves behind her with a smile as Bleu turns back towards me, "What the fuck did I do?"

I let out another laugh as I lean my forearms onto the table, "You touched her."

Bleu sits down in the chair next to me, "She doesn't like to be touched?"

I give him a devilish smile, "Oh she likes to be touched. Especially by you."

Bleu's eyes blow wide as he turns to the door then back towards me, "You telling me you think she has a thing for me?"

I smile again, turning my arm back and forth, testing the range of it, "I am telling you I am positive she has a thing for you."

Bleu's eyes light up like Times Square on New Year's Eve. I put a hand up, "But beware, she has been seriously hurt before. Mentally, physically and emotionally. She is not the one to fuck and dump. Plus, I think if you were to hurt her at all, Maeve would pretend you were Lane."

Bleu shakes his arms out like a chill has run through them, "I really don't want a kitchen sponge shoved into my ass. By the way, what the hell was that about?"

I let out another laugh as I stand up, "She had me heat up the tongs, then she used them to pry his asshole open and shoved a sponge doused in bleach in there. Every single move he made he could feel the bleach burning into the open wounds."

Bleu stands up looking at me in amazement, "Where in the fuck did she come up with that one?"

I shake my head back at him, "I have no idea, and I pray I never find out."

We both laugh as we step back into the kitchen. I look out the back door but don't see Maeve anywhere. I turn back to Bleu, "I am gonna go check on my girl then we can get to clean up."

Bleu nods back at me then starts towards the living room, "I am gonna go find Sarah."

I let out another chuckle, "Remember, you have been warned."

He flips me off as he leaves through the door leading to the living room. I step up to the sink to get a glass of water when I finally spot Maeve. She was standing at the fence watching the horses galloping through the moonlight. I down a glass of water quickly then make my way outside.

Maeve is smiling at the horses as I step up beside her. She doesn't even turn to look at me but still leans her body into mine. She lays the side of her head on my arm still staring at the wild beasts roaming in front of us.

She lets out a sigh, "I feel like this weight has been lifted. Like I am breathing for the first time in 3 years."

I lean down and kiss the top of her head, "So your work here is done then?"

She lets out a soft chuckle as she stands up and turns to me, "Definitely. Time to move onto bigger and better things. Like being your baby momma."

I burst out laughing as I wrap my arms around her and pull her body close to mine. I hold her tight, "I love you so fucking much Maeve." Her grip around me tightens as she squeezes me closer to her.

"Are you ready to do this?" Bleu is standing next to us. I don't even hear him approaching. I look up towards him, seeing Sarah over his shoulder standing on the back steps.

I let out a heavy sigh, "Yeah. Let's get this over with."

Bleu nods his head then turns towards the barn. Maeve looks up into my eyes, "What are you going to do with him?"

I kiss her forehead, "Take him to a place he will never be found."

She nods her head then gives me another quick hug before walking towards Sarah on the steps. I take another glance towards the horses before starting my journey towards the barn. I glance over at Maeve one last time to see her hopping in place with what seems like excitement. Sarah is very animated, telling her some story. She is grinning from ear to ear and her face is beet red.

It has Bleu written all over it.

I slide the barn door shut behind me as I make my way inside. Bleu is crouched over what is left of Lane, "Is his dick in his mouth?"

I step up to the pole and lean against it, "Yup. His balls too."

Bleu doesn't even look up at me, "Jesus fucking christ. What happened to his nipple?"

I start looking at the ground around the pole, "Yeah, we should probably find that and get rid of it too. It should be on the ground around here somewhere."

Bleu stands up shaking his head at me, "I have never been this terrified of someone so small before."

I laugh, looking up at his face "I completely understand and agree with that statement."

Bleu shakes his head again, "I'll grab the tarp."

He starts to walk to the other side of the barn, scanning the ground for the rouge nipple. I heave off the pole, "I will get the barrel."

I walk to the far side of the barn and grab the empty metal barrel I have been saving to make a water trough out of. It is going to be Lane's final resting place. Once it is buried deep in the mountains, we will never have to think of this man ever again.

I wrap my arms around it and start carrying it towards the center of the barn. Bleu throws down the tarp and large bag of lyme next to Lane's corpse then yells out, "Domino Mother Fucker!!! Found it!"

I look up just in time to see him displaying the nipple in the air. It is disturbing just how not disturbed I am with the smile on his face. This man has seen and done more shit than most. None of it ever talked about again. Him flinging the rogue nipple into the empty barrel is just another memory we will never speak of.

We quickly wrap Lane's body in the tarp then stuff him into the barrel. We empty the bag of lyme into the barrel then seal it shut. We quickly carry it out to the back of the truck then head towards the mountains. I let out a heavy sigh knowing in just a few hours I will be back home, making plans for the future with my gorgeous little psychopath.

It doesn't take nearly as long as I had thought to bury the barrel. Bleu has slept the whole way there so he is invigorated with energy by the time I stop the truck at the dump site. We take turns digging the hole and cursing ourselves for only bringing one shovel.

Not 45 minutes later, we are on our way back down the mountain. Bleu is staring out his window when I turn the radio down and take a quick look over at him, "So what happened with you and Sarah?"

I can see him smiling but he continues looking out the window, "I am sure I don't know what you mean."

I throw a glove at him, "You fucking know exactly what I mean Jackass. What happened?"

257

He is laughing as he turns to face me, "Nothing too big. Promise. I just kinda cornered her in the living room and made sure she was aware of what I was feeling for her at that moment."

I laugh, nodding my head as I look out the windshield, "Mmhm."

Bleu laughs out loud again before turning his head towards me, "She is a little spitfire. I was just trying to put some feelers out there but she reached down and grabbed my dick man. She just grabbed it and squeezed then moaned into my neck. I just about cum all over her hand like a fucking school boy."

I am laughing so hard the truck is swerving, "Sarah? Little, domesticated Sarah?"

Bleu turns to me completely in the truck, "Fucking exactly! I thought I was going to give her a little nudge but all I did was lean into her barely and she was on me like a piranha at feeding time. It was fucking hot!"

My side is hurting, I am laughing so hard, "So I guess this means Maeve and I were right in our observations."

Bleu is nodding his head now, "If your observations were that she is a fucking freak then yes. You are right. It was so fucking hot man. I had to walk away before I fucking destroyed your living room destroying her."

I laugh out loud again, "Well thank you for that. My mom decorated that living room."

Bleu belts out a laugh as well, "It took massive amounts of restraint. But now, I am not gonna lie, I am fucking intrigued. I may have to stay around awhile. See what might come from this."

I nod out the windshield then let out another heavy sigh, "Just remember what I said earlier. She has been through a fucking lot. Be easy on her or you will have Maeve to deal with.

And I will not stop her cause you have officially been warned already."

Bleu throws the glove back at me, "Some kind of friend you are."

We return home just as the sun is starting to come up. Sarah has pulled the couch out to a bed and is sound asleep. I quietly sneak around her and up the stairs. I take one last glimpse down the stairs as I see Bleu lay down next to her and gently put a strand of hair behind her ear.

I smile to myself at the gesture then turn and head up the stairs. I quietly open the bedroom door to see Maeve also sound asleep on her side of the bed. She has laid out clean clothes and a towel for me on my side of the bed near the pillow.

I smile down at her before emptying my pockets then heading towards the bathroom to take a shower. I am so exhausted I nearly fall asleep standing up. I finally head back to the bedroom to a still sleeping Maeve. I slowly slide into bed closing my eyes before my head even hits the pillow.

I wake up hours later. I noticed Maeve is gone as I stretch and roll over to face the bedroom door. I look at the night stand seeing the clock reading 1:30. Fuck I have slept all day. I let out a loud yawn then sit up, rolling my shoulders.

My forearm is still burning from the stabbing last night but I will live. I have lived through much worse actually. I stand up and grab some clean clothes out of the dresser to quickly get dressed.

I step barefoot out into the hallway, hearing laughter rolling up the stairs from what sounds like the kitchen. I smile at the sound of the 3 closest people in my life enjoying the company of each other.

I look towards my mothers bedroom door. I step up to it slowly, opening it to see the sun flooding its rays into the room. I look at the picture on her night stand and smile. She would have fucking loved Maeve.

I glance around the room again and notice there is one ray of light that is shining directly onto her jewelry box on top of the dresser. I immediately know what mom is trying to tell me. I smile as I feel a tear run down my cheek.

I pad over to the box and slowly lift the lid. Sitting front and center is my mother's ring, which had once been my grandmother's ring. It isn't anything fancy but it means the world to me. It is the only priceless thing I have ever owned.

I look at the pictures sitting on the dresser and smile, "You're gonna be a grandmother, mom. I wish you were here to see it."

I look back down at the ring then pick it up and slide it into my pocket. I collect my thoughts and emotions then slip back out into the hallway then down the stairs. I round out of the living room into the kitchen and see everyone sitting at the table with the remnants of what looks like lunch.

Maeve instantly smiles up at me, "Hey sleepy head. Are you hungry?"

I smile back as I pull out a chair at the table, "Starving actually."

She nods and jumps up. She immediately starts to make me a sandwich. Sarah smiles from me to Bleu then walks over to talk to Maeve while she prepares me some lunch.

Bleu leans over, "I think I am in love."

I smile back at him as I lean back in my chair, "With who? Sarah or Maeve or yourself?"

He chuckles at me, "Well of course myself but this time I actually mean Sarah. This chick is fucking phenominal. I have never met anyone like her before."

I smile and look up at the girls at the counter, "She is pretty fucking special."

Bleu follows my gaze and smile as Maeve turns around to hand me a paper plate. I devour the sandwich in about 4 bites. The girls continue their chat about something they saw in town while we were gone. Bleu and I just sit there in silence watching them, smiling the entire time.

With lunch finally over, we all grab our drinks then head out to the back porch. Bleu and Sarah sit on the swing while Maeve and I sit on the back steps. Maeve leans into me, watching the horses in the pasture.

I kiss the top of her head, "Wanna go for a walk with me?"

She smiles up at me and nods. We sit our glasses on the top step then walk down towards the pasture. Maeve wraps her arm around my waist as I settle my arm over her shoulders. I let out a deep breath, "So what now?"

She lets out a matching sigh, "I am not sure. I think I am wanting to just come clean to everyone though. Let them know I am alive. Just maybe not on everything I have been doing since I have been back."

I let out a laugh, "Yeah that sounds smart. You can just tell them you met me and have been here the whole time."

Maeve smiles and looks up at me, "You would be okay with that?" I give her a soft kiss, "Of course I would be okay with that."

Maeve pulls her arm from me leaning up onto the top rung of the fence and rests her chin on her forearm, "I really want to see my parents. But I don't really want to go to California. I think I am kinda over it there."

I close my eyes and mentally cross my fingers, "Maybe they can come here then. Like for the wedding or something."

Maeve turns around quickly and her breath catches in her throat when she sees me holding out the ring to her. Her eyes blow wide and she stares at the ring for what feels like forever then looks up at me, "James, what the fuck are you doing?"

I instantly start to second guess the situation. I fidget a bit looking from the ring to the ground then finally back to her eyes, "I am asking you if you would marry me. Maeve, I know you are not perfect. You know that I am not perfect. And I am not doing this because of the baby. I would have done this either way honestly.

"I want to marry you because you are my best friend. I can't fucking breath when you aren't here. The first time you left me, when you met Sarah, I was fucking miserable. I didn't know how I was going to go on without you with me. Now that we are here and we are happy and you are done with everything, I just want you to know that I am yours. Forever. There will never be anyone else for me."

Maeve's eyes are quickly filling up with tears. I reach up to wipe one away as she leans her face into my palm. I am dying with anticipation. I let out an anxious sigh, "Please say something baby."

She smiles and looks into my eyes, "Can we get married before I get fat?"

I feel a crushing smile come over my face. "Is that a yes?"

She smiles back at me nodding her head, "Yes. That is a yes."

I quickly slide the ring onto her finger and then devour her in an emotion filled kiss. I can hear laughter and yelling behind me but I just continue to kiss Maeve with reckless abandon. When I finally pulled away from her, Sarah quickly hip checks me out of the way and wraps Maeve in a death grip of a hug. They are both giggling as they jump up and down. I have never seen Maeve act so feminine before.

It is scarier than seeing her stick that sponge up Lane's ass.

Bleu clamps his hand on my shoulder, "Looks like she is making an honest man out of you."

I smile back at him, "I wouldn't go that far."

He pats my shoulder laughing along with me. I turn to him, "You gonna stick around long enough to be my best man?"

Bleu smiles at me then turns back to Maeve, "You bet your ass I will."

Maeve steps up to Bleu and wraps him in a surprise hug. Bleu looks scared to death. Sarah leans into me and we both start laughing at the look on his face.

Maeve pulls back, smiling and crying up at him, "Bleu, thank you for everything you have done for me. You got yourself involved in something that anyone else would have just walked away from. You have no idea how much I appreciate you. You keeping this man alive for as long as you have, is the best gift you could have ever given me. I will be forever grateful to you. And I guess that means, now I owe you one."

Bleu doesn't look away but just smiles down at Maeve and gives her another hug. My heart instantly goes to my throat.

I know what it means to owe someone something. I know he will call in that favor at some point. And with him knowing what she is capable of, I am scared what that favor will be.

I take a deep breath deciding to cross that bridge when it presents itself. Right now, I am just going to celebrate with my friends and with the woman I love.

24

Maeve

Roses – Awaken I am

I have not been this nervous in a long fucking time. Maybe, this is even the most nervous I have ever been in the history of my life. We are going to claim amnesia. That is the going lie.

That I somehow survived the attack on us in South America then made it to a safe haven. My mother is standing for me, claiming that I had reached out to her during one of my few lucid moments and she sent me all of the civilian documentation I would need to get back into the states. She also claims that I stayed with her and my father hoping that I would recover my memory totally. She states that she had woken up one morning and I was just gone.

That is where James steps in. He states he picked me up as a hitchhiker. That I had no clue about where I had been or what had happened to me. He kept me safe until my memories started to come back. That is when I reached out to my family and decided I needed to come forward. So the military would not continue to list me as MIA.

There are so many rounds of questions that at one point I feel like my head is on a swivel. At the end of it all though, I am allowed to leave on my own. Honorably discharged. The most disgusting moment of my life though is when I am awarded the Medal of Honor. And there isn't a damn thing I could do to stop it. Refusal was not allowed, I tried.

I make James hide the medal from me. Actually, I beg him to throw it away, toss it in a river, smelt it down, anything to remove it from my life. He refuses but never speaks to me about it again. Finally after weeks of questions and paperwork I am allowed to come back home. Back to the ranch.

I smile as we turn down that familiar driveway. I feel James' arm tighten around my shoulders as I sit up, smiling out the windshield "Mom and dad are here. There is Sarah's car too."

James grunts his acknowledgement and I turn to him, "What's wrong?"

I can hear the concern in my own voice. He catches my glance quickly then turns back towards the windshield, "Nothing Maeve. Everything is good."

I know from his tone that he is lying. Everything is not good. He slows to a stop and throws the truck in park. He lets out a heavy sigh as he turns the key off and leans over to grab the door latch. I quickly dart my hand out, grabbing his thigh. He turns to me with a worried look in his eyes, not holding my stare, "James. Something is wrong. Tell me."

He places his hand over mine and lets out a heavy sigh, "It really is nothing Maeve. It's just my own head fucking with me is all."

I scoot back over to him and lay my head on his chest, "Tell me please."

I can feel him slowly running his coarse rugged hand over my hair. He kisses the top of my head gently, "They are going to want you to leave with them. I don't want you to but I am not going to force you to stay either. I just don't want you to have to choose. You have been through enough already."

I sit up, placing a hand on each side of his face and turning him towards my own, "If they want to be a part of my day to day life then they can move here. I am not going anywhere James. You are my home and my home is here. Yes, I love them. Yes, I want to be close with them but you are my family now. You and this little chaotic gremlin inside of me that

265

makes me want to vomit 8 hours of the day. You both are my future. Again, I am NOT going anywhere."

James smiles wide at me, trying to hold back his own emotions. He leans in and kisses me deeply before turning to the door and sliding out. He holds the door open as I grab my bag then slide out the driver's side right behind him.

I look to the front porch and see my dad standing at the door with my mom hovering over the top step. I smile at them and hand my bag to James then run over to hug them.

My mother holds me tight, "Oh sweetie. I only dreamed that someday I would be able to hug you again. You have been through so much. It is just so damn unbelievable that we are here."

I smile into her neck, deeply taking in the scent of cocoa butter and the sea. My mother has always smelled like a tanning lotion commercial and I love it. I feel two strong arms come around us and know my father is now wrapping us into a group hug.

Ten minutes have passed before we all pull away from each other. Mom and dad are both crying but all I have for them is a huge smile. I love them so much and thankfully they will never know the things that I have done to get to where I am today. They will never know the full extent of what happened to me.

Even though they lied for me, there is no way I can put the burden of the truth on them. They deserve to be able to live in the bubble of trust we have all created with one another. I feel James step up behind me and see my mother's eyes go to him.

She smiles at me again then looks at James, "You are the one that saved my daughter aren't you?"

I hear his gruff sigh, "Actually ma'am. She saved me."

266

My mom's eyes fill with tears as she moves around me and then wraps James in a crushing hug as well.

I turn to watch them, my mother and my soon to be husband. James really does look like he needs the hug he is receiving. My dad puts his hand on my shoulder and squeezes gently.

I lift my head to meet his gaze and he gives me a quick wink then reaches his hand out to James, "It really is great to finally meet you son. I cannot thank you enough for helping Carrie. I truly believe we would have lost her forever if she had never run into you."

James smiles at my father as he proudly shakes his hand, "I am not kidding. I think she saved me just as much as I saved her. You have raised an amazing person."

I hear my mom giggle and I give her a quick glance. She is wagging her eyebrows at me then gives me a quick wink. I let out another laugh, "Okay everyone. Let's go inside. I would love to sit on a chair that isn't metal for a little bit."

We all make our way inside. As soon as the door opens, I can smell coffee and something that smells an awful lot like apple pie.

My stomach instantly growls and I bashfully look at James, "Apparently I am hungry."

He smiles back then looks towards the kitchen, "I wasn't hungry before but now I will definitely eat whatever that is that Sarah has made."

Before he can even get the whole phrase out, Bleu comes walking out of the kitchen wearing an apron that says "This Bitch Can Bake". We both let out a loud laugh.

Bleu puts his hand up, "Don't say a fucking word. Sarah made me wear it." We continue laughing out loud.

My mom lets out a chuckle as well, "I haven't met Sarah but I am kinda in love with her right now."

Bleu lets out a chuckle as well but before he can say anything Sarah walks around him with flour all over her face and hands. She is also wearing an apron that reads, "Now Watch Me Whip" with a picture of a whisk beside it. I let out another loud laugh then walk over and give her a hug, "Hey sweetie. I missed you."

Sarah hugs me back tightly, knowing damn good and well that she is getting flour all over me but I don't care. I missed her so much.

She pulls back and smiles at me, "How are you feeling? Are you still doing okay?"

I let a look of fear fall over my face. She is unaware that my parents don't know that they will soon be grandparents.

My dad steps up quickly, "What do you mean still doing okay? Maeve, have you been sick? What happened?"

I can hear the fear in his voice. I smile at Sarah, "I will deal with you later."

She mouths the word sorry before I turn to my parents. I grab James' hand tightly and then smile at my mother, "I am feeling fine. I have just been under the weather on and off for a few weeks. Apparently, that is what morning sickness does to a person."

James squeezes my hand tightly like he is afraid they are going to rip me from his clutches. My mother's eyes start filling with tears and her jaw falls slightly. It takes my dad a few more moments to really comprehend what I have said.

Mom runs up and smacks James in the bicep, "You fucking devil! You could have said something!"

268

She instantly turns and hugs me tightly again, "Oh my god Maeve! I am gonna be a grandma? How far along are you? Why didn't you tell me?"

I am unable to get a word in, she is asking a million questions a minute while at the same time crushing me in a hug. I watch my dad step up to James and shake his hand again forcefully, "Congratulations son. This really is a great day. You gave me my daughter back and now there is gonna be a baby too. I don't know how to thank you!"

James seems just as shocked as me. I didn't really know how my parents would react but this is not what I had envisioned at all.

My mom finally pulls away from me, still smiling as she turns to Sarah, "And you must be the best friend I have heard so much about!"

Sarah smiles back, "Yes Ma'am. My name is Sarah."

Mom waves her hand at her, "Don't give me that ma'am shit. Call me mom."

She then makes it Sarah's turn to struggle for air as she crushes her in the next hug. Dad has finally stepped back from James so I lean into his side, feeling his arm slip around my waist. Dad turns and steps up to Bleu, "And who are you young man?"

Bleu instantly stands up straighter and shoots a glance over to James. With a smile on his face he speaks up for the both of them, "This is Bleu. He is my brother. We served together overseas."

Bleu turns back to my dad and sticks out his hand. My dad leans into the offering, "Thank you for your service. All of you. I hold the deepest form of pride for anyone willing to fight for our country." Dad turns his head to me then smiles, "That means you too kiddo."

I smile as I feel a tear run down my cheek. My father has never told me he was proud of me before. He has told me a

269

million times I am gonna break my neck but never that he is proud of me.

Mom has finally released Sarah from her death grip and she leans over to me putting her hand on my still flat stomach, "I think I smell apple pie. Let's go feed my grandbaby."

I smile back and lead her into the kitchen.

25

Maeve

Daylight - David Kushner

5 years later

I swear to fuck if I have to chase down another god damn mare this week I am going to force James to sell this fucking ranch and move to the desert or something. My bones are fricken sore. I am so tired. I didn't even know that could fucking happen.

3 fucking times this week I have found myself chasing rouge fucking mares down the drive, out of the neighbors field and back over the fence on the back of the property.

And it is only Thursday!

It doesn't fucking help that Bleu come for visit this week with Sarah and just stands back laughing his ass off at Sarah and I trying to wrangle in a 1000 lb mare.

James loves it when Bleu comes through every few months, but right now I am planning his demise in my head. He has 3 fucking seconds to wipe that smirk off his face before he is wearing a sack full of horse shit.

As if finally catching my glare, he quickly stops smiling and turns around to find Maggie standing there lifting her arms up to him. Bleu reaches down and tickles her, making her squeal in only a way he can do.

Even while working I can hear Maggie, "Uncle Bwue, spin me again! Pwease spin me again!" Sarah and I both turn around to see him propelling her in a wide circle, watching her feet fly out behind her.

271

She is never happier than when everyone is home. Finally getting the horses squared away, we decide to get cleaned up and figure out some dinner.

I lean onto the fence, watching Bleu and James, "Hey boys? Since I did all the work with the horses you guys gonna cook tonight?"

James cocks his head to the side and gives me a half smile, "Beef or chicken?"

I give Sarah a half glance then turn back to James with a smile of my own, "Half and half."

He nods at me as I step up into his space. He leans down and gives me a deep kiss, causing Maggie to promptly step between us and push us apart, "Stop it daddy. I am hungry."

I smile into his lips, "Yeah daddy, she's hungry." I feel his hand grip my waist tight when the word daddy leaves my mouth. He smiles back down at me as he pulls away, "We'll talk about you calling me that more often."

I laugh at him and head inside to wash my hands. I clean up fairly quickly then get a glass of sweet tea, downing it in 3 gulps. I can see everyone still in the grass between the house and the horse pasture.

Maggie seems to be forcing them all into a makeshift game of tag. I really do have it all here. Mom and dad will be in next week for Maggies' birthday. I can't wait to see them. I have only seen them a few times a year since the wedding.

I fill up my glass again and sit it on the table when I hear a knock at the front door. I look out the window but no one else has seemed to notice a vehicle.

Is someone on foot? All the way out here?

I turn walking from the kitchen to the living room. There is a man standing there, facing back down the drive. He is tall, maybe 6'4" or hell even taller. Skinny as a rail too. I have no fucking clue who this dude is.

I gently push the screen door open, "Can I help you bud?" I step out onto the porch as the stranger turns towards me.

He is still looking down towards the wood floor, "Man, it has been a long time since I heard that voice."

My blood instantly runs cold. I know that voice. I know those eyes as soon as he forces his gaze to meet mine.

Kevin Lang is standing right in front of me. His face is sunken in and his eyes look like two pools of death, anger. He looks as though he has aged 20 years in the last 8. Why is he here?

I can't force words out of my lips. My mouth instantly goes dry and fear ripples down my spine. Kevin squares his shoulders, "Where is the captain?"

Everything happens so fast. He is on me before I can even scream. His filthy hands are over my mouth, but there is a sweet smell to them. Like his shirt sleeve is drenched in kool aid or something.

I start to feel myself drifting. He is dragging me backwards down the drive towards a truck I have never seen before. I can't scream. I can't cry out.

He has chloroformed me or something.

The last thing I see is Bleu running down the driveway towards us and James jumping off the porch steps with a shotgun in his hand before the world goes black.

www.ingramcontent.com/pod-product-compliance
Lightning Source LLC
Chambersburg PA
CBHW010515100726
47903CB00009B/2763